BOOK
2

The John Morano Eco-Adventure Series

MAKOONA

A NOVEL
BY JOHN MORANO

grey gecko press

Text & Illustrations © 2017 by John Morano
Cover art by Diana Buidoso
Design © 2017 by Grey Gecko Press

Published by Grey Gecko Press, Katy, Texas.

www.greygeckopress.com

Printed in the United States of America

Library of Congress Cataloging-in-Publication Data
Morano, John
Makoona / John Morano
Library of Congress Control Number: 2016917367
ISBN   978-1-9457600-4-4
First Edition

For John Tyler and Vincent

See Clearly
Smile Brightly (and Often)
Feel Deeply
Touch Gently
And Give Thanks . . .

Mother and Padre Love You
Sooo Much . . .

Introduction

by Kathryn S. Fuller, President
World Wildlife Fund

"Out of sight, out of mind," goes the old saying. And nowhere is that more true than with the world's oceans—those vast and magnificent environments of which human beings see only a tiny part.

Sometimes, it takes a book like John Morano's *Makoona* to remind us just what amazing sights are lurking beneath the surface. In the undersea world of Makoona, octopuses, dolphins, sharks, turtles, blowfish, gobies, stargazers, and moray eels all combine to create a teeming tableau of life.

Far from being a fantasy kingdom, this coral reef and its denizens are typical of the life that flourishes in our seas. Oceans sustain a dazzling array of species—from jawless fish to giant squids, from microscopic phytoplankton to mammoth blue whales. It's no exaggeration to say they are the largest wildlife "home" in the world.

But oceans don't just harbor life; they make life possible. Covering two-thirds of the Earth's surface, they absorb three million tons of carbon dioxide a year. They also provide lifesaving medicines and the world's largest single source of animal protein. They are irreplaceable parts of a functioning planet.

And now they are in danger. Overfishing, coastal development, pollution, and illegal trade in endangered species have imperiled these precious marine environments . . . along with the plant and animal life they sustain.

Consider these statistics:

- Ten percent of the world's coral reefs—reefs just like the one portrayed in *Makoona*—have vanished. Another sixty percent are at risk.

- Nearly half the planet's salt marshes and mangrove forests have been drained or cleared.

- Many of the world's fisheries are overfished and at risk from destruction.

- Populations of tunas, swordfish, marlins, sharks, and other large oceanic predators have dropped more than eighty percent in the last two decades.

And that's not all. Manmade chemicals are preventing marine wildlife from surviving and reproducing. Land-based pollution is killing off huge numbers of fish and spreading massive oxygen-draining blooms of algae across our waters. And destructive fishing practices like the ones described in this book are driving endangered species to the brink of extinction.

Time is running out for our oceans. And it will take a concentrated global effort to save them.

That's why the World Wildlife Fund has launched its Planet Campaign, an ambitious effort to save the Earth's most biologically important habitats.

Using special computerized mapping technology, our scientists have identified some two hundred of the world's most outstanding environments. Nearly a third of these are marine: places like mangroves of east Africa, the Philippines' Sulu Sea, Australia's Great Barrier Reef, and the legendary Galapagos Islands (a setting aptly used by the author in his first eco-novel, *A Wing and a Prayer*), where Charles Darwin first developed his theory of evolution.

Drawing on this framework, WWF and its partners are now working to apply conservation principles across entire ecoregions. One of our projects, for instance, is targeting Alaska's Bering Sea, a remarkably productive marine ecosystem that boasts 450 species of fish, crustaceans, and mollusks, 50 seabird species, and 25 mammal species.

We hope that by finding new ways to manage natural resources here, we can create models for saving marine resources on even larger scales.

Unfortunately, much of what we are trying to save is out of sight. So although our oceans are, in some respects, even more threatened than our lands, many people may not know it. That's one of the reasons why *Makoona* is so important. It brings the ocean and its life to us, lifting it above the surface of the sea and reminding us of its value and what needs to be done.

How many of us realize, for instance, that during the late 1970s and 1980s, nearly 80 percent of the grasses in America's Chesapeake Bay disappeared? You can be sure that if 80 percent of America's forests had disappeared over the same period, there would have been a massive outcry. But here, it went relatively unnoticed.

So the World Wildlife Fund is working to sound the alarm. Through our Living Planet campaign and our Global Marine Initiative, we are working to protect not just marine species, but also the biological processes that have kept our oceans alive for millions of years.

We still have much to do . . . and much to learn. In the last few years alone, scientists have discovered whole new groups of organisms living in deep-ocean vents—organisms that flourish without sunlight and resemble no other life form ever encountered. Perhaps they will one day be characters in another John Morano story. And who knows what other mysteries are waiting to be unlocked?

That's why it's so critical to educate people about our marine systems and the threats they face. I hope, as you read *Makoona*, you'll understand just how important healthy oceans are to a healthy planet. And I hope you'll become one of the millions of citizens who have dedicated themselves to restoring oceans for future generations.

No Good Deed

They were no more than a community of crabs, turtles, and small fish floating on the foam—fifty-six boat people. While several lied about their nationalities, the majority were Vietnamese, along with a few Chinese and one Cambodian, a boy named Kemar. In addition to sharing the boat—an old bucket of bolts—the occupants were all refugees, having fled their respective countries for a variety of reasons. Most were tired of war.

Kemar was running from the Khmer Rouge. It's not that they were looking for him specifically. They didn't even know the sixteen-year-old was alive. They were more preoccupied with other things. One of their twisted political sayings was, "To keep you is no benefit. To kill you is no loss." It was a saying all Cambodians were familiar with. And so, like countless others, Kemar fled. He was luckier than most.

The whistle blew—one long blast, one short. It signaled that the boys would have to dive again. Kemar had already stashed enough fish for himself and Son Ba, but ignoring the call was a dangerous thing to do. Reluctantly, Kemar rose and put his wet clothes back on so that he'd have a dry set waiting for him when he returned.

Son Ba was a girl of Cambodian-Chinese descent who made the mistake of letting the Vietnamese know her heritage. Old prejudice and hatred ran deep. Son Ba was lucky that she wasn't tossed over the rail, as she was reminded daily. She and Kemar were allowed to stay on the boat as long as they performed the most unpleasant tasks. The two had a deal: Kemar would steal fish and prepare them, and Son Ba would steal everything else. Together, they would survive, always watching each other's back.

Kemar had no family on the vessel. He lived above decks in a lifeboat that had more holes in it than a fishing net. It could be cold and wet in the lifeboat, but it was also roomier and usually smelled better than other places on the rickety tub. The lifeboat was actually a very comfortable home, unless, of course, heavy weather or a tsunami crossed their bow, in which case Kemar would get onto a main deck and lash himself to the boat.

Although he was probably the best swimmer among his peers, Kemar was fortunate to come away with a handful of fish livers at the end of the day. He didn't dare complain. Discipline was doled out by several of the older men on board. Anyone who stepped out of line would be forced to kneel on a length of bristly sun-dried rope while being beaten with an old bamboo fishing pole. It reminded the boy of the monks' rattan switch that creased his back when he was a child at school in Cambodia.

But as bad as the boat might be, Kemar knew it was much better than existing under the Khmer Rouge. He had the ocean, Son Ba, and a meal or two each day, and he didn't worry about dying. Life was good.

Kemar made his way to the bow, where the boys would gather their gear. A canvas awning strung over the forward section of the deck shielded the elderly from the afternoon sun. Above the wheelhouse, dirty laundry waved in the breeze like flags in a regatta. At the stern, women cooked rice on charcoal stoves next to vats of boiling fish.

Filthy coops held fowl and pigs. Across from the stoves and livestock, a lean-to was draped over the aft deck with two "toilets." Though many people neglected to use them, there was no end to jokes about the toilets' proximity to the galley.

The boy was handed a scare line from a smiling elder named Mir Ta. Mir Ta was the tallest, largest man on the boat. He was perhaps the only elder who liked the boy. No one knew more jokes than Mir Ta. It was said that his spirit was so full of joy and love that he had to constantly tell jokes, laugh, and embrace others to prevent his body from bursting with cheer.

"Last trip of the day," Mir Ta chuckled. "Be careful out there."

"Yes," Kemar joked, "I wouldn't want anything to happen to *your* dinner."

"It's a shame . . . a real shame that I don't have to jump in that ocean. And what makes it worse—yes, it certainly does—is that I eat better than those who do. But I don't make the rules, no I don't."

"When you find out who does, will you let me know?" Kemar asked facetiously.

The dozen boys Kemar fished with were good workers. They had more energy than the adults, ate less, drank less, took up less space on the boat, and were easier to discipline. It was not unusual to make ten or more dives a day. This was their twelfth, and the day wasn't over yet, although for Kemar, it would be soon.

Just as they had done previously, the boys began to launch themselves over the rail as the boat passed over a reef that looked like promising fishing ground. The youngsters usually worked in water anywhere from fifteen to forty feet deep. Often, they would have to save one of their comrades from drowning, especially toward the end of the day when everyone was tired.

Some of the older boys swam to the far end of the reef, where they secured a large net to the base of the coral and stretched it up to the surface. In the meantime, Kemar and his cohorts spread out in a line at the other end of the reef.

Each boy held a length of rope weighted at the bottom with a heavy stone or brick. White plastic strips were tied about a foot apart along the ropes. When the lines were stretched out underwater, the two-foot-long plastic strips would come to life, swaying and bouncing as the boys shook their ropes up and down. Slowly, the youngsters would swim toward the net, herding the fish, who were too frightened to swim through the ropes.

Even fish who lived in underwater lairs would be driven from their homes by the scare lines. The fiercest among them would fall prey to the illusion. Panicked by the swaying plastic strips coming at them, they swam from the perceived danger right into the netting, which was untied and raised from the sea before the victims could escape.

It would usually take a few minutes to winch the net out of the water and swing it over the stern of the boat. Large wicker baskets were used to remove and sort the catch. Perch, bass, coral cod, grouper, rays, sharks, eels, angels, grunts, octopuses, snappers, and even crabs and turtles were all dumped on the deck. Valuable fish would be packed in ice and sold. The "junk" fish would be boiled or salted. Some would be smoked, dried, and eaten.

The boat people used almost everything they caught, needed no bait, and could generally support themselves without much help from others. But there were secondary effects produced by their lifestyle that eluded their attention. They created a high level of incidental death. Sea life that didn't suit their needs often died on deck. Size and species limits were ignored, devastating fish populations, removing animals before they could reproduce, and altering the ratios of predators and prey.

Even their method was problematic. Fish perished in the process of being netted. Weighted scare lines crushed the coral it crashed down upon, destroying not only the backbone of the coral community that took thousands of years to form, but ultimately, the foundation upon which the boat people's own way of life was built.

Because the boat people were generally seen as a nuisance, no country would allow the refugees to dock and disembark. The closest they came was when Captain Phan would run the boat ashore near a port, knowing the host country would supply water, fuel, a few parts for the engine, and a tow out to sea if the refugees would sail off quietly. For the boat people, it was the only way to survive.

As Kemar began what he hoped would be the last pass of the day, he slipped a cheap pair of swimmer's goggles on. To him, they were priceless, because they kept the stinging salt water from irritating his eyes. He'd fought more than once to make sure the cheap plastic goggles stayed in his pocket.

The boys hit the water, swam into position, allowed their lines to uncoil, and began to chase whatever lived beneath them into the net. It was Kemar's job to veer in and close off his flank to prevent the fish from escaping out the sides. The other boys were all cued to Kemar's movements. Although none of them would admit it, once they hit the water, Kemar ceased being "the Cambodian" and became their leader.

Kemar liked to look under the water. He tried to see beyond the sooty clouds that the scare lines created in the sand. The colorful coral and the incredible variety of sea life always amazed and amused him. He could see that this dive was going to produce a good catch.

Transfixed on what was happening below, he watched the fish flee just as they'd always done. A grouper, a parrotfish, several clownfish, a pair of porgies, a cluster of grunts, coral trout, a black-barred garfish, a gray shark, and a white-tip all raced toward the net.

Then he saw something flash beneath him. It was moving swiftly and changing colors as it swam, from pure white to cobalt blue to angry orange to terrified red. Kemar had seen hundreds of octopuses in his life, but this one held his attention. For the first time, the boy could sense the fear, the desperation this animal felt. It reminded him of how he'd fled. And then he wondered, if that octopus was like him, had he somehow become its Khmer Rouge?

Suddenly, the octopus shot up from the bottom and hovered right in front of Kemar's face. The boy's dark stare met the mollusk's yellow eyes. It had long, black, rectangular pupils. Kemar had never noticed an octopus's eyes before. These were bright, full of life, and petrified.

The creature hovered in the water. Its tan flesh was smooth, with yellow and orange flashes pulsing through its body. The colorful streaks seemed to emanate from the rear of the octopus's large mantle. The streaks stretched over the top and around the sides and stopped at the eyes, where the orange and yellow met in a burst of color.

Kemar was mesmerized. The octopus gently reached out two of its arms. One stroked the red sash, called a kremar, that was tied around the boy's waist. The other arm touched Kemar's hand,

the one that held the dangling scare line. The creature creased its mantle, and then Kemar thought—or imagined he thought—the sound of a single word reverberating in his mind: *Why?* A moment later, the octopus turned black, released a cloud of black ink, and jetted off toward the net.

The confused Cambodian dropped the scare line and contemplated his hand. It felt cold and numb. Was it his imagination? One can think strange thoughts after a dozen trips into the sea. The water was cold, he reasoned, and he'd probably gripped the line a little too tightly, cutting off his circulation. Perhaps he grazed it against a stinging coral or a meandering jellyfish.

Regardless, his hand was empty. The line was draped over a stand of fan coral beneath him. The fish were quick to spot the opening. They began to pour out of the exposed flank, the corner that Kemar hadn't sealed.

"You idiot!" the boy treading water next to Kemar shouted. "Now we'll have to dive again for sure. How could you be so stupid?"

All Kemar could do now was watch the fish racing past him. He pictured himself kneeling on the hard rope with Phan standing behind him swinging the bamboo pole. Others would enjoy watching his punishment. However, Kemar was mistaken. This time, it would be different. He would be punished, but not with rod or rope.

The mushroom coral sat majestically at the entrance to the reef. Its tentacles were expanded so it looked more like an anemone than coral. The clownfish, however, knew the difference. They preferred the anemone.

Like most parts of the reef, this little outcrop was inhabited. A half dozen cleaner shrimp, almost invisible were it not for minute strands of purple and pink running through their translucent bodies, worked furiously, tending the coral. They were a tiny speck among the living mosaic of corals, sponges, ascidians, and algae, all teeming with life and activity. If ever there was an underwater city, it would be found hidden in the coral.

Just beyond the mushroom coral and the little shrimp sat a violet sponge flecked with white. At least it appeared to be a violet sponge flecked with white. Actually, it was an octopus. And her name was Binti.

There isn't another creature on Earth more skilled at camouflage than the octopus. In addition to being able to change color instantly, they can also emit an underwater smoke screen that's actually made of ink. And what few other creatures realize is that many octopuses can also change their shape as well as the texture of their skin. At the moment, Binti looked exactly like a violet sponge. That was good news for Binti but bad news for the crab who was chasing an injured goby.

Panicked by the crab and so fooled by the octopus masquerading as a sponge, the wounded fish chose to hide in Binti, who was waiting for the crab to pursue its meal. Fortunately for Binti, the goby didn't mimic the pearlfish, who often seeks sanctuary by swimming up the rear end of a sea cucumber.

When the crab brushed against the octo-sponge, Binti came to life, reared up, and dropped on the crustacean like a living net.

She worked the crab toward her mouth, bit through the shell with a small, sharp beak, and delivered a powerful poison that would immediately end the struggle.

The injured fish, a young goby named Dakada, swam up to Binti and said, "Thanks for saving my scales."

Binti replied, "I'm the one who should thank you for delivering my dinner."

"Better to deliver dinner than be dinner," Dakada pointed out. And then he swam off, hiding under some platter coral.

Binti inched up to him and assumed the color, shape, and texture of the coral so that she didn't give either of their locations away. She whispered, "Did you hide in me because you knew I was an octopus and I'd eat that crab or because you thought I was a sponge?"

Dakada peered out from under the coral, winked, and responded, "I thought you were a sponge. I had no idea you were actually an octopus."

"Good answer," Binti said as she crawled away with the crab tucked beneath her, held tightly in a large sucker.

Now, Binti was faced with an important decision: to eat the crab there or take it to her den. Either choice involved enormous risk, because although the octopus is the queen of camouflage, beyond that, the creature is virtually defenseless to those who prey upon it.

Having no bones, no claws, a diminutive beak, and being a relatively slow swimmer in open water without much swimming stamina for the long runs, Binti was constantly concerned about being spotted and attacked. Those she feared the most were sharks, barracuda, grouper, sometimes snappers (especially in packs), the occasional dolphin, and, of course, humans. But more than any creature in or above the sea, Binti feared the moray eel.

So the question remained: what to do with the catch? There were three choices. One, take the crab into a nearby hole or crevice and eat it there. The problem with that choice was that Binti didn't know if something dangerous was already in the nearby hole or crevice.

Two, eat the crab under some coral awning or rocky overhang, the problem with that solution being that Binti was perilously open to predators, especially with remnants of crab floating all around her. On the reef, that's a real attention getter.

Three, hold the crab tightly, bury it under her so it would be virtually sealed, and move slowly along the bottom back to her hollow.

After careful consideration, the octopus decided to take her meal to go. Binti moved slowly, rhythmically, pausing often to test the waters. She could sense danger and had the ability to feel minor ripples against her smooth flesh. Binti also had the ability to identify chemical traces in the sea. In fact, her body functioned like a super-sensitive giant tongue. She literally tasted chemicals in the water and used that to help determine what shared her reef. At the moment, Binti tasted nothing out of the ordinary. She felt safe.

She swam under a rocky overhang. In the shadows, she turned black. But Binti couldn't see very well, so she crawled out from under the rock and climbed on top of it. When she reached the summit, the octopus disappeared, replaced by a bright orange sponge that swayed in the current like several others clinging to the rock. Convinced that she was unseen, Binti was surprised to hear, "So, my friend, will we be eating when you get home?"

"Shhh," she answered. "Sponges don't talk."

"True, but octopuses do."

"Well, if you give me away and I'm forced to run, neither of us will get to eat."

"Ah, but if I give you away and a barracuda comes down here... By the way, there's one right up there trying to hover in the glare of the sun. Do you see him?"

"Yes . . ."

"Good. If he was to swim down here and you were to flee, you'd have to drop that crab. And while that barracuda chased you all over Makoona, I'd take good care of that crab for you. I would definitely make sure no one else got it, I promise."

"But then, little blowfish, what kind of friend would you be?"

"One with a full stomach, but also one with one less pal."

"Well, Hootie, the question is what's worth more: a friend or a crab?"

"Tough question. Might depend on who the friend is. Ah, I suppose I'll sacrifice a full stomach in the name of our august association."

Suddenly, involuntarily, the octopus changed its color to an alarming red. The smaller blowfish puffed and extended its fins. Danger had arrived.

A pair of horrified red snappers shot past Hootie and Binti. It was evidence of trouble—big trouble. When a fish that might normally eat you swims by without so much as a nod, it usually means it's swimming for its life. Usually, this is the result of another predator—a bigger, nastier, meaner one. A predator that might very well change its mind and have you for dinner instead. So when the snappers are panicking, it's wise to err on the side of caution. Both Binti and Hootie concluded instantly that whatever made them flee like that was probably pretty nasty.

Then the two friends heard it. They felt the unmistakable surge underwater. The octopus and the blowfish knew what was happening, and like the snappers, they, too, fled.

There was another vibration in the water. A school of tuna raced past them. An agitated gray reef shark darted by, followed by a scrambling young turtle. To the casual observer, it looked like the shark was fleeing from the tiny turtle, when in reality, they were all running from the same thing.

The vibrations became more pronounced. There was no mistaking it. The man-tide approached. Nothing churned the water up quite the same way. The humans swam so clumsily, yet their arrival was so deadly. As they'd done many times before, Binti and Hootie ran from man.

Caught up in a chaotic mass of terrified ocean dwellers all swimming with one goal in mind—to survive—Binti spotted some of her friends. She saw the goby cleaners Fin, Gill, Wiff, Ditt, Ya Ya, and Dakada. They were led by Paykak. She spotted Fraco, the ancient, wise, and gentle grouper (when he had a full belly) fleeing for his life. Rising to the surface, she spotted Jaqu the turtle, no doubt trying to size up the situation by slipping his head above the water.

Binti was also swimming with predators. Barracuda, bonita, and a stone fish raced by her, paying no attention to the opportunity she and Hootie presented for a quick meal. The man-tide had a way of galvanizing the residents of the reef. Even mortal enemies came together when united in fear against man, all part of a full-blown swimpede.

Binti could see the humans now. Their awkward limbs kicked and thrashed as they moved slowly and deliberately forward. Even though they were so obviously out of place in the water, the humans were, in their own way, masters of it. One need only see a reef shark flee in terror to understand that.

Binti spotted a pearl perch named Sa Rah. The octopus called out to her friend, "Where should we go?" The scare lines were almost bumping Hootie's tail fin.

Sa Rah yelled, "The turtle! Ask the turtle!"

"Jaqu!" Binti called. "Where should we swim?!"

Looking down from the surface, Jaqu shook his head. "They are everywhere! Ask the tuna!"

Several tuna darted back and forth between the scare lines and the net. If there was an escape route, these swift open-sea swimmers would surely have seen it.

Hootie chased one, screaming, "How do we get out?"

The tuna paid no attention. They blew by the blowfish and then swept past again from the opposite direction. It was clear they were as terrified as the others and didn't know how to get away either.

Binti could now see the scare lines and the nets which would sweep her from the sea. She stopped swimming and turned her fate over to the spirit-fish. Immediately, without any thought on her part, Binti found herself following the advancing perimeter of the man-tide. She stayed out of reach and out of sight and measured its expanse. The longer she spent studying the wall, the tighter its grip on the ocean creatures became.

Binti heard a voice. It was a voice she'd heard before, an articulation from within that was her own, yet she didn't know for sure where it came from. It was the voice that all creatures possessed, though many were skilled at ignoring it. Binti, however, believed that her inner voice revealed the truth of the spirit-fish. And while she didn't always understand the message, she always listened.

The octopus swam along the encircling mass of man-tide. Deep in her mantle, she heard, "You are the most skilled at deception in the sea. If you do not fall prey to one of your own devices, you will be un-tide."

Not quite given the answer, Binti had received guidance. Sometimes, that was all you got. And sometimes, that was all it would take. The octopus pondered the message. Was the spirit-fish, if indeed that's who sent the message, suggesting that this entire event was a charade of some sort, that it's not what it appears to be? Binti hesitated, uncertain. She'd seen what the man-tide could do. She'd lost friends. She'd seen ruined reefs. And they were no charade.

Rooted in her reflections, deaf to Hootie's howling, Binti suddenly realized the approaching wall was upon her. She panicked, scrambling away. A moment later, she grazed against the massive net and then jetted away from it as well. When a rock tied to a scare line crashed down on her arm, Binti shot herself off the ocean floor. She landed quietly and sat on a broken clam. And then it hit her— she had just passed through the moving wall!

Carefully but quickly, the octopus swam back through the scare lines, which were now moving away from her. She passed through the wall again. Had the spirit-fish bestowed her with special powers? Binti reached out two arms and touched the shaking lines. They didn't hurt, and they didn't hold. The wall was a façade! It didn't exist, at least not to the degree the fish believed. The answer wasn't to run from it but rather run *through* it. Just as she was never actually a sponge, this wasn't actually a wall.

Binti jetted herself through the faux wall one last time as she swam back to find her friends. When she saw Paykak, Hootie, Fraco, Sa Rah and Jaqu all gathered together, she shouted, "I have the answer! Pass through the wall! Swim through it, not away from it!"

But the others continued to flee.

Binti pleaded, "Listen to me! Trust me!"

As the shaking curtain closed in, the fish were too terrified to listen to the octopus. Through the chaos, none of them even noticed her swimming in and out of the lines. Now Binti became panicked. She understood what was happening. She understood that at any moment, a net would rise up from the bottom and claim the lives of all her friends, her family, and even her enemies. Everyone would be gone.

That was when Binti decided to take matters into her own arms, swimming toward a single human who floated with the outermost scare line that was approaching the net. Rising to the surface, the octopus faced the creature. Their eyes connected for an instant while Binti stretched out two of her powerful arms. With one, she stroked what looked like red seaweed dangling from the human's midsection. It fascinated and mesmerized Binti. Then she gently laid the tip of another arm on the human's hand, the one that grasped the scare line.

Her intent was to hold that hand and then pull the line free with two of her other arms, but Binti never had the opportunity to complete her plan. She didn't have to. Her eyes stayed locked on the human's eyes. Binti saw deeply into the creature and was surprised how much they appeared to have in common. The human tilted his head up, closed his eyes momentarily, and then released the line, floating where he was, expressionless.

The octopus dove below and called to the creatures of Makoona, who were now herded into a tight ball as the net began to rise.

"The wall has collapsed!" Binti bellowed. "Escape! There is a hole!"

Fraco saw the hole and rushed through it. Immediately, Sa Rah and Jaqu followed. Soon, the entire community poured through the opening. Binti was rolled and bounced like a shell in the surf under the surge of the swimpede. As she rose up and dusted herself off, Binti was pleased to see an empty net being pulled from the water.

Hootie, who'd stayed to help others flee, was the last one out. He swam calmly up to Binti and asked, "Still got that crab? I'm pretty hungry."

When the octopus didn't reply, Hootie quipped, "What good are you?" And then the disgusted blowfish swam off.

Although he knew he'd pay for his mistake, likely with the rod and rope, Kemar was strangely amused by his decision to drop the scare line. It was something he'd never done before, and it was such an open act of defiance, it quietly pleased him.

He was also struck by his confrontation with the octopus. Kemar knew it was nothing but chance—a mere coincidence—but swimming face-to-face with the strange octopus caused him to wonder. Had he actually felt something from the creature? Had it touched him? It was as if the octopus had understood what was happening and realized that Kemar had the power to stop the catch.

He floated, reflecting on the bizarre circumstances, until he concluded it would be best to return to the boat. Swimming back to the vessel, Kemar could already hear the boys talking about what had happened.

Phan, the captain, was at the railing. He wasn't just the captain of the ship; Phan was the chief of the boat community. He was tall and thin. His hair was cut short in an effort to accentuate a scar on the side of his head. He claimed it was a badge of honor that he'd received in battle and that the one who'd inflicted it came out looking much worse than him, but Kemar doubted the story.

In his mind, Phan was a coward and a liar who cared only about getting his hands on whatever valuables people managed to bring onto *his* boat. Although Phan rarely meted out punishment himself, he always seemed to enjoy the spectacle, especially when Kemar was on the receiving end. Today, Kemar was sure the rod would rake his ribs. Phan would be pleased.

Kemar swam slowly toward the rope ladder that hung from the rail, thinking how much the salt water would sting his wounds when he returned to fish tomorrow. But the ocean could also help clean and heal. It was one of the powers that drew the Cambodian to the sea. It might be painful at times, but the ocean also healed.

Before Kemar reached the ladder, Sambath, the boy who fished next to him, climbed on board. Phan grabbed Sambath, struck him, and demanded to know why all the fish had escaped from his side of the scare lines.

Sambath, who'd never liked Kemar that much to begin with, wasn't going to be punished for Kemar's mistake. He pointed to his comrade and said, "It was Kemar. He dropped his line, and the fish rushed out before they hit the net. Look, he returns without his line."

Phan released Sambath and turned to Kemar. He looked down from the deck and asked, "Tell me the truth, you barnacle. Did you cost us our catch?"

"I'm sorry, Phan!" the boy shouted. "The line got caught on something and slipped from my hand."

"That's not true!" Sambath countered. "I saw Kemar wrap the line around his wrist when we started. We all do that so we can't drop them."

Phan scanned the deck. Everyone had gathered, waiting to see what would happen to Kemar. The captain didn't want to show weakness. Unfortunately, he wasn't someone who understood that strength is often the ability to show mercy and weakness is more likely found in cruelty. It was the same disease the Khmer Rouge suffered from, and Kemar knew that again, he would fall victim to this distorted reasoning.

The boy reached the ladder. As he opened his hand and stretched his arm out, Phan pulled the ladder out of his reach and over the rail. He yelled down to the puzzled youngster, "Your value was as a fisherman. And since you don't seem to be able to do that anymore, I'll quote your Khmer countrymen, 'To keep you is of no benefit. To kill you is no loss.'"

Sambath helped Phan secure the ladder. Then the boat chugged off, away from the setting sun. Kemar was abandoned on the open sea. When the stern swung around to face the boy, he could see Son Ba calling to him, but the wind snatched her words away before they reached him. She hefted a large red box on the rail. Then Mir Ta ran up to her. She struggled with him, probably thinking he was going to stop her. But Mir Ta merely wanted to help. He held a tin can in his hands, kissed it, and dropped it into the red box.

Kemar's two friends strapped the container closed, and then the large, powerful man threw it overboard to the boy. The box hit the water, bounced in the boat's wake, and began to float away from Kemar. The boy tried to swim toward it, but it was difficult to see just where the box was. Most of it was underwater, and sea foam washed over the lid, obscuring it. Like the voice of Son Ba, the box rode a current that carried it away from Kemar.

Beneath the boat, fish returned to Makoona to see what was left of their home. Although they lived in a large reef and the man-tide hadn't fished this spot many times, the single pass of the scare lines had taken its toll on the precious coral. Beautiful stands of staghorn were reduced to rubble. An exotic patch of orange, yellow, and pink sea fans fell broken and lifeless on the sand.

The humans had cut their path of destruction through the heart of Makoona and through the hearts of all of those who loved their home. Those who'd once lived in snug coral cracks and crevices now desperately searched for some shelter to spend the night. As the sea darkened and shadows became long and fuzzy, nocturnal hunters would appear, a fact that only added more urgency to the displaced creatures' quest.

Binti was lucky. She could fit almost anywhere, so she wasn't as frenzied as her friends. Others, like Fraco, the large grouper, had little to fear from most sea creatures. But they were the exceptions.

Just as Kemar had done, Binti took some time to reflect on what happened earlier. She found a spot among a group of yellow brain coral, the perfect place to think. Binti changed her color, rolled herself into a tight ball, wrapped her arms around her mantle, and shifted the texture of her skin to mimic the pattern of the coral. The octopus had become a brain.

She also slipped two arms around a rock that jutted up underneath her, making it almost impossible for another to pry her loose, since Binti could lift many times her own weight with little effort. The octopus liked the idea of being anchored, especially when she was outside her den. Relaxing and reflecting among the brain coral, she scanned the area for food or foes before she started to move back to her home, which she hoped the scare lines hadn't destroyed.

Directly above, Binti heard a loud splash, the kind of noise a large fish makes when it breaches. But when she looked up, all the octopus saw was some type of garbage floating on the sea. The swimming island that carried the man-tide was paddling steadily away from it. Binti watched the box roll and bob on the waves, waiting to claim it for a home should it sink and prove worthy. As the box drifted away, drawn by a weak current, Binti noticed something else. She could feel the vibrations in the water. A human was plodding along slowly on the surface.

It appeared as though the creature was chasing the garbage or perhaps the swimming island. But Binti could see that he would never catch either. The octopus smiled. For the first time, she understood an expression that she often heard on the reef: "I felt like a human off of land." It suddenly made sense to her how out-of-place a human must feel in the sea. It was almost like being a fish out of water, she guessed. Binti reasoned that she belonged on land about as much as they belonged in the sea. Fish hadn't been given feet and lungs, and the man-tide certainly didn't have fins or gills.

It occurred to Binti that this human must've come from the swimming island. Perhaps he was fighting for his life. She watched to see if he'd cut himself on the sharp coral. If that happened, things would get really interesting, she thought. The way the human thrashed around probably kept him from sinking, but it certainly called attention to his presence and might even signal that he was injured or panicked—either of which was dangerous at dusk on the reef.

She saw the red seaweed waving from his torso. Was this an indication that this human was poisonous, like the conspicuous colorful gills of a nudibranch signaled? And then Binti realized that this might be the same human who released his line and saved the reef. She guessed that his school or pod or whatever the man-tide called it had abandoned him. Binti wouldn't do the same.

The octopus assumed that for whatever reason, the floating container was important, so she changed color to an olive drab with flecks of sand sprinkled along her body, hugged the sea floor, and crawled under the floating box. She reached it easily, changed color again, and swam to the surface. Holding it tightly in her suckers, she towed it to the human who cared.

Kemar watched the red container drift off. It moved much more slowly than the boat, which was now nothing more than a speck on the darkening horizon. Things didn't look good for the boy. He smiled to himself as he realized Phan had dropped him not unlike the way he'd released his scare line. However, Kemar's action gave life, whereas Phan's was intended to take a life.

Kemar hoped he wouldn't sink as quickly as his weighted scare line did. The boy had seen his family and his country die. But deep down, Kemar had always believed that he might rise above the mess that was happening in his homeland, that one day he would live a truly wonderful life, a tribute to all those who perished too soon to live their own dreams. It seemed to him now, floating on the quiet, cold sea, that there would be no tribute. His young life would end here.

He was bumped hard, jarred from his thoughts of doom. He couldn't see what it was, so Kemar backed away, paddling slowly but deliberately. It felt like a large, muscular fish, one that would surely find him an attractive target. The boy was afraid to look at it, afraid that he would see the open jaws of a great white coming at him. He hoped it would just go away, but instead, it slammed into him a second time.

The creature knew Kemar was there, and it seemed to be pursuing him. It was becoming difficult to see in the deepening darkness. The boy hoped it might only be a nearsighted turtle bumping into him. He'd heard of turtles getting stung in the eyes while they eat jellyfish and then mistaking people for other turtles. Whatever it was that found him was unquestionably large and hard.

Finally, Kemar mustered enough courage to face the creature. He turned and saw a large, hard . . . cooler. It was half submerged. Kemar threw himself on top of it. The container was buoyant enough to support the boy's thin frame. The red cooler had a white lid. It was old. The plastic had been patched, and the lid was held in place with a tattered green bungee cord. Kemar had seen this cooler before. He was the one who'd patched it. It was the box Son Ba used to store some of her most precious possessions.

Kemar remembered what his mother had told him when she lost her closest friend, a woman named Ba Elle. "True friends are hard to find and harder to lose," she'd said. Son Ba and Mir Ta were true friends.

The boy threw his arm over the box. He could feel the bungee cord swollen with salt water beneath his fingers. He stroked it for a moment. It felt secure, solid. And then the cord stroked him back! It was an octopus's arm!

Kemar gasped, whipped his own arm away from the cooler, and slid back into the water. Then he saw Binti. She'd turned bright red, like the box. An involuntary wave of blue pulsed through her body. The octopus reached out three arms and pushed the cooler toward the boy. Shocked, Kemar grabbed the cooler's only handle. When he grasped it, Binti turned brown and jetted off, disappearing into the dark deep.

Although Binti did have quite an impressive array of defenses, they were most effective when she was in a reef or on the ocean floor. An octopus is extremely vulnerable in open water. Binti had taken a huge risk for the human because she sensed he'd taken a risk for her. It was a principle that she lived by, one of the basic teachings of the spirit-fish: "When one acts honorably, one should be treated with honor."

Binti dropped to the bottom and began her slow crawl home, a wonderfully tight crevice nestled between two rocks that opened into a snug little den. Only another boneless creature—or one so small as to not concern Binti—would be able to access her den. Even though the octopus knew this, she always paused before entering. She liked to study the surroundings to see if there was any evidence that something had visited her lair, or worse yet, that something was inside or waiting nearby.

The octopus could tell if the stones or shells she piled outside the coral crack had been disturbed. The sight looked as pleasingly pristine as she left it. Still, Binti lingered. Something told her not to enter. It was the voice. Lately, the octopus was working hard to pay attention to it. She found that her inner voice often gave her good council, so she began to listen for it. It seemed that the more Binti sought the voice, the more she found it. "Listen, and you shall hear," Fraco had once told her.

There was one predator who might be able to enter Binti's home. It was long and slender, sporting a huge, gaping mouth lined

with twisted coral-sharp teeth. It was, unfortunately, her most lethal enemy, the moray eel. The morays were loosely tribal. They
lived amongst themselves, never socializing, never using the same
cleaning stations as the rest of the reef. They were mysterious and
aloof. And they were deadly, especially to an octopus. The fear of
the moray swam deeply within her, so Binti waited.

It was a good thing she did. When Binti saw the two eyes peering out of the crack, she knew she had a problem. Something was
in her home. And it probably wasn't afraid of her, because by now,
it certainly knew it was in the home of an octopus and had chosen
to remain. Binti watched. The eyes slid back into the shadows, and
then they reappeared. Was it looking for someone? For her?

She studied the creature. It didn't have a moray eel's eyes—
tiny, red eyes with narrow slits set closely together. The intruder
seemed to be smaller than Binti. Her territorial 'tude took over,
and the octopus decided an eviction was necessary.

She approached the entrance to her home, rose up slowly,
and stretched her body across the crack. Making sure the intruder couldn't escape out the emergency exit, Binti reached an arm
around the rocks, stuffed the tip into the escape hole, and attempted to scare the interloper into fleeing out the main opening.

The creature didn't move. Binti reached her arm deeper into
the rocks. She slapped a sucker on the creature and felt that it was a
fat fish. But as she tried to tug it out, it wouldn't budge. The animal
was wedged solidly between the rocks, apparently having grown
dramatically larger since it had entered.

At that point, Binti knew who was in her home. She was in no
danger. Only one fish could make itself thin enough to slip into her
coral hollow and then swell into a size that could not be removed—
a blowfish. It had to be Hootie.

Binti heard a muffled monologue vibrating off the rocks. She
withdrew her body from the opening.

Hootie was screaming at her quite clearly and rather loudly.
He emerged, shouting, "What is wrong with you? This goes beyond
reefanoia. Now you're worried about blowfish?"

"I didn't know who was in there," Binti explained.

"I'm in there, that's who. You were expecting a whale shark?"

"Well, what were you doing in my home? What do you need?"

"Need? What do I need? So a visit from me means only that I must need something?"

Embarrassed by her suggestion, Binti backpaddled, "No, I . . ."

"What do I need? Isn't that just beautiful? And why shouldn't I be in your home? It's a lot safer waiting in there than waiting out here—that is, of course, unless some demented reefanoid octopus overreacts to a little social call. You don't mind that I rest in your rocks instead of floating out here in the open where any predator with a craving might be enticed by my tender tailfin?"

"Trust me, your tailfin is the last thing anyone would bite."

"This is precisely why you don't have many friends!" the blow-fish bellowed. "You treat us like sand."

"I don't have many friends because I'm an octopus. I'm a solitary creature."

"You say that's the reason, but that's just an excuse. What came first, the turtle or the egg? Do you not have friends because you're solitary, OR are you solitary because you don't have friends? Think about it . . . I'm telling you, eight-arms, you don't know how to act around coralized fish."

Binti could see that Hootie was going to swim with this as long as he could, so she decided to submit to the clambasting rather than fight it. It was the only way it would ever end. She managed to tune out the boisterous blowfish until she heard him say, "So, that's the thanks I get. I find the shell *you're* looking for and you *hunt* me?"

"You found my shell?"

Trying his best to stay away from the coral, Kemar floated with the cooler beneath him. The coral frightened him as much as anything in the sea. While it was stunning to behold, Kemar had also seen what coral cuts could do.

Wounds from corals on his former shipmates often infected quickly. Many corals also dispensed toxins that could easily cause one to drown. And blood in the water from fresh cuts was the last thing Kemar wanted. He found it difficult to kick his legs and still avoid striking the hard pillars below.

The rapidly setting sun didn't make the boy's situation any more hopeful. The darker it became, Kemar worried, the tougher it would be to see him (not that anyone would be looking for him). And that would decrease his already slim chance of rescue.

Like the cooler he clung to, the boy's thoughts began to drift. He saw irony in the fact that when he lived on the boat fishing the sea, he was the ultimate predator. But now, exposed, alone, and totally without defenses, Kemar had become the ultimate prey. For the first time in his life, he began to see just who actually ruled the sea and how precarious man's place at the top of the food chain really was.

Kemar hugged the cooler. It was his lifeline, and he didn't want to lose it. Since he had no idea where he was going, he gave up splashing and kicking. The boy tucked his legs against his body. It kept him a little warmer, kept his appendages away from the coral, and most importantly, diminished the appetizing appearance that two dangling legs with ten tasty toes could present. He floated quietly with the current and prayed that he'd make it to morning. After that, he didn't know what he'd do.

The nighttime wasn't a bad time for Binti. Almost impossible to be seen in the daylight, at night, the octopus was even more difficult to spot, but so were the predators. Yet at the same time, night could also be an easy time for the octopus to eat and a more difficult time to be eaten. While she couldn't go so far as to say she liked it, Binti didn't mind the night.

Usually, she preferred to sit in a crevice or a cave, unseen and unnoticed, which makes sense when the sun is out, but at night, the octopus often got bolder. That's when she'd move along the reef, venturing out to the deep drop-off where the coral disappeared. Along the way, she'd dine mostly on crustaceans.

Sometimes, she would stop and chat with a friend or two. It was a good way to hear if a new shark or a family of barracudas was in the area. Binti always asked about moray eels too. She could usually taste traces of slime in the water or feel their ripples when the eels were roaming, but a little extra research never hurt.

Fish who rarely left their small patch of reef, certain gobies, damselfish, clownfish, and others liked to hear what Binti encountered during her nighttime feeding forays. However, there really wasn't much that she could ever tell the cleaner gobies. They were the kings of gossip. No creature in the sea knew more about what was happening than the gobies, and yet the little fish never left their home.

The gobies knew so much because information came to them. They ran the most successful cleaning station on the reef. And everyone knows how much chatter goes on while fish wait in line to have their gills raked. The gobies heard everything first and often repeated it first as well.

Binti slipped under a broad table coral, hugged the edge of a giant clam, slid across a sponge, and emerged within fins of the fields of one of her favorite friends, Ebb the damselfish. Ebb was the original underwater farmer. Aquaculture was his thing. His kind had been farming the seas while the man-tide still had tails.

The territorial algae agronomist was busy chasing off a much larger rainbow parrotfish, who actually had no interest in the damsel's crop. But that made little difference to Ebb. He had no intention of allowing anything to get close enough to his precious algae to express an interest.

Ebb screamed, "Swim clear of my algae, Parrot-pirate! I see that look in your eyes! Never seen algae this green before, have ya?"

The indignant fish could only muster, "Well, I never."

"I know, that's what I said. You never seen algae like this." Then Ebb thrust himself at the solid parrotfish and tore a scale from its belly. The fish raced off into the reef. Ebb, poking fun at the fish's sleeping habits, taunted, "Cover yourself in mucus and go back to sleep! I'll have no squatting on my rocks!"

Binti dropped down from a large purple sponge, turning brown as she settled on the ground next to Ebb. "Relax, Ebb. That fish isn't interested in your crop. You know it prefers coral."

"Sure, it's easy for you to just go with the flow," the cranky cultivator countered. "But I need to set an example. Otherwise, that parrot will wander back, and I know she'll bring others, and *they* might nibble my crop. Then I'd have to drive several fish away instead of just one. It's a slippery slope."

"I doubt it's really that serious a situation."

"I've seen it before!" Ebb cried. "They always come back—never alone—and they never leave my pasture the way they found it. Clam it! I owe it to my algae!"

Ebb rarely got worked up about anything other than crops. He did, however, get worked up about his algae quite often. Binti understood that there was nothing either of them could do about it. The cantankerous damselfish was created to be crazy about his algae; it was the way of the water, part of the spirit-fish's grand design. So, in spite of her friend's protests, Binti went with the flow anyway, enjoying Ebb's enthusiasm.

"Well, *I've* never brought anyone out here," the octopus pointed out.

"Oh, yes you have."

"Have not."

"Have too." Ebb smiled.

"Who then?" Binti demanded. "Name names."

"Hootie. How's that for a name?"

"I never *brought* Hootie here."

"That's open to interpretation, my friend. You came to see me, and Hootie followed you. Now he comes here all the time."

"But I didn't *bring* him. You said it yourself. He followed me."

"I'm the last fish to split scales, but isn't that bringing him? I mean, if he follows you, then wasn't it *you* who brought him here?"

"He follows me everywhere."

"That may be true, but it's not really the point at fin. Allow me to explain more simply . . ."

Binti was annoyed at the implication of the statement. She didn't enjoy condescending damselfish. Ebb knew this, which was precisely why he made the statement. The farmer continued cultivating Binti's ire.

"You were, in effect, the one who led him to this place. Were it not for you, he would not have come here. Hence, *you* are guilty of bringing, perhaps unwittingly, another here, yet guilty nonetheless." Ebb smiled, proud that he could point out what the brainy octopus had missed.

"But you love Hootie."

"I think the word 'love' is a tadpole strong. I *like* Hootie. But again, not the point."

By now, Binti's pride was bruised. She flushed a deep pink with wisps of pale blue. As one of the most intelligent creatures on the planet, it was disconcerting to be intellectually toyed with by a farming fish. How could a scale-covered creature who spends all day tending algae growing on sponges and rocks talk whirlpools around her? And then it happened. The mollusk's monstrous mantle went to work and found an idea Ebb hadn't considered. She returned to a confident rusty brown color and went on the offensive.

The octopus queried the fish, "Ebb, didn't you say—and correct me if I'm wrong, I know you will—that visitors always return with others? And that they never leave your farm as they found it?"

"Yep, those were my words."

"Well, let me ask you . . ." Binti paused for effect and took a slow, deep breath, releasing the water through her siphon beneath her mantle, which she aimed directly at Ebb's face. A stream of disorienting bubbles popped all around him. "Who has Hootie ever brought here? And when has he ever disturbed your field?"

Ebb leaned over and trimmed some algae below. He looked up and replied, "But that's exactly why I like him so much. He doesn't eat my algae or disturb the sponges. And unlike yourself, he's a brilliant conversationalist."

"Now who's avoiding the issue?" Binti teased. "The larger principle is, I believe, that visitors are not inherently trouble. Some, like Hootie, may actually turn out to be friends. Rather than a hindrance, visitors could, in some cases, actually be a benefit."

"Maybe," Ebb mumbled. The farmer, suddenly quite interested in his chores, looked up at the octopus and smiled sourly. "But some *friends* can turn out to be a real pain in the anal fins, if you catch my drift."

Binti did, so she moved on to another topic, asking, "Have you seen it?"

"No, I haven't. But you've got half the fish on the reef out searching for your shell, and none of us are really sure what it looks like."

"If I knew, I'd find it myself. But when I see it, I'll know."

Ebb pointed a stout fin as some loose rocks rolled onto his algae. The friends froze for a moment and looked for danger. Seeing none, Binti stretched out one of her long arms and brushed the stones away.

"Thanks," Ebb said.

"Don't mention it," she replied. "Now, where were we? Yes, it's important, Ebb. At least to me, it is. Just as the spirit-fish showed you how to find your harmony, I need to find mine."

"And you really think the shell is the answer?"

"I think so. I'm a mollusk without a shell."

"So?"

"Imagine if you were a fish without gills," the octopus suggested.

"Well, maybe the spirit-fish will tell you where that special shell is."

"Wouldn't that be nice? But maybe I need to find it myself."

"To hear the blowfish tell it, sounds like he might've found it for you."

"He's supposed to take me to it tonight."

Ebb looked skeptical. "How many times has that blowfish told you he's found *the* shell? I hope he's not just blowing water up your siphon."

"He's trying to help."

"Just don't get your hopes up."

The octopus clammed up, feeling disappointed before she'd even seen the shell, remembering how many times she'd already been disappointed. But really, it didn't matter how many times she was led to the wrong shell. When the right one washed up, that would be it, once and for all. It only had to be right one time. Yet something was becoming obvious to Binti: she might have to find the shell herself.

Like a lizard clinging to a log, Kemar floated with his cooler. Half asleep and getting cold, the boy rolled with the gentle waves, prepared to go wherever they carried him. Perilous uncertainty was fast becoming a way of life for the young Cambodian, who gazed at the crisp stars overhead.

Again, something large and solid bumped up against Kemar's thigh. It felt like a fish, but not one with large scales. It had smooth skin. Whatever it was, Kemar hoped it would take no notice of his precarious position and continue on its way so they could remain just two things that go bump in the night.

But the fish continued to nudge the boy. Something splashed behind him off to the right. On his left side, a few feet away, he spotted a triangular gray dorsal fin crease the sea and then disappear into the dark. With only dim starlight and a sliver of a moon, Kemar couldn't tell whether he was in the company of sharks or dolphins.

The boy's heart jumped when he felt something grasp his foot in its mouth. He whipped his leg away, avoiding an actual bite, but he could feel teeth against his ankle. Lifting his foot out of the water, he was terrified by what he saw, a slight, steady trickle of blood dripping into the sea. Although the injury itself wasn't going to kill him, it could easily cause his death. It might also explain the increased presence of the gray visitors and their apparent interest in him.

Kemar tried to keep his foot out of the water, but his blood still found its way into the sea. The boy thought about wrapping the wound in his kremar, but it was too late to do anything about the cut. The damage was done, the blood had found the ocean, and it seemed the ocean was about to find him.

Suddenly, Kemar was thrown sideways. His cooler popped several feet into the air. The lid flew off, and the box took on sea water. It began to sink. The boy scooped up the lid and frantically swam to the cooler, knowing that without the buoyant box, he wouldn't survive. When he reached the topless cooler, he threw his arms around it, drained the bilge, and snapped the lid back in place.

Then he realized why the fish might've been so interested in him. Several dried flounders, a smoked perch, and another salted fish of some sort were in a bag, semi-submerged next to a plastic gallon jug filled with what he assumed was fresh water. Son Ba had obviously stolen some food and some very valuable water for her friend. Kemar figured that she must've grabbed the goods while Phan questioned him. It was an act that could easily have cost Son Ba her life.

Kemar grabbed the jug, which was still capped, and the bag of fish. He spotted an old blue coffee can floating near him. As he placed it into the cooler, he reasoned that it was the object Mir Ta had added to Son Ba's survival kit. Kemar found the old bungee cord dangling from the one handle. He stretched the cord around the cooler, secured the lid, and held on, wondering if he'd ever see his two friends again.

His thoughts drifted back to his mother's words, "Good friends are hard to lose." And the boy reflected, *Unless they're my friends.* He'd already lost so many in his young life. Once again, he was alone, without direction, family, or companions. But the boy smiled as he considered that perhaps he did have one other pal, the octopus who'd earlier helped him retrieve the cooler. He noted, ironically, that this would also be a friend he'd probably never see again.

A high-pitched laugh jolted Kemar from his thoughts. It startled the boy. Right in front of him, a large, gray dolphin emerged from the sea, looked him over, and laughed its squeaky, whistle-like giggle before dipping beneath the surface and swimming below the boy. Although Kemar didn't perceive it, the dolphin was telling the boy its name.

Again, the cooler shot into the air, the lid popped free, and a dolphin swam off with one of Son Ba's flounders. Gathering the cooler and its contents once more, Kemar was relieved to see that he was surrounded by mischievous dolphins rather than dangerous sharks. In fact, the dolphins might actually be able to keep the sharks at bay.

Kemar watched the beautiful creatures as they swam, ate, and cavorted all around him. The night air was filled with their chuckling, clicking, and splashing. They seemed so happy. Kemar had always liked dolphins, but he did get a little nervous when one after another rubbed up against him. The boy didn't know if it was accidental or whether they were merely having fun or perhaps planning something more sinister.

At one point, he reached down and stroked a large adult who floated next to him. In the shimmering moonlight, he could see lines on its smooth hide where others had run their teeth across its skin. He scratched the lines, hoping to soothe the dolphin, then ran his hand along its back, tracing the outline of white spots and brown patches.

He reached out and gently grasped the prominent dorsal fin, and as he did, the dolphin began to tow him slowly. The animal didn't dive or try to shake the passenger free in any way. It seemed to the boy that the dolphin was leading him somewhere.

Kemar couldn't decide whether or not to let go. Another smaller dolphin appeared on his other side and nudged up against him. The human understood that he was at the mercy of these beasts. It was clearly their ocean. But he reasoned that as long as he held on and allowed the dolphins to pull him, he could save energy and wouldn't drown.

So Kemar held one dorsal fin, slipped an arm through the bungee cord wrapped around the cooler, and grasped the other dolphin's fin as well. He felt the power of these mammals as they cut through the water, ignoring currents and waves. With some of them almost ten feet long and several hundred pounds of muscle, the dolphins commanded the human's respect.

Moving along effortlessly at a steady clip, Kemar fell into a light sleep. In his restless dreams, he returned to memories of Japanese and Korean tuna boats. He recalled the massacred dolphins hanging from enormous fishing nets, raised by cranes above massive decks. It reminded him of Cambodia's killing fields and, in a strange way, helped him bond with his finned friends. Both were very familiar with terror.

But then the boy began to worry. Were these dolphins holding him responsible for the carnage of their species? Could they actually be dragging him somewhere to enact their own vengeance upon him? They certainly could do it if they wanted to. They had the brains and the brawn to accomplish such a dark design. Still, the boy didn't relax his grip, yet he was unsettled by the thought that something horrible might be in store for him at the end of this journey.

Truth be told, the thought of his own death didn't move the young Cambodian the way it once might've. At a tender age, he'd witnessed too much death. Before he'd escaped, he'd seen his countrymen execute many of his family and friends. Some were dispatched quickly, others died more slowly, and still others just disappeared.

As far as Kemar could understand, no one had ever been killed with good reason, and many who continued to live under the Khmer Rouge might've been better off dead. That was the realization that had caused Kemar to plan his escape. His family and friends were gone. His home was gone. He no longer went to school. He was a starving child slave in a rice paddy, waiting for his turn to collapse or be escorted for a final journey into the bush.

By the time he left Cambodia, Kemar felt he was already dead inside. For him, life ended when the Khmer Rouge was born. So if he actually perished escaping or on the boat or out at sea with the dolphins, it really didn't mean so much to him. Kemar would fight for his life because instinct dictated he should, but if he lost the fight, it wouldn't matter.

And so he held on to the dolphins, numbed by the cold water, numbed by the threat of death, numbed by being alone on a dangerous sea. He closed his eyes and tried to rest, wondering what he might find when he opened them again.

It was night on the reef. Just as Binti would be difficult to see, the same was true for those who hunted her. And there were many predators who didn't need to rely on sight to hunt. In fact, the night signaled the release of an entirely different population of hunters.

Dolphins and whales use a form of radar—echolocation—so light or dark doesn't really have an impact on their ability to feed. Other creatures sense movement in the water or in the sand. Still others are able to pick up minute electrical impulses that flow within a prey's body, an ability the hammerhead shark has more or less perfected. Many species combine several senses with their own unique forms of cunning and stealth. There was no end to the way prey could be identified, and so, day or night, one had to be careful.

Without question, the most dangerous times on the reef were dusk and dawn, the times of a thousand shadows. When the sun rose and fell, predators embarking on their hunt crossed paths with predators concluding their feeding. The result was twice the number of predators on the prowl, many of them quite famished.

By the time the sun began to breach the horizon, Binti hadn't made it all the way to her home. She'd shot the current with Ebb much longer than she should've. As she ducked into a coral crack near her den, she saw that it was occupied. A parrotfish, covered in mucus, was breaking out of its bedtime bubble to start a new day.

The bubble was an interesting defense, Binti thought. It wasn't strong enough to keep a shrimp out, but it did seal up the parrot's scent, masking it from would-be predators. It probably also provided the creature with a relatively silent slumber.

The nautical napper looked up at the octopus and yawned. "I'm just leaving. Feel free to use the crevice until I return."

"Thank you," Binti replied. "That's very kind."

"Yeah, I'll probably have a bite to eat." The parrot yawned. "OoouuuAHHHhhhh. Then I'll lumber off to, ooouuuAHHHhhhh, the cleaning station for a while. Have 'em take a little off around the gills."

"Yes, I've seen you before. You get trimmed at the goby cleaning station over by the purple sponges, right?"

"I do. Nobody cleans like those little gobies. No, indeed . . . aaaAHHHhhh . . . Well, maybe I'll go a little later. Why be first in line?"

"What's the rush?" Binti agreed.

The parrotfish picked up what was left of his mucus sack and slipped it back over him, saying, "I got a lot to do today. Most fish think that means you better get an early start. But the way I see it . . . aaaAHHHhhhh . . . when you have a lot to do, the best thing is to go to sleep. Then, when you wake up . . . aaahhhaaa . . . you'll have enough energy to take on your chores with vigor. Maybe I . . . aaaAHHHhhhh . . . Maybe I better rest up a little more. Got an ocean of work ahead of me."

"Okay, I'll see you at the station sometime," Binti said as she abandoned the cozy crack.

"Save me a place in li . . . AHHHhhh." The parrotfish was back asleep before the octopus cleared the opening.

Binti's lair was close by. She wanted to dash for her entrance, but two seemingly minor details prevented her from doing so. The first was that the brown sponge that she always placed in the entryway after she left was lying in the sand a few fins from the rocky recess. This wasn't a good sign. It suggested visitation. And that worried the mollusk.

But even more distracting was the passing of a nudibranch. The wonderful creature was swimming right at Binti, who froze, adjusted her camouflage, and watched. The small animal rocked and flailed her decorative fan-like lungs for all to see. It was an elaborate display of color and grace, one that Binti would never dare make. The nudibranch swam in the open water, bright, bold, breathtaking, and without any fear. Indeed, her defiant colors demanded attention.

For a creature with no teeth, no spine, no speed, and no camouflage, it had a very potent defense, one that enabled it to travel anywhere on the reef with impunity. The nudibranch had no food value, and it couldn't be eaten even if it did. The prancing dancer was packed with poison. Its bright colors warned all others to treat it with respect. Look, admire, even joke—but don't touch.

Binti loved nudis for their attitude. They grimaced at groupers, smiled at sharks, and blew kisses to barracudas. They lived on the edge confidently. It was a concept that was totally foreign, totally exciting for the octopus who, quite literally, turned green with envy.

The sunlight disappeared momentarily while a fifty-foot-long, two-ton whale shark lumbered overhead. As the gentle giant continued on its way, the sunlight returned, and the coral shimmered once again.

Intoxicated with the bravado of the exotic nudibranch, Binti burst into her lair, prepared to meet whatever might be there. It was a foolish thing to do, but the octopus was feeling surfy. Luckily, her home was empty. Binti quickly slapped a sucker on the brown sponge and sealed herself from the rest of Makoona.

With an entrance only a few suckers wide, her lovely little lair opened into a more spacious abode once she was safely inside. It was the perfect place to lay her eggs and protect them, the most important part of any female octopus's life.

Binti glanced at the brown sponge she'd stuffed into her doorway and tried to remember when she started using it. As she strained her mantle, furrowing it with deep lines of thought, even though her powerful brain was located closer to her neck, she realized that she'd never consciously decided to use the sponge.

The inspiration had come to her from somewhere else, somewhere inside her that was not actually thought. The same was true for her home. No one had ever told her what to select or where it could be found, and yet here it was, and here she was.

For a relatively young octopus of only two years, Binti knew a lot about life on Makoona. How did she know so much? Was she simply very intelligent, or was it something else? By now, Binti's internal dialogue was running like a tidal wave across the sea, sweeping over one observation after another. And then she realized something else: that she'd never actually seen an old octopus. A couple of times, she spotted large males at the edge of the reef who looked pretty old, but Binti couldn't ever remember seeing an old female.

What was the reason for that? she wondered. Was there some disease that affected only mature females? Was the man-tide involved? Perhaps she was missing something. It was a topic she'd love to talk to the spirit-fish about, but without a proper shell, she believed the discussion would never happen, that only wearing the right shell would enable her thoughts to reach the spirit-fish.

Time and Tide

Kemar opened his eyes as the sand brushed against his skin. It was good to feel the soft earth beneath his feet. He stood. And then it hit him: he stood! He was on dry land!

Kemar looked around. He was standing on a small sandbar, small enough for him to know without taking a single step that he was alone. A dozen paces wide in any direction, the small patch of sand barely split the surface of the vast water. He stood on a whisper, a quiet little spot that the ocean hadn't heard, for surely if the

ocean knew about this subtle interruption, it would've swept over the sandy intrusion and washed it from existence. But the island survived, and so did Kemar.

Looking out to sea, the young Cambodian spotted a flurry of dorsal fins slicing through the deep green beyond the pale blue that ringed the sand. The boy guessed that having done their good deed, his dolphin saviors were heading back to their own corner of creation.

Kemar sat down comfortably on the red cooler to ponder his fate. For some reason, he seemed to ponder better when he sat. The boy was happy to finally feel dry. However, he had no idea how he was going to find food or water or get off this barren patch that was little more than a sandy life preserver. Kemar began to tap the cooler with the heel of his foot, another movement that increased his ponder power.

Maybe it was the sitting, or maybe it was the tapping, but the boy's neurons started to fire once again. The cooler! He remembered that Son Ba and Mir Ta had filled it. He remembered that he retrieved fish, water, and other goodies when the lid slipped off.

Not quite sure what was still in there, Kemar knelt in front of the plastic box, which seemed more like an altar at the moment. He flipped the white lid open and looked inside. Some salt water had seeped in, moistening a dried flounder fillet and several salted perch. Overripe fruit tumbled along the bottom. There was a plastic jug with drinking water, an extra kremar wrapped around a fillet knife, and a cheap, waterlogged compass, as well as a tin can that looked like it might store rice or beans.

Little more than a swatch of cloth, the kremar could be very useful. The boy spread it out on the sand and arranged his booty to dry in the steadily rising sun. Any trace of the lingering cool night air would soon be burnt away.

After a hearty glug of water and a modest morsel of fish—since it was unclear how long these provisions would have to last—Kemar began his work. At first, he thought it would be good to erect some type of signal flag or fire that a passing boat might see. But all the island offered in the way of materials was sand and water.

And since there was no vegetation, there was also no shade. The boy knew he would have to escape the sun if he was going to survive any length of time, so he moved to the center of the sandy plot and began to dig.

Like a ghost crab, he burrowed, figuring that he would dig as deeply as he could until he struck water. Then he'd construct sand walls a foot or two high if they'd hold. He'd tie the ends of his two kremars together and drape them, along with his clothes, over the top of the shelter. If it didn't get too windy, he might find relief from the sun and the heat.

After a little more than a foot of digging, the sand became cool and hard. The digging hurt the boy's raw hands, which were water-logged and sore from his dolphin rickshaw ride. Kemar picked up the coffee tin, thinking it could make a suitable scoop in the more densely packed sand. He popped the plastic lid. Frozen by what he saw inside, the canister slipped from his hands and landed upright in the supple sand.

The vessel contained neither coffee nor beans. And although it was quite full, there was nothing in the tin for Kemar to eat. In fact, with his present situation in mind, there was nothing in the tin of any use at all. Still, it was an incredible sight—gold. Lots of it.

Mir Ta, as generous as he was large, had filled the can with gold taels—thin, leafy sheets of the precious metal that refugees used to pay for their passage on the boat or to bribe officials as they escaped from their homelands. They were more valuable than currency, even U.S. dollars, in that virtually no one would refuse to accept them.

Kemar knew where these came from. Three days ago, he'd told Mir Ta that he found Captain Phan's stash stuffed in a section of unused pipe. The pipe was mounted vertically from the ceiling to the floor in a remote corner of the engine room. A façade, the pipe led nowhere and did nothing other than house Phan's blood money. Often extorted from vulnerable shipmates, other times taken as a bribe or gratuity, more than occasionally stolen, there was a lot of gold in that pipe.

It had been a coordinated effort, the boy guessed. Son Ba filled the cooler while Mir Ta raced to the engine room, knowing that everyone would be watching Kemar's demise. Mir Ta seized the opportunity to be alone in there. He was so large, he could've popped the pipe out in an instant.

The boy wondered if he'd stuffed all the gold into the can. Did he give the entire treasure to his waterlogged friend, or did he keep some for himself? Kemar hoped he'd held on to some of it, but whatever his intentions, Mir Ta had thrown his friend a golden lifeline. Little did he know that Kemar would gladly have traded the whole can for a leaky raft and a paddle with a hole in it.

Placing the taels in the cooler, Kemar used the empty can to continue digging. He scooped out a cozy crater and used the heavy, wet sand to construct two-foot walls. He made them two feet thick as well, pouring a little sea water on the sand to mold and pack it solidly. Next, he stretched out his two kremars over the top and piled sand along the edges all the way around. A frisky wind would surely whip the fabric from the sand, but for the time being, the primitive shelter would protect him from the sun. There was, however, something else the shelter was powerless against, something the boy had optimistically overlooked.

It was a busy morning for the gobies of Makoona. Everyone was up to their pectoral fins in work, and still, clients were lined up. Paykak, the leader of the station, didn't have time to chat with his friend. Knowing the octopus as he did, he was pretty sure she'd be asking him and several of his patrons what shells they've seen. On a slow day, that wasn't a problem, but Paykak and the gobies prided themselves—actually, they were obsessed—with providing fast and efficient service.

The coral reef cleaning station was one of the most remarkable places in the sea. It provided an unparalleled example of mutual trust between species. Tiny gobies hovered above their station, flashed their neon stripes, and waited for customers to swim in.

The clientele consisted of virtually all the larger fish of the reef and many of the smaller residents. Groupers, bass, rays, eels, jacks, triggers, and even barracudas would stop in for cleanings regularly.

Lined up in single file, they'd slowly approach, one at a time. An old sawfish named Shnozz loved to swim in and point her head down at the sand, almost bowing to the gobies. She'd raise her fins, open her mouth, and spread her gills wide. Then a pair of gobies would look Shnozz over, discuss their findings, and get to work. One or two cleaners would enter the sawfish's mouth, completely disappearing inside the creature, working on teeth, mouthparts, and beyond. Anywhere else in the sea, the gobies would be snapped up and swallowed, but at the cleaning station, that never happened.

According to the law of the reef, the gobies were expected to give any fish a thorough cleaning, eating all the parasites that lived in and on it. They also consumed lesions, scar tissue, and remnants of past meals as they attended to the general hygiene of the fish. The fish benefited from the cleaning, while the gobies got plenty of free food without having to search very hard to get it.

But all this was based precariously on one very important rule: neither the gobies nor the patrons could be eaten or harmed while they were at the cleaning station. However, once a fish cleared the bounds of the station, it was back to survival of the fittest. The rule was generally obeyed by all.

Binti enjoyed visiting the cleaning station. Occasionally she'd get in line for a little nip and pluck around the suckers or the siphon, but Binti was really there more for the interaction than the actual cleaning.

There were two other things the octopus liked about the station. The first was the unique sense of cooperation and relaxation. Since no one worried about being eaten, it presented a rare opportunity to relax. Makoona always seemed more beautiful when Binti saw it from the cleaning station. The coral colors seemed deeper, sharper. The fish were more interesting. The water was easier to breathe. For Binti, the cleaning station was a special place. There were always excitement, rumors, and news.

The other thing she really liked about visiting Paykak was meeting new fish. In that sense, she was unlike the rest of her kind, who tended to be a solitary lot. Because no one was very concerned about being eaten, Binti could actually converse with potential predators, sometimes even as friends.

The predators, however, usually fell into two categories, neither of which could be described as friendly. Either they wouldn't interact with you at all, because it's harder to eat an acquaintance, or they'd talk to you all day, finding out where you lived and where you fed. They'd get your scent. They'd study you in a friendly way. And then, after you both left the cleaning station, they'd look for you.

Without a doubt, the most remarkable behavior of predators at the station was their restraint. Imagine how simple, how enticing, it would be for a barracuda to bite a goby or for a gang of snappers to butcher a bass waiting to be cleaned. It didn't happen, and there was a very good reason why. Everyone in Makoona knew the story of Sledge, a hammerhead shark who didn't follow "the rule."

As the legend was told, Sledge was waiting in line one afternoon. The line was rather long, and the shark had already been warned about finning to the front. He was a rather selfish, impatient creature who would fin his way in front of others as if his time were somehow more valuable than anyone else's.

The gobies worked diligently but slowly. The sun started to set, and all the other fish had been cleaned except Sledge. When it finally came time for his cleaning, the shark approached the pair of gobies who waited for him. The two were tired and full after cleaning fish all day, but since Sledge had waited so long, they agreed to clean him anyway.

Rather than be appreciative that the gobies were tending to his needs, the hammerhead complained, "I waited here all afternoon. I haven't eaten, and now everyone else is heading out to feed. You're getting your meal from me, and *I'm still here*, SO HURRY UP!" As if his tantrum wasn't annoying enough, Sledge added volume to his complaints. He was one loud shark.

Gobies don't enjoy being yelled at, especially when they're cleaning, so one of them, Yhtac, calmly said, "Sledge, there are other things that we would like to be doing too. And you know as well as we do that we don't have to clean anyone after sunset. The only reason we're still here is that we want to make your wait worthwhile so you don't have to take more time from your very important life and return here sooner than necessary."

While the former part of the goby's statement was somewhat fish-etious, the latter part about not wanting Sledge to return sooner was as true as the tide. The pair knew that the better they cleaned the hammerhead, the longer he'd be out of their lives, so they worked quite gilligently.

Then Sledge barked, "You're not trying to help me out. You're just slow. I could do better rubbing up against barnacles!" The feisty fish was suffering from a classic case of cleaning station rage.

Having heard quite enough, the gobies emerged from the hammerhead's gills and said, "Fine, go rub up against some barnacles."

And as they turned to swim off, Sledge swallowed one of the cleaners.

Yhtac screamed, "Spit Laup out! Don't be stupid! Come on, he's Paykak's cousin!"

Sledge smiled, Laup's tailfin hanging from a space between his jagged teeth. The shark sucked it in and swallowed, saying, "Oops, too late." Then he stared at Yhtac and asked coldly, "Who's next?"

The remaining goby dove under a rock while Sledge, humming to himself, swam off into the darkening blue.

When Paykak heard about Laup's demise, knowing that all the cleaners of the reef were united in this principle, he decreed that there would be no cleaning anywhere on Makoona for two days. This didn't ingratiate Sledge to the rest of the reef's residents, who had all types of raw wounds and parasites that needed tending to. But Paykak went a step further, declaring Sledge an "uncleanable." It might very well be the worst fate that can befall a fish.

Oh, it might take a little time, but eventually, Sledge would return to the cleaning station and beg to be cleaned, a request no goby or any other cleaner would honor. As an "uncleanable,"

Sledge's wounds would fester, parasites would abound, disease and bacteria would proliferate, and ultimately, Sledge the mighty and ungracious hammerhead would die a slow, horrible death.

And that is why no fish, no matter how mighty, wanted to ignore the rules of the goby cleaning station. Sledge provided an apt reminder to the rest of the reef as to just how powerful the little fish could actually be.

After a refreshing rest in his most humble of abodes, Kemar woke and decided he'd dine on a piece of overripe fruit, figuring he'd eat the foods most likely to spoil first. The boy crawled out of his hole, stood, and bent over the red cooler. He removed a soft mango, took a bite, looked down, and noticed that the tide was rising. As a matter of fact, it was rising quite rapidly. While he'd dozed, at least a third of his island sanctuary had been reclaimed by the sea.

The tide was definitely a problem, but in order to know just how much of a problem it was, Kemar would need to know exactly how high it would rise. If the tiny patch wasn't completely engulfed, this would be little more than a survivable annoyance, but if the tide washed his footing away, it could cost the boy his life.

Kemar gazed at the sand beneath him. He knelt down and rubbed his hands across the hot, dry surface. His knees and toes sunk into terra that was not so firma. Kemar poked around, hoping to find evidence of a diminutive plant that might suggest the salt water never reached its sensitive roots. He didn't find any.

It wasn't long before the tide covered the island. Kemar's hut had washed away. He was left sitting on his cooler, praying that the water had reached its apex. The boy turned the cooler on its side, which added about six inches of height to his precarious perch. He certainly could've stood on the sand not too far below the water, but it was safer and dryer to sit on the cooler. Kemar hoped that the high-water mark had more or less been reached.

Over an hour later, the boy was no longer sitting on his cooler. It was underwater, and he was standing on it. Had he stepped off the plastic box, he would've had to tread water to keep his head above the sea. The boy could feel the rising tide wet the top of his neck. And as the ocean rose, the sun set. A sliver of sun clung to the sky, while sparse tufts of thin clouds veiled faint stars and a moon that seemed to shove the remaining daylight beneath the horizon.

Boom! The sound of a nearby explosion cracked through the still air. Thunder, perhaps even a distant volcano, Kemar thought. With the run of luck he was having, Kemar felt that it could even be both, or maybe some nation was test firing nuclear weapons nearby. Yet the sky was cloudless. The noise didn't appear to be weather related. There'd been claps of thunder earlier in the day, but they were much more distant, and Kemar had taken little notice of them as the tide demanded more and more of his attention. *Boom!* This explosion was so close, it couldn't be ignored.

At this point, the tide wet Kemar's earlobes. Where there was once a claustrophobic crease of sand, there now appeared to be a boy's face floating like a coconut on the calm sea. In just a few moments, Kemar would be forced to abandon his perch, hug his cooler, and cast his fate to the currents once more.

Another problem occurred to the boy. As a fisherman, he knew that when the water returned to the sand, predators followed to see what had emerged for them to feed on. Kemar wondered if something might find him.

And just as Kemar slipped off the cooler and started to tread water, something did find him. A bright light hit his eyes, blinding him temporarily. The boy heard the distinctive sputter-putt-putt, sputter-putt-putt of a slow-moving outboard motor.

The light grew brighter as the sound grew louder. The beam bounced up and down with the tiny swells. When the light struck his eyes, Kemar saw nothing, but when it broke away for a second or two, the boy could glimpse a small boat, under twenty feet, with what appeared to be one person on it, approaching slowly.

Kemar shouted and waved with nervous delight—delighted to be found, yet nervous about who had found him. He'd been a boat person. He'd seen firsthand just who the people were who inhabited the ocean—who they could be. He knew there was no shortage

of pirates or criminals or opportunists on the sea. On the boat with
Son Ba, one of their biggest fears was being targeted by pirates who
knew that boat people were usually very easy marks.

Then someone called, "Is a body beneath a head?"

All the boy could say was, "Help me … please take me aboard."

Even though Binti was very safe at the cleaning station, she continued to use her camouflage. She couldn't help it. She didn't really know how to turn it off. Her posture, her shape, and her color
would all change automatically based solely on her surroundings.
The only time her primary defense system could be short-circuit-
ed was during intense emotional situations—terror, birth, mating,
or anger to name a few.

In one sense, Binti was lying to herself. She pretended that the
reason she came to the cleaning station was to socialize, but that
wasn't the whole truth. Deep inside her mantle, she hoped that
she'd meet a creature who knew where she could find her special
shell. Both Paykak and Hootie had seen enough to know that any
conversation with Binti inevitably touched on the topic of shells at
one point or another. The octopus was obsessed.

While she gabbed with a grouper named Fraco and a snail
she'd never met before, the discussion turned to shells.

"I don't think the odds are with you on this," Fraco said in his
waterlogged baritone.

"Why not?" Binti asked. "You don't think I'll find my shell?"

"Well, you don't really have a shell. You've evolved without the
need for one. So why waste your time looking? Just go with the evo-
lutionary flow. You know, in a way, you're almost violating the intent of the spirit-fish."

"That's not true," Binti countered. "I may not have a shell, but
I'm a mollusk, so I should have one."

"Squid's a mollusk. It doesn't have a shell. I never heard one of
them complain."

"They're squids! It's different."

"So what? You want to be a nautilus? A cuttlefish, perhaps? They're kinda like octopuses with shells."

"You're on another species again." Binti blushed deep red in frustration. "It's about an octopus and a shell. Not squids. Not nautiluses. Not cuttlefish. An octopus. Me. Get it?"

The grouper shook his large head. "Well, you're the one who mentioned mollusks. I'm just following your thought." Fraco didn't buy her argument at all, but he did enjoy the discussion. "You should have what you have. Let me ask you this. Have you ever seen an octopus with a shell?"

"But that's not the—"

"Oh yes, it is the point. You're an octopus. Your kind don't have shells. You just want what you can't have. The algae's always greener on the other reef."

Speaking as much to herself as she was to the grouper and the silent snail, Binti blurted, "I just want one! Think how beautiful it'll look on me. Think how difficult it'll be to eat me. I'll be stronger *and* more beautiful. I *need* a shell."

The snail finally spoke up, although a little tentatively because some octopuses love to eat the little gastropods. "The name's Noril. I hope you don't mind, but you've got one big problem." The snail carried instant credibility, carried it right on her back.

"I'd love to hear from an expert," Binti said. "So what's my big problem?"

The snail studied Binti with her eyestalks. Then she said, "Size. You're too big for a shell. Believe me, I know from shells. And I've never seen a shell that would fit you."

"Snail's got a point there," Fraco echoed.

"No, she doesn't. What does she know? I don't have any bones. I could fit into lots of shells."

"Next!" a goby called.

"Well, that doesn't sound very practical," the grouper observed.

"NEXT!" the impatient goby shouted. "Come on, Freako, move those fins!"

"It's Frac-o," the grouper grunted. "Sea ya, Binti. I think you're wasting your time, but if I see any good shells, I'll let you know . . . Nice to meet you, Noril."

"Thanks, Fraco. Have a good cleaning." Binti turned to the outspoken little snail, who was sifting through the sand looking for a snack, and asked, "Honestly, do you think I'm wasting my time?"

Noril held out her head, stretched her long, slender body, blinked her eyes, and said, "It's not for me to say. It's your time. Do what you want with it."

Binti pressed, "But you live in a shell. This should make sense to you."

"When a little snail who needs protection slips into its shell, that, bubble-uh, makes sense to me. I have a cousin who wears an anemone on her back. That even makes sense to me. But you're an *octopus*. You don't need a shell."

Frustrated and disappointed, Binti quipped, "You don't understand."

Noril flashed a knowing smile and said, "Maybe I don't. I'm not a mollusk or an octopus. But let me tell you what I do understand. I wear a shell. All day, every day. And believe you me, it's not as wonderful as you think it is. This thing is heavy, it's hard, it slows me down. It's lonely too. I'm in here all by myself. I'd love to swim around naked like you and everyone else in Makoona, but if I did that, I wouldn't live too long. I can't be you any more than you can be me."

"But I don't want to be you."

"Yes, but you want to be like me. Listen, let me tell you something my mother told me. Maybe it'll help. What you are is the spirit-fish's gift to you. What you make of yourself is your gift to the spirit-fish. Think about it, my friend."

As she swam away, squeezing water through her siphon, Binti reflected on the logic of the gabby gastropod. *Why should I swim against the current?* she wondered. *I am what I am, a shell-less, boneless camouflage creation. I should accept what I've been given and make the most of it.*

But even with those thoughts swimming inside of her, Binti knew, out of the corner of her eye, she'd always be looking for a shell. And, although she told no one, she believed it was precisely what the spirit-fish wanted her to do. Hopefully, the shell, the quest, or both would reveal some larger truth to her.

Binti swam along the landward side of Makoona, where she could usually find an easy meal. Ironically, she was hunting for snails slightly larger than the one who just counseled her. And when Fraco was done with his cleaning, he might be hunting for an octopus, among other things. It was reefality, the law of the sea.

She felt it as soon as it washed across her, a slight chemical change in the water picked up by her highly developed senses. She could taste the caustic bitterness against her body. Then she felt a subtle crease in the current waft against her supple skin. It didn't occur to her that had she been wearing a shell, her skin might not have registered these clues. But she wasn't wearing a shell, and she did pick up on them. Binti was being hunted. The octopus had three choices: freeze and blend, hide, or flee. And she had to decide quickly.

The chemical disturbance, stronger now, stroked her skin again. Binti's greatest fear as an octopus was realized—a moray was hunting her. Without thinking, she froze under a stand of green table coral and waited while her body turned dark green and took on the texture of the thicket. If the moray had already seen her, it would strike quickly. If it had only caught her scent, it would try to sniff her out, something most morays were quite capable of doing.

Binti hoped she had lost the predator, but the nerve endings on her suckers suggested that the moray was still on the prowl. The octopus wondered if it hunted her specifically or if it was just hunting in general. She raised her eyes slightly above her mantle so she could see almost three hundred and sixty degrees around her. Binti couldn't locate the moray, but she could taste the slime in the water.

Suddenly, something sharp clamped down on one of her limbs and began dragging her out from under the coral. It was the moray.

It, too, had changed color, sliding through cracks and hugging the sea bed until it found one of Binti's arms.

Instinctively, Binti slipped three other arms around the base of the coral and held on tightly. If the moray managed to pull her out into the open water, she'd be dead. The predator tightened its grip on her arm and tugged. Binti felt searing pain as its twisted, spiny teeth cut through her flesh. The teeth were angled so they would dig into and cling onto whatever they clamped down upon.

Binti felt her arm tearing from her body. Although she'd never lost an appendage, she'd met other octopuses who had. With their powers of regeneration, the arm would eventually grow back, but an octopus with seven arms instead of eight might be less able to feed and defend itself. In some situations, like her present circumstance, a missing arm could decide the delicate balance between life and death. And the fact that the arm would grow back did nothing to diminish the pain Binti felt at the moment. Besides, the arm would only grow back if the rest of the octopus survived.

The moray began to roll over and over, hoping to twist Binti loose. Her arms held the coral, but the pain caused her to lose focus. She tried to slip another pair of arms around a rocky outcrop to stabilize the twisting of the moray. As she reached for the rock, the base she was already anchored to snapped. The coral collapsed on top of her, and the moray dragged her out into the open water while the shards cut into her soft flesh. Binti's blue blood began to trickle into the reef. Soon, other predators would investigate.

When she emerged from the rubble, the moray, still locked onto her arm, began to spin itself again. This disoriented Binti, prevented her from anchoring herself or escaping, and allowed her attacker to get a better grip on another arm. Without having something to hide in or hold onto, Binti knew she'd die. The moray would never unlock its jaws. It wouldn't settle for an arm when it could eat an entire octopus.

In an act of desperation, Binti fired a blast of dark ink into the water between her and the moray.

An octopus doesn't like to release ink unless it's an emergency, because it can take time to build up a fresh supply. Normally, the ink would serve as a distraction and block the moray's senses of sight and smell, but Binti was already in its mouth. It didn't need to or smell her. It could taste her. Binti released the ink anyway, hoping the moray might ease its grip for a moment. It didn't.

The octopus was exhausted. They were surrounded by a cloud of silt, sand, black ink, and blue blood. The struggle had gone on as long as Binti's strength would allow. Camouflage could do nothing for her now. She couldn't jet away. She had no ability to hurt the moray. Her puny beak had little effect on the thick length of muscle that twisted and shook her. Poison that would have paralyzed lesser fish was essentially useless against the moray.

Binti began to think about how quickly her life had passed, how little she'd accomplished. She had no mate. No young would survive her. She hadn't found the shell that would unite her with the spirit-fish. Her life on Makoona was less than a ripple on the sea.

Binti knew that it was over, that she was experiencing her final moment, but for some reason, she couldn't accept that her life had ended. Making a final attempt to free herself, Binti released her chewed-up arm from her body, hoping it might give her an opportunity to flee.

Before the octopus could retreat, a sudden surge of water rolled over her and slammed her onto the sandy floor. Pinned to the bottom, she was pushed down into the sand. It was as if the moray had somehow felt the need to bury its meal. But the predator's jaws no longer held her. Binti emerged from the sand, jetted off into a patch of sponges, squeezed under one, adjusted her color, and froze.

With no idea why the predator had released its death grip, the octopus was afraid to even breathe. She tucked what was left of her severed arm beneath her, doing her best to keep her blood from marking her position.

The moray had disappeared. *Where did it go? Why did it vanish?* the octopus wondered. Perhaps the spirit-fish also didn't like the timing of Binti's demise. And then she saw it hovering inside a wide, dark coral cave, staring in her direction. At the moment, it was dressed in gray with black spots. As she watched him, Binti

realized that it wasn't an eel at all. It was Fraco from the cleaning station.

Dangling from the corner of his mouth was the green tail of the moray. What Binti saw next literally caused the octopus to turn white. Hanging from the other side of Fraco's mouth was Binti's arm. The massive grouper chomped down one time, sucked in both the tail and the arm, shook his head side to side, and swallowed hard.

Just as the moray had transformed Binti from hunter to hunted, Fraco had transformed the moray. Binti had never been so happy to see the grouper before. *He must've grabbed it the moment it was about to finish me off,* she thought.

But even though Fraco had rescued Binti, seeing her arm disappear down her savior's throat provided good enough reason to be careful and to stay hidden. The octopus wasn't at the cleaning station any more. The rules were different out here. Binti would wait—she had all the time in the ocean. After all, she'd just been reborn. Binti turned herself a sandy yellow and hunkered down among the sponges. Life suddenly had a new sweet flavor, like lobster in her lair.

The son of highly educated parents, Kemar spoke several languages. Fluent in his native tongue, he was also comfortable speaking

French and English. He could stumble his way through a Chinese dialect or two and some Vietnamese. It was one of the main reasons the boy had been able to survive for so long on his own.

The man in the boat who extended his arm to Kemar was a middle-aged Chinese fisherman. The man smiled and helped the boy into his launch. As he climbed into the boat, the cooler popped up from beneath Kemar and started to float away unnoticed. When he hit the deck, Kemar dropped to his knees, exhausted. The fisherman handed him a water bottle, and the boy drank from it.

Barely an inch taller than the boy, the fisherman wore stiff, dirty pants that reached below his knees but came up well short of his ankles. His arms and legs were thin but seemed quite strong. A pack of cigarettes was stuffed into his soggy shirt pocket. The man's eyes virtually closed whenever he flashed his narrow, tobacco-stained smile.

Grinning at the boy and nodding approvingly, the fisherman said in passable English, "Am Bao." He gestured around him. "My boat . . . my reefs."

Kemar handed back the water bottle. "I think you came just in time . . . Do you know if the water would have gotten much higher?"

Bao looked up at the rising moon, allowed the breeze to blow over him for a moment, and then shook his head. "No, not much higher."

Kemar mumbled, "I could have made it."

Bao pointed to the spot where the boy had been perched and said, "Could put you back."

Suddenly Kemar's eyes went wide and he shouted, "The cooler! The gold!"

While the word "cooler" had little effect on Bao, the term "gold" seemed to register. He waited anxiously for the boy to expand on the statement.

"It was in the cooler. I was standing on it."

"Gold? In cooler?" Bao reached for a diving mask and a large lantern.

"It's in a blue can. It must be floating around here somewhere."

Instantly, Bao switched the lantern on and combed the swells. He and Kemar leaned over the side, shuffling from stem to stern and starboard to port, hoping to spot the treasure. Off in the distance, Bao locked the bouncing beam of the lantern on something sloshing in the swells.

"There!"

Kemar rushed to Bao's side. "That's it!" he yelled.

"Hold light, boy. Bao get boat there." Bao raced the vessel toward the object like he was chasing a school of tuna on the open sea.

"Hurry! It's sinking!"

Bao pulled alongside the cooler, gaffed the handle, and pulled it on board all in one smooth motion. The boy picked up the box, turned it upside down, and then faced Bao.

The fisherman said it for him. "Empty."

The two spent the next forty-five minutes trying desperately to find the gold. All they recovered were a mango and an orange. Dejected, Kemar peeled the orange while Bao turned the boat toward home. Focused on the fruit, the boy didn't notice his rescuer slip a bleach bottle buoy over the rail to mark the spot.

By the time they reached the crude bamboo structure that served Bao as a dock, the two had learned a few things about each other. Bao had heard an abridged version of Kemar's story, listened very carefully about the lost gold, and had formulated some plans for the boy. Kemar had learned that Bao usually liked to come in from the sea under cover of darkness so that others couldn't see what he'd brought in, or more importantly, how he'd come by his catch.

The boy saw that Bao was fishing with surplus grenades, which explained the explosions Kemar had heard just before Bao appeared. It seemed to be an effective way to fish. Working alone, Bao had returned with a very impressive catch. Kemar helped him unload fish and gear. For the boy, it felt strange to be on land again.

When they were done, the Cambodian asked the fisherman, "Where is this place?"

Bao grunted and said, "Makoona."

Responding to Kemar's blank stare, Bao continued, "Knowing name not really help much. Still have no idea where you are."

"Well, I have an idea," Kemar countered.

"No, you don't," Bao interrupted. "You nowhere." Then he picked a few loose items off the sand and casually strolled off.

Kemar called out, "Is there somewhere I can get work? Do you know anyone who will hire me?"

Bao turned back. "I just save life."

"Yes. Thank you again."

"Say 'thank you,' but ask, 'Is anyone I work for?' No debt to Bao? Now you safe from sea, and Bao have served purpose? Boy say 'thanks' and yet ask to work for another? Has Bao done nothing for you?"

"Well, what would you have me do?"

"No need to give back to Bao?"

"What do I have to give? Would you like my kremar, my shorts, my shirt? That's all I have."

Bao was setting the boy up. He knew exactly what he wanted. The time to strike had arrived. "Owe Bao a great debt, agree?"

Reluctantly, Kemar assented. "I guess I do."

"Since have no gold, why not give Bao labor? Could do that. Bao old and weak. Boy young and strong."

"It is something I could do, but without food or shelter, how much labor could I provide?" Now it was Kemar's turn to work Bao.

"If Bao not let boy drown in ocean, would not let boy starve on land. Will provide for you as long as you provide for Bao."

Kemar nodded. "I will give back, but when will my debt be paid?"

Bao shrugged. "Talk tomorrow."

With that, Bao threw Kemar the canteen, a crust of bread, a piece of fruit, and a fish from a green bucket. The fish looked more like bait than dinner, but Kemar had eaten much worse before. Then Bao and the boy pulled the boat onto the shore. Together, they flipped it over on the sand.

Kemar asked, "Do you mind if I sleep here under the boat?"

Bao smiled, pleased that he had someone to watch over his property. "Feel free. See boy in morning."

Kemar propped up the bow with a weathered log and crawled under the boat. Salt water dripped from the sides. The boy smiled to himself—once a boat person, always a boat person. And before he could think another thought, he was in a deep sleep.

Perhaps it was the trickle of water slowly stroking his thin forearm or the sound of the surf sliding across the sand, but while he slept, Kemar dreamed of the sea. He found himself swimming and breathing like a fish, moving through a reef he'd never seen, not realizing that he'd arrived at the other Makoona, the one beneath the surface of the sea.

In his dream, the fish he encountered didn't flee from him, nor did they attack him. Instead, they greeted the human as though he were a citizen of the reef. Kemar was searching for something, something that he might find in the coral of Makoona. Whatever he found would be the key to the rest of his life, or so his dream led him to believe.

Off on the seaward side of the reef, Kemar spotted a familiar face, someone he'd hoped he'd meet again one day. Son Ba was walking toward him. She grinned, stepping carefully over and around the corals that grew and bloomed everywhere. Although he couldn't see her clearly, she dredged up little puffs of sediment that caught the moonlight and fell sparkling back to the ocean floor.

Son Ba seemed to be waving him over. She apparently knew that this fish was actually Kemar. Excited to see Son Ba, Kemar swam to her. But as he got closer and saw her more clearly, Kemar hesitated. He became frightened.

Getting closer, he could see that Son Ba wasn't actually waving at him. She was reaching out to him. She stood in a decimated coral clearing, where the man-tide had dragged nets or dropped scare lines. The colors were faded. The stalks were broken. The corals were bleached. The fish were gone. Son Ba was the only living thing on the barren reef.

On her head, however, she had hair like a Medusa, but in this case, the undulating snakes were replaced with the coiling arms of an octopus. The creature's eight arms reached out of Son Ba's head, swaying back and forth like soft coral in a current. And even though he was frightened, Kemar felt compelled to reach out and accept Son Ba's extended hand.

When he touched her palm with his fingers, she clasped them firmly with both her hands. An octopus arm extended itself from behind Son Ba's ear. The bright orange limb stretched and wrapped itself around their hands, tightening like a constrictor.

Son Ba leaned over, kissed Kemar's cheek, and whispered into his ear, "Come with me."

Kemar shook his head no. "Come with me!" he heard again.

Light struck his eyes. Kemar woke. Bao stood over him, tipping the boat up.

"Come with me," the fisherman said again. "Time to make money!"

They dragged the boat back to the surf and loaded it up with gear, and while Kemar ate an extremely modest breakfast, Bao gently placed some wooden boxes in a bin near the stern, where he

hoped they wouldn't bounce around too much. The boy took no notice. His thoughts were still swimming in the coral Makoona. He
wondered what the dream meant and what Son Ba was about to tell
him.

Once again, Kemar was stirred from his thoughts by Bao, who
instructed the boy to drop anchor. Neither realized, nor did they
care to realize, that when the heavy metal anchor struck bottom, it
would crush and destroy a small patch of living coral that had tak-
en tens of thousands of years to form. This destruction, however,
would pale when Bao revealed how they were going to fish that day.

Anchored securely, the boat barely bounced on the diminutive
swells that tickled the hull. Bao was pleased.

"Won't it be difficult to net fish if we're anchored?" Kemar
asked.

"Not use nets today."

A pair of terns began hovering over the boat, anticipating free
meals of bait and throw-backs. They were joined by several other
birds. Bao didn't welcome the visitors, knowing that other fishermen always took note of where the birds gathered. He preferred
that no one notice where he was or what he was doing.

"Well," the boy probed, "if we're not netting, how do you expect to catch anything? Are they supposed to just jump into the
boat?"

"Are other, easier, more money ways to fish." Bao opened a
ragged umbrella and handed it to Kemar.

The boy was about to point out that there wasn't a cloud in the
sky until Bao raised his index finger to silence him. The older man
reached into the weathered wooden crate near the ancient outboard motor and pulled out a vintage American hand grenade.
Kemar had seen them before.

Bao bounced the sphere in hand once or twice, grasped it firmly, and scanned the area. Then he pulled the pin, tossed it overboard, reached out, took the umbrella from the boy, and sat down.
Kemar fell to the deck and covered himself.

BOOM! The sea exploded with the same sound Kemar had
heard while he stood on his cooler, up to his ears in ocean. Water

erupted, fizzed, and fell from above as if they were under attack from Thai pirates. The boat rocked. The birds scattered.

"Ha haaaa," Bao laughed, clutching his dripping umbrella. "Now get fish."

Kemar responded like a Labrador retriever. He jumped over the side and began bringing a variety of fish back to the boat. They all rose to the surface, dazed or dead. And then Kemar came across an angelfish that was conscious but floating sideways on the surface.

"Grab fish!" Bao screamed. "Quick, before get away."

Kemar scooped it up and swam back to the boat. "Why would you want this?" he asked. "We've got much better eating fish, and we don't need this for bait since we're not using any."

Bao said quietly, "Understand part of payment from Bao is knowledge. Already show you better way to fish. Now tell you something useful. Is man on Makoona who buy fish from Bao." He pointed to the stunned angelfish.

"But why?"

"Sell to another man from Philippines, who sell to someone from America or Europe or place people pay lot of money to have swim in tanks in homes."

"Why?"

"As possession."

"These fish are colorful, but don't they have colorful fish in America or Europe?"

Disgusted, Bao said, "Have no time with such question. But always have time take fool's money. Another lesson for boy. Someone has money to give, you take and not so many question. Otherwise, money go away."

Kemar nodded. He understood the logic.

"Gather all fish. Small one too. Keep alive and sell as well."

The boy did as he was told while Bao prepared another blast. Kemar didn't like the explosives. They seemed out of place on the reef, but more than that, the grenades reminded him of something he was trying to forget.

An Octopus's Garden

Binti had worked her way to the outer reaches of the reef, where she busily consumed crustaceans for her morning meal. She would've preferred to crawl into her den and nurse her wounds, safe from predators, but wounded or not, the octopus had to eat.

A spider crab had just slipped into a crease between two rocks, thinking that Binti wouldn't see him. The octopus didn't need to see him. She could feel him, sense him. Binti approached the rock carefully. She shrouded the entrance with her body and felt that the crab was sliding deeper into the crevice.

As the crab hunkered down, Binti cloaked herself in a dusty gray-blue, with bolts of green streaking her body. She'd become the reef. She was imperceptible—not from the crab, who was well aware of the octopus, but from anything else that might take notice of her activity.

Binti slid one of her remaining seven arms around the rear of the rocks and felt for another opening. When she found one, she worked her boneless arm into the crack. Then she reached a second arm around and felt for another opening. When she found it, she wedged her arm into the hole. She used a third arm to search for additional escape routes and found none.

Binti pushed the two arms that were already in cracks deeper into the rock. The crab panicked and rushed out the main entrance, where the octopus waited for her meal, which she quickly engulfed, paralyzed, and carried off to eat.

Reclining under the hull of a coral- and barnacle-encrusted lifeboat, Binti dined. She gave thanks to the spirit-fish for all her blessings; for her escape from the moray eel and for the bounty and beauty of Makoona. The world always seemed better to Binti when she had a crab to eat. It was her favorite food. She could eat it every day, every meal, and be totally happy. It fact, that's almost what she did.

But Binti also understood that she had just ended another creature's life in order to continue her own existence. It was a truth that the octopus took no joy in. Surely that crab was also a child of the spirit-fish. It, too, loved and lived Makoona. Binti considered Ebb, the farmer who ate algae, and wondered why she hadn't been created to live that life instead.

The octopus also pondered how she knew so many hunting and survival skills. She'd never known her mother or father, so how did Binti and other octopuses learn their social and survival skills? Retracing her brief life, Binti concluded that she'd somehow *remembered* the skills. They'd come to her as memories. But how, she wondered, could she remember something that she hadn't previously known?

And then Binti made another realization. For her, instinct and memory were related. What other fish might call instincts were actually memories passed on to her from her ancestors. Their collected truths seemed to live somewhere inside the cephalopod. Had her ancestors given her their knowledge, or was it more than that? Were they actually talking to her, she wondered.

Since she could certainly remember survival skills, Binti believed that if she tried hard enough, she could possibly remember aspects of her forerunners' day-to-day lives. She hoped that these memories might also be stored in some corner of her massive mantle, waiting to be tapped. The octopus had no idea how to call them up but believed if she could access these thoughts of the past, truths would be revealed.

Binti concluded that the spirit-fish could show her how to unlock the thoughts of eternity that lived within her. She finished her meal, and with a full belly, she continued her search for the singular shell that she believed would carry her questions to the sprit-fish.

As she cautiously crawled out from beneath the sunken boat, the ocean erupted. Coral, sand, rock, wood, fish—whole and in pieces—tore through the water in a thousand different directions. Binti was spun, bounced off a canyon wall, and crashed back into the wrecked boat along with a green sea turtle that was hurled on top of her. She took several coral and wood splinters, her flesh ripped by the intensity of the blast.

The agitated sea settled reluctantly. Bubbles, foam, and fizz rose to the surface as if the water itself were looking for a way to escape the mayhem. Everything that was alive and could move had only one purpose—to flee. Sea life raced off in every direction. Injured animals fought to collect themselves, taking toll of the terror.

Many floated to the surface, conscious but paralyzed, joining scores of dead who were already belly up. Others could only flap a single fin and wandered aimlessly in the open water, fighting for control of their bodies. Makoona, Binti's underwater Eden, had exploded.

Off in the distance, the octopus saw the ominous shadow on the surface. She hadn't noticed it earlier, the shadow that interrupts the sky and the sea. It was the shadow that carried the man-tide on the water. It was the shadow that enabled the man-tide to wash away the children of the reef. Then Binti saw him. A human was swimming, gathering fish in a small net.

Binti moved toward this human. When she got closer, the octopus knew she'd seen him before. He was the one who'd saved her from the nets a few days earlier. *Such difficult creatures to figure out*, she thought. *They are capable of such extremes. The man-tide can be so wonderful and yet so horrible.*

It probably wasn't a very smart thing to do, but Binti wasn't in complete control of herself at this point. Still numb from the blast, she wasn't sure whether she was swimming or merely being carried by a current. Binti had something to say to the human. She wasn't exactly sure what it was, but the octopus was going to give him a piece of her mantle.

The closer she drifted, the angrier she became. Binti surveyed the carnage, the pain and destruction of a section of reef that had been living in peace for thousands of years. What moments before had been paradise, an untouched example of the spirit-fish's perfect balance, was now obliterated. It was disgusting, a senseless waste to any creature who could claim the sea as home. The man-tide were invaders, desecrating something they couldn't comprehend, blind to the boundless beauty of Makoona.

To add insult to injury, one of the barbarians swam around joyously gathering the defiled inhabitants of the reef, who were paying with their lives for this madness. Seeing the pulverized pillars of coral all around her, Binti decided she would show this human, in the only terms he seemed to understand, that the creatures of the water wanted him to leave their sacred reef. The octopus would take up arms—seven of them—against her oppressor.

Swimming completely on her own now, she regained her strength. The man-tide had struck fear into Binti's three hearts, and she would try her best to return the favor. Even though the octopus was no match for the human, this was one of those times when it didn't matter. Binti didn't care that she was risking her life in this foolish attempt.

Her plan was to turn bright molten orange, the color of lava bursting through rock. It was the most intense color she'd ever seen. If she could get close enough, Binti intended to slap an arm or three around any available appendage, sucker down on the human, pull herself close, and try to slip in a quick bite from a beak sharp enough to cut through a clam.

If she could do that, she might even be able to slip a little venom the man-tide's way. She knew it would devastate a crab or a lobster, but she didn't know what effect it would have on a human. This seemed like a good time to find out.

Binti was, however, a little unsettled by the idea that this behavior was unthinkable for any creature of the sea who possessed the spirit. She certainly didn't intend to eat the human, and she made no attempt to flee his aggression. Using her venom for something other than hunting didn't float so well with her.

Hesitating for a moment, Binti reasoned that this actually was a matter of survival, a case of self-defense. In a larger sense, she *was* fighting for her life, fending off an attacker. Under those conditions, she believed the spirit-fish would see the need. Once she delivered her bite, Binti would ink him up and jet away. Her point would be made.

Within arms' length of her target, Binti burst into a searing orange and thrust out four of her arms. They missed the human, who at that instant climbed out of the water onto the floating shadow. But two of her arms managed to grab something . . . the little net. The octopus held fast and pulled it back into the sea.

A second later, something crashed through the surface, reaching down into the water. It had no suckers, no claws. Instead, one long arm with five little ones on the end of it wrapped themselves around the net and began to tug. It was the human. Several little fish trapped in the mesh escaped. But one unlucky goby still had a gill entangled in the mesh.

The human lifted the net out of the water with an enraged orange octopus still holding on.

Both Kemar and Bao cried out in surprise when the hand net emerged from the sea. They never expected to find an infuriated octopus waving its arms, looking, quite literally, like it wanted to pick a fight with them. Bao, initially shocked, began to laugh at the feistiness of the creature.

Kemar, however, was affected much more deeply. His thoughts immediately went to his dream. He saw, in front of him, the octopus that had seemed a part of Son Ba, just as it appeared the night before. And this octopus before him had also risen from a dead sea, just as the octo-Medusa had done in his dream.

Kemar couldn't drop the net fast enough, which only caused Bao to laugh even harder. Binti, net and all, returned to the sea in a sloppy splash. This was too much fun for Bao, who'd always found other people's discomfort amusing. The fisherman's delight subsided when he realized he'd lost a perfectly good hand net.

The outboard motor sputtered and pinged as the pair moved on to their next fishing site. Bao spent the time lambasting the boy over the loss of the net. Eventually, Kemar made it clear that he wasn't fishing with hand grenades, nor would he go back into the water to search for the net with that crazy octopus around, so Bao decided to try yet another method of fishing, eventually declaring, "Is fine. You will find way to replace net."

The suggestion, however, never registered with Kemar, who was deep in thought. The sight of the agitated octopus had thrown him. Why, he wondered, was he crossing paths with so many of these creatures? He'd seen two the day Phan abandoned him. He'd dreamed about an octopus. And now he'd been visited by yet another.

Then it occurred to the boy that it might not be several. Perhaps all the encounters were with one specific octopus. They were all the same size and in roughly the same place. What could it want? No, that wasn't possible. Kemar convinced himself that it was all merely coincidence.

Binti placed a heavy stone inside the net to help secure it to the bottom and then stuffed it under a huge rock. She wanted to ensure that no other creature might meander into the murderous mesh. Even without a human grasping it, the net could kill. Sadly, there was no need to release the entangled goby, but after a moment's thought, Binti removed the carcass so as not to tempt any other creature to explore the lethal net. Then she used her beak to snip a few holes into the mesh.

There were many things that the octopus was aware of that other reef dwellers didn't understand. Some creatures viewed great intelligence as a tool that enabled them to get what they wanted by fishipulating others, presumably less intelligent. Binti, however, saw her great mind, her awesome awareness, as a fishdate to do the right thing.

Anything less, she felt, disrespected the source of the gift, and she didn't want to offend or anger the spirit-fish. That wouldn't be the action of an *intelligent* creature. So Binti buried the dangerous net, which obviously wasn't part of Makoona.

Tucked securely into an old green bucket that was toppled, half submerged in the sand, and encrusted with yellow sponge, Binti rested. At first, she liked the idea of sitting in the plastic bucket. It was smooth and clean inside, almost like having a spacious shell. The octopus was relaxed and quite comfortable until she heard a voice.

It had the same tenor as the voice she heard within herself. It was soft and so clear, it could easily have been mistaken for a thought. But this voice didn't come from Binti. And since the bucket wasn't really a product of the sea, it could never be a conduit to the spirit-fish. Still, Binti heard a voice.

She lifted her eyes above the rim of the container. She listened to her senses. Binti couldn't locate the source of the sound, but a few seconds later, she knew exactly what produced the vocalization.

The speaker whispered, "Dressed myself in green, I went down to the sea. Try to see what's going down, maybe read between the lines. Had a feeling I was falling, falling, falling."

Binti heard the words yet couldn't quite figure out what they meant. She detected a slight shuffle at the base of the bucket and looked down. That's when she saw a large male octopus who, like the container, had dressed himself in seaweed green. Binti had never actually spoken to a male before. She wasn't exactly sure she wanted to speak to this one, but since it was a unique opportunity, Binti grinned, turned a demure shade of violet, and introduced herself.

The male replied, "You've got an empty cup only love can fill, only love can fill."

Confused, Binti pointed out, "This is not really a cup. Actually, it's a man-shell. And why do you speak of filling it with love? How could one put love into this?"

"Let's see with an honest heart these things our eyes have seen and know the truth will still lie somewhere in between," the male responded. Then he slipped up and under the encrusting sponge, flashed bright red, and settled into dull yellow with streaks of green.

By now, Binti perceived him as no threat. She was amused by his playfully bizarre way of speaking. "Do all males talk like you? You're not very easy to understand."

He laughed, returned to red for another instant, flashed scarlet with a touch of gray, and then became yellow and green. He carefully extended one arm toward Binti, saying, "See how everything led up to this day? And it's just like any other day that's ever been. Sun goin' up, and then the sun it goin' down. Shine through, and my friends, they come around, come around, come around." He waved several arms to accentuate the phrase "come around."

Confused, Binti asked, "What are you talking about?"

The male touched her mantle softly. It was a very intimate gesture. Binti could feel a single sucker gently take hold of her flesh and then release. The male mollusk whispered, "Maybe you'll find direction around some corner where it's been waiting to meet you . . . When push comes to shove, you're afraid of love." Deep, passionate purple and pink raced through Binti's arms.

In an instant, he turned blue with a touch of gray and jetted off, giggling, "Run and see, hey, hey, run and see!"

Binti had no idea what he meant. She wondered whether he was inviting her to follow him. She also wondered whether he might be a few fish short of a school. Binti had heard of reef dwellers who spoke circumspectly because they knew things and tried to hint at deeper meanings, although she didn't quite see this male fitting into that category. Perhaps he'd been in the reef when it exploded, she thought, which could scramble any octopus's mantle. She decided not to chase him.

Binti left the bucket and crawled along the bottom, changing color as she touched upon gray rocks, tan sandy patches, colorful corals, and spectacular sponges. She arrived at her home and paused to look for intruders. Not far from her crevice lived an anemone. In and around the anemone lived a pair of clownfish named Agora and Ozob.

"Hey neighbor," Ozob called. "What do you hear? What do you say?" Ozob never hovered more than a body length or two from his host anemone. His plantlike benefactor provided powerful protection. Only the clownfish could survive among its poisonous tentacles, so the anemone kept all predators at bay. In return, the clownfish cleaned their host, who wasn't mobile enough to visit the cleaning station. It was a wonderful example of cooperation in Makoona.

Binti didn't feel like recounting all the tribulations of the day, so she answered, "Nothing special. I did meet another octopus earlier."

Agora popped her head out. She was even less adventurous than Ozob. "He was here before," she said. "His name's Molo."

"You met him?"

"I know Molo," Ozob declared. "He was poking around your lair. But don't worry, I kept an eye on him."

"Really?" Binti flashed bright green, her curious color. "How do you know he's okay? Have you ever spoken with him?"

Ozob laughed. "He's definitely weird, not exactly normal, but he's okay . . . kinda like you."

"What?" Binti wailed. "*I'm* weird? You live in an anemone, and you call me weird?"

"Are we discussing you or Molo?" Agora asked. Then she disappeared deep into the anemone.

When Ozob did the same, the octopus picked up on the signal, slid behind a rock, turned brown, and disappeared. Something was coming.

A brief bubble later, Hootie drifted in puffed with excitement. "Binti! Binti!"

"Over here," a brown lump of rock replied.

"Binti, Ebb's got something for you."

Flushed with green, Binti asked, "What's that farmer got that would interest me? I don't particularly relish eating algae."

"Oh, it's not algae," Hootie puffed.

"Then what is it?" Ozob said as he slid his head beyond the anemone's tentacles.

Hootie looked to Ozob and then back to Binti. Satisfied that he commanded their rapt attention, he said, "I believe our friend has unearthed the shell that you've been looking for."

Binti turned mother-of-pearl blue and trembled. She lowered her mantle until it almost touched Hootie's snout. "Tell me about it."

Ozob squealed skeptically, "Don't let him get you excited again."

Agora added, "How many times has he claimed to have found your magic shell?"

"It's not magic," Binti corrected him.

"Whatever. It's a shell. And octopuses don't have shells."

"But mollusks do."

"And so will you," Hootie howled. He puffed himself up even further. "Allow me to escort you to your shell."

Binti paused and asked, "What about the other shell, the one Ebb claimed you had found for me?"

"Oh, that didn't clam out. I couldn't convince the conch to leave it. Anyway, don't worry about that. This is the one. I can fin it."

With that, Hootie swam off slowly. Binti followed as though she were in a trance.

As they left, Ozob yelled, "Don't be a sucker! I'd hate to see you get shell shocked again!"

On the way to their afternoon fishing site, Kemar began to think about his current situation. Where would he go? How would he fend for himself? The boy wondered if he could survive by fishing with Bao. Finally, he asked the man, "Are you going to pay me for my work today?"

Without looking at Kemar, Bao said, "Have not discussed already?" He quickly added, "After losing net and wasting explosives, boy should pay me."

The motor's distinctive sputter-putt-putt, sputter-putt-putt punctuated their discussion. Even though the water was calm, Bao's boat always seemed to run rough.

The fisherman hissed, "Ah, must bring motor to old American witch. Fix anything, but Bao hate hearing her stories and stupid ideas about reef. Not even on Makoona can escape crazy Americans."

"You know, neither of us is actually from Makoona either," Kemar pointed out.

"Neither of us is old woman."

The boy brightened. "Do you think she'll have work for me?"

Bao bellowed, "Is no other work! Not see? Only fishing. If there other work, don't think Bao be doing it? On Makoona, is only catching and selling fish."

"This person you speak of has found something else to do. Will you introduce me to her?"

Bao considered the boy and his suggestion. The way Kemar pursed his lips, the way the sun shone on his face, for an instant, he looked like a sea bass. Bao smiled. His demeanor changed. He had an idea. Bao told the boy that he'd introduce him to Meela and that when they returned, he would introduce him to all his friends on the island.

Kemar also looked differently at Bao. He recognized that not only had this man saved his life, but he had also sustained him for the last twenty-four hours. All he asked in return was that Kemar fish with him. *Is it possible that Bao is my friend?* the boy wondered.

Kemar had not had many true friends. Life in Cambodia and on the boat didn't produce situations where strangers—or, for that matter, even some family members—could be trusted. For the first time since he met Bao, Kemar began to trust that the fisherman would do right by him.

Although deep down, Kemar knew it might be foolish to believe in someone who fished with dynamite, the boy reasoned that he'd certainly seen others do much worse, not only to fish and coral, but also to friends and family. Bao had saved him. Bao was trying to make a living. With any luck, Kemar would do the same.

The ancient Evenrude outboard wheezed and sputtered, sounding like it was going to seize at any moment. Bao was frustrated because there were several solid hours of fishing left in the day, and he'd hoped to make good use of both the time and the boy.

Even without grenades, bait, or a decent net, he had another sure-fire method for catching the type of fish that the Filipino middleman would pay good money for. Indeed, the whole system of wasting money to keep fish in a tank that would never be eaten seemed absurd to Bao, but he never allowed absurdity to inhibit commerce.

The project, however, would have to wait one more day. At the moment, if the modest, leaky boat with the wheezing, pinging engine could make it, instead of fishing, Bao would be introducing the Cambodian boy to a somewhat senile seventy-something-year-old American woman who just happened to be the best—albeit the only—outboard motor mechanic within three hundred miles of Makoona.

The two fishermen drifted into the little lagoon where the American woman had set up shop. Her small hut was shaded by tall palms and lush mangrove trees. A dozen rusty oil drums, each filled with salt water, housing a mounted outboard of one type or another in various stages of disrepair, flanked the east side of the shack.

In one sense, the engines looked like a mechanic's version of the Evolution of Man chart—if it featured Heidelberg Man, Piltdown, and Peking along with Lucy, Neanderthal, and Cro-Magnon. The outboard equivalent of *Homo sapiens* was conspicuously absent, as there was nothing quite so evolved in Meela's shop. Her evolution line featured fossilized Hondas, Evenrudes, Johnsons, Yamahas, Mercuries, and several other motors whose pedigrees weren't so clear.

There were two or three large tables made out of old doors mounted on empty barrels. A bench consisted of an abnormally long door laid across three weathered sawhorses. Tools were scattered over the tabletops like shells strewn along the shore by the surf. Four or five tidy little fishing boats were tied to a small dock. They all had fresh paint, floated high in the water, and appeared to have reliable outboards. These crafts, however, weren't for the locals. They were rented to tourists or fishermen on those rare occasions when a paying customer visited the shop.

A thin elderly woman leaned over one of the barrels. An engine rocked the huge can, and water burst from the barrel when the mechanic tilted the prop down into the oil drum. Then she cut the power, kicked the cask, and threw a screwdriver at a toolbox.

Before Kemar stepped into the surf to pull both Bao and the boat onto the beach, the fisherman whispered to him, "Listen to Bao. Old lady as mixed up as tern in tornado. Out her mind . . . Boy say nothing. No telling what set her off. Bao need motor fix and know how to handle her. Boy just smile. Say nothing. Understand?"

Kemar answered, "I know how to say nothing."

"Then do," Bao hissed while stepping onto the soft sand.

Bao's sour countenance changed quickly and drastically as he approached the woman. He smiled broadly, displaying an assortment of crooked yellow teeth.

"Meela, what fisherman lucky enough have you bent over his motor?" Bao began.

The old woman remained hunched over the prop, maintained her focus, and muttered, "Put it in storage, Bao. Don't play me like some innocent reef fish. It's insulting."

"Really, Meela, no need hostility. Know each other too—"

"What's wrong with your motor?" Meela asked. She ripped a soiled scarf from around her neck and wiped grease from her hands.

The woman struck Kemar as a plain-speaking, no-nonsense mechanic who had no time for insincere pleasantries, perhaps because she'd endured a lifetime of them, or possibly because she felt she didn't have enough time left in her life to play such useless games. Whatever the reason, Kemar's first impression was that he liked the honesty of the woman. To him, it suggested intelligence, and that was something the boy respected.

Kemar was also amused by Meela's physical presence. She looked to be in her early seventies. She was definitely American. She reeked of it. Slightly hunched, her posture was still more upright than the old Cambodian women Kemar remembered hauling wood, water, fruit, rice, and laundry. Meela was taller than those women, but she was as skinny as a bamboo shoot, probably just as tough too.

She kept a ratty cigar stuffed in her breast pocket. A shorter version hung from the corner of her mouth, at the moment unlit. However, the thing Kemar liked most about Meela was the gaping space between her coral-white top front teeth. For some reason, her smile made him smile. Although all these thoughts were streaming through Kemar's mind, he did as Bao instructed and said nothing.

Meela went straight to the engine, hopping into the boat and climbing to the stern. She pried the metallic blue cover off and examined the ancient, dirty motor, poking here and pulling there. Bao chased behind her, explaining the symptoms.

After a moment or two, the expert looked over her shoulder, rolled the stubby cigar in her mouth, and said, "Take it off and mount it in that can over there."

Bao said, "Can't fix?"

"Of course I can fix it."

"Why must Bao remove?"

"That's what you need to do so I can fix it."

"Need motor now. Have to fish."

Meela poked a boney finger at the man. "Listen to me, Bao. If you want it fixed, mount the motor in that can. You're grounded. You got it? I'll do what I can. You just better pray that I have all the parts."

Bao didn't like this at all. He suspected that Meela wasn't being straight with him. Not that she would cheat him, but she didn't approve of the way he fished or the way he treated the reef. Meela had rules: no anchors near coral, no excessive wakes, light sinkers, tie-ups, and other requirements she expected from her clientele. Bao was well aware of Meela's rules, and because he followed none of them, he suspected she would take advantage of the situation to keep him from the fish.

Regardless, Bao softened his tone and asked humbly, "Could borrow motor while Meela work on mine?"

Meela flashed her gap-toothed grin. "Sure," she said, "I'll lend you a motor that's better than this bag of screws."

Bowing to her, Bao said, "Thank you."

"No problem. But you gotta do one or two things just so I feel better about this."

The fisherman cocked his head, squinted, and waited to hear the conditions.

"First, you still owe me for two spark plugs, a spool of wire, a connecting rod, and for the work I did the last time you had trouble. I haven't even thought about rent for the motor you're asking to *borrow* . . . I'd actually be willing to forget that stuff, but there's one thing that's just really started a fire in my fuselage."

Meela bent down and casually plucked a grenade from the box in the boat. She bounced it recklessly in her hand as she continued, "You disgusting fool. You call yourself a fisherman, and this is how you fish? You're a criminal. I will not be part of it, you lazy bucket of bilge." Meela climbed out of the boat. "Let someone else fix your motor."

"Is no one else. Bao swear, Meela, never again. Never use grenades for fish again. Must fix motor."

The old woman turned back to Bao. She took a step toward him, pointed to the grenades, and said, "Take those out of the boat and leave them over there, away from my shop. Mount the motor in that can. Pay me every cent you owe me, and take care of this for me." Meela held out the grenade in her hand, offering it to Bao.

When he wrapped his fingers around the explosive, Meela released her grip and pulled the pin. As long as Bao maintained his grip, the grenade wouldn't explode, but if he let go . . .

Bao choked, "What?"

"And don't you dare throw that into the lagoon or anywhere near my shop; otherwise, I'll drop the next one in your boat."

The mechanic returned to her chores, uninterested in Bao's dilemma. The fisherman stretched his hand out to Kemar, offering the grenade to him. The boy shook his head and backed off quickly.

Bao called out, "Where Bao put grenade?"

Meela smiled, lifted her head from a toolbox, and said, "I do have a suggestion, and I'll even help you put it there, but you'd probably come up with a more comfortable place than what I have in mind." She bent back into the toolbox and resumed her work. Kemar could hear her quietly cackling to herself while Bao splashed around the boat, desperately searching for the missing pin.

When Binti and Hootie arrived at Ebb's algae farm, the diligent damselfish was hard at work cultivating his crop. As soon as he heard his friends, he stopped working.

"Show her! Show her!" Hootie hooted.

Ebb gestured with his right pectoral fin and nodded toward a stand of staghorn coral. Binti and Hootie followed him to a spot just beyond the thicket. There, sitting on top of a broad yellow sponge near a cluster of mussels, was a trident shell, the largest one any of these three had ever seen. It glistened in the twisted, bouncing rays of sunlight that pierced the sea.

Binti reverently raised four arms to stop her friends from going any closer. She smiled and flashed pink, blue, and finally red. Then she reached out and gently stroked the speckled smoothness of the trident.

"Oooohhh, it's magnificent," the octopus cooed. "Smooth, clean, large—it's everything I dreamed my shell would be. This is the shell that will put me in touch with the spirit-fish. I can feel it. I can see it."

"Pretty nice, isn't it?" the blowfish asked rhetorically as he puffed with pride.

"I stumbled on it when I was chasing a grunt from my field," Ebb explained. "He hid in the shell, but I got rid of him. No room for squatters here."

"It's so beautiful," Binti said as she slipped other arms around and into the shell, exploring every corner, every contour.

"Well, it wasn't this nice when I first spotted it, but I cleaned it up a little."

"The gobies couldn't have done any better," Hootie added. "When I saw it, it just screamed *Binti* at me."

"Really?" the octopus asked. "It said my name?"

"Not really. I mean, I thought of you. The shell didn't talk."

"It'll speak to me." The octopus hugged the trident shell and proclaimed, "Today, I am a true mollusk."

"Uh, you've always been a mollusk," Ebb said matter-of-factly.

"No, I haven't been. Would you be a farmer without your farm? Now I'm a mollusk. Now I'm complete."

"Why don't you try it on for size?" Hootie invited.

"Yes, yes. It's just so exciting." The boneless Binti backed into the shell's crevice, slowly inserting herself. It appeared to be a very tight fit, like trying to fit a whale into a whelk, but Binti squeezed into the trident anyway. The constricted octopus had a difficult time breathing. With her arms dangling from underneath the shell, it looked like seven snails all shared the same home. Her eyes

peered out of the small space just above her arms. Her huge mantle was crammed into the interior.

A breathy Binti asked, "How does it look?"

Ebb and Hootie made eye contact, not quite sure what to say. The blowfish deflated a bit and then said, "Well. Uhhh. You look, marvelous."

"Yeah, you're a regular gill grabber," Ebb echoed.

"But how does the shell look?"

Ebb hedged, "I've never seen an octopus in a shell before. It takes a little getting used to."

"You sound kinda funny, Binti. Are you sure it's comfortable?" the blowfish inquired gently.

"It's a bit of a tight squeeze, but isn't that how a shell is supposed to feel? It does feel hard. But I'm not so worried that something will just sweep by and swallow me, like I am without a shell."

"That's good, but you can't really change color in that shell, and it doesn't look very mobile," Ebb said. "Are you sure this is the one?"

"You're the one who told me that this was the shell I was looking for, that this shell would change my life! It *is* beautiful, right?"

Both her friends chimed their agreement.

"Oh, yes. Spectacular."

"Stunning, positively radiant."

"And you know it's better to look good than to feel good."

After a few moments of shell kissing, Ebb asked, "Are you *sure* this is the one?"

"I know. I'll just crawl around in it for a while and see how it feels. Maybe the spirit-fish will speak to me or give me some sign. Then I'll know for sure."

That said, Binti began to crawl awkwardly away. Swimming was out of the question. Even crawling was difficult, with several arms all bundled up under the hulking husk. The shell slipped off the octopus once or twice. She was forced to throw two arms over the trident with suckers locked down to keep the carapace in place, which didn't really enhance the effect.

Hootie asked, "Where are you going?"

"Home."

"How are you going to get into your lair wearing this huge thing? I mean, now that you have a shell, doesn't *it* become your home?"

"I guess you're right," Binti muttered. "Maybe I'll just sleep in it right here and see how I feel in the morning."

"Maybe by tomorrow, you will have heard from the spirit-fish. Then you'll know whether this is the shell you've searched for. That's what'll happen," Hootie predicted.

The optimist in Hootie always seemed to float to the surface. It was a trait that could be very encouraging, but it was also a trait that could make Hootie—and those who swam around him—more susceptible to disappointment.

That night, Binti wedged herself, shell and all, under a rocky ridge. She felt pretty safe, but she was also getting rather hungry, probably because it was next-to-impossible to hunt with the heavy house on her boneless back. She felt numb in several arms and endured the meanest mantle-ache of her life. But Binti was determined to give the carapace a chance, so she kept it on and stayed where she was.

Then, finally, Binti began to nod off. It was the type of sleep where one is half passed-out, half awake, bouncing back and forth between the two states. As she dozed restlessly, she heard the familiar voice that she couldn't identify, the voice that came from within but was not her own. The octopus listened carefully. The voice was faint and fuzzy.

What could she do to make the murmur more clear? Should she sleep or should she rise? Unable to decide, she hovered in the in-between state, waiting for guidance. And it came. Carried by a cool current, it came out of nowhere, a whisper on the reef. There were many words being spoken at once, all with the same voice. But Binti could decipher only one message.

The voice sang softly in her mind, *In wickedness of pride is lost the light to understand . . . Without love in a dream, it will never come true.* The octopus strained to hear more. She asked the voice, *What are you saying? Are you the spirit-fish? Have I made the right choice? Can't you tell me?*

Then she heard, *"Well, well, well, you can never tell."*

The voice faded away as the light of morning rinsed it from the water. Only one last thought floated in the current: *Miracles happen when everything else fails.* And as the sun lit up the morning, Binti knew only that she hadn't yet found the singular shell she searched for. She suddenly suspected that she'd embraced her quest for the wrong reasons. Binti believed there was a shell she was meant to find; however, it had nothing to do with establishing her identity as a mollusk. Cramped, cold, and hungry, the octopus emerged from the barren husk, abandoning the trident on Makoona's sandy floor.

Binti turned tan with brown blotches and streaks of green. She was pleased to taste the water against her skin. She was an octopus, and that meant she was also a mollusk. She did not need to wear another's shell to become what she already was. The animal accepted the truth, hoping it would lead her to another.

The Ends Justify

Bao had managed to hold the grenade all the way to the dump, where he tossed it into a pile of garbage. The exploded trash created a fresh buffet for Makoona's lazier fauna.

Later, the determined fisherman borrowed a motor from a colleague who was too ill to go to sea. The man who supplied the motor made Bao swear that Meela wouldn't hear about the loan. That, however, wasn't a guarantee Bao could make if the rumor on Makoona was true, that the engines spoke to Meela. Many times, she'd merely listened to an outboard—some claimed without it being started—and diagnosed the engine's problem and its cause.

Before they left to fish, Bao brought the boy to meet many people. He smiled as he introduced Kemar and seemed genuinely pleased with their association. Like a proud father, Bao boasted of the valuable help Kemar gave him. He explained, in great detail, many things the boy had done to help him, including several feats even Kemar couldn't remember performing.

The boy began to see that he might've found not only a friend, but also a place where he could belong and feel safe. It was one reason why Bao's sudden sullenness later that day perplexed the young refugee.

As they motored through the soft swells that rocked the small boat with the borrowed motor, Kemar hesitatingly asked Bao what was bothering him. He was shocked when the man replied, "You what bother Bao."

Kemar thought he understood the problem. He reassured his companion that he was fine, that he was happy to have ended up on Makoona with him.

Bao laughed. "Don't care you fine or happy at Makoona. You worthless."

"Worthless? Why? Because I lost a net? Because I don't enjoy fishing with hand grenades?"

"Worthless because no one buy you."

"You tried to sell me?"

"Why think Bao show to everyone? Boy have no value. Should have let sea keep you."

Kemar slumped against the rail. For a moment, he'd allowed himself to be weak, to trust. He'd indulged a desire to live a normal life. He was thankful to Bao. The fisherman reminded him that he could never have a normal life. You can't exist under the Khmer Rouge as a youngster and then forget the horror; you can't be thrown from a boat into the sea to die; you can't be sold by your savior and live a normal life. Happiness and trust, it seemed, were no longer possible.

Kemar returned to the numb callousness that had protected him in the past, failing to comprehend that a life without a dream, a goal, a challenge is not a life at all. The boy pushed his pain into a place deep within him that housed all the pain he'd ever felt. Every time he added another experience to the vault, a rare shred of what remained of his innocence was torn away.

Finally, Kemar stated, "You don't own me. You can't sell what you don't own."

"Not really *selling* Kemar. Bao choose wrong words. Trying to help boy. Try to match skill to someone who needs."

"And who will pay."

"Pay boy too. Boy, Bao, merchant all benefit."

"When were you going to tell me about all this?"

"Boy one who put idea into Bao's head. Boy one who ask for work with mechanic. *You* abandon Bao." The older fisherman was practiced at deceit. He knew exactly how to bend the truth to fabricate believable lies.

"Maybe you could let me know what you decide for me before you do it. I might have something to say about it."

"Not think boy mind."

"Not mind that I'm being sold?"

"Not sold! Not sold! Wrong word."

"What if I decide this is the last time I will fish with you?"

Bao liked the idea of sitting dry in the boat while Kemar did the dirty, dangerous work. But Kemar might not be worth feeding, paying, or using extra gas to transport, especially since he was proving to be somewhat annoying company. So Bao replied, "Then this will be last day. Can sleep under boat if like." The benevolent Bao knew it would be difficult for anyone to disturb his property while Kemar slept under it.

The boy thought for a moment. "I will work for you today. You will give me dinner and two dollars."

Bao smiled. Now they were playing his game. He would give the boy a lesson in making deals. "Is fair to Bao, if fair to boy." Bao pointed a finger at Kemar, adding, "If anyone Bao introduce you to give work, you give Bao half of wages for first month. Only be pennies. How much could boy be worth? Boy give money for all Bao do for you."

The words rang in Kemar's ears. This was something that Phan would've negotiated, the type of language and logic those who believed in the Khmer Rouge would've employed. Kemar knew this game, and he knew where Bao would've stood had he been in Cambodia when the trouble started, when the cities were evacuated and the educated were murdered.

Kemar paused and presented a counter-offer. "You will give me dinner tonight and two dollars for my work today. For every night I sleep under your boat and keep it safe for you, you will give me either seventy-five cents or breakfast. I will give you one quarter of my first month's pay if one of the people you introduced me to hires me."

Bao was amused by the thought that perhaps the youngster wasn't as worthless as he appeared. But he dismissed both the boy and the thought as he responded to the latest offer.

"One-third of first month money. Twenty-five cent for taking care of gear at night." Since he'd introduced the boy to most of the merchants on the island, Bao knew that Kemar might wind up working for several of them. In his mind, Bao believed he'd be entitled to money every time Kemar worked for a new employer. It was a possibility the boy overlooked and the man banked on.

"Very well, Bao." Kemar offered his hand to the man.

Bao accepted the small, thin fingers and the sincerity of their grip. He returned the grip but not the sincerity.

When they reached the stretch of ocean that Bao was looking for, he gunned the engine and then glided to a spot where a weathered plastic bleach bottle bobbed on the water, anchored to the coral below—a marker, not a mooring. Bao had Kemar toss the boat's anchor over the side. The boy knew that gunning the motor and tossing the anchor would alert and disperse many of the fish but wasn't very surprised at Bao's sloppiness.

Although Bao thought a lot about money, he typically expected more from others than from himself. Bao tended to be lazy in that he'd do whatever was easy to make a quick profit. Other, more sophisticated ventures—potentially much more profitable—usually eluded him.

What eluded both of them was that the heavy anchor was crushing and ripping large patches of living coral. It could take a thousand generations before any of Kemar's offspring would see similar coral configurations in this spot again.

With the boat secure, Bao briefed his new employee about the day's activities. Since Meela had confiscated the grenades, Bao had prepared another very effective and equally lethal method of coaxing fish from the coral. Bao popped open a compartment under a seat and produced several plastic squeeze bottles. They were filled with liquid that, when viewed through the cloudy plastic, looked more like opaque, dirty water.

Bao handed two of the bottles to Kemar, saying, "Don't drink. Would be better off sucking down sea water." The older man handed his associate a small orange hand net. "Not belong to Bao. Don't lose, or maybe Bao lose your two dollar."

"Really?" the boy asked. "Well, I might lose your boat one night." He picked up the net and dropped a bottle into it. Holding the other container in his hand, Kemar asked, "How do you fish with water in water?"

"Not water. Cyanide. Have more if need."

Kemar stared blankly at Bao.

Sighing, the man explained, "Swim up to a coral with plenty place for fish to hide. Spray in cracks. Scoop what come out. Even if look dead, grab. A few minutes in bucket, many wake up. Good way to catch tank fish. Fun."

"Lots of fun when *you're* sitting in the boat," Kemar mumbled under his breath.

The anchor line snapped free, and the boat bounced and rolled. Kemar tripped over a bucket while Bao reached for the rope. The dislodged anchor slid along the bottom, plowing down sponges and corals, causing quite a disturbance below.

The coral crashed onto the sandy floor, producing plumes of smoky silt and debris. The residents of Makoona scattered instantly. There were several, however, stunned by the collapse of their homes, who hesitated before fleeing into the nearest shelter they could find. Fish flew into holes, hoping that they were deep, twisted, and uninhabited. Many of them knew what would happen next.

A minute or two later, the splash came. It was the unmistakable sound of a human disturbing the sea. Those already huddled into crevices squeezed into the deepest corners they could fit into, hoping to elude the man-tide's venom. In one of those cracks, Binti's home, the octopus had thrust her boneless body behind a smooth rock. She breathed softly, taking small, shallow breaths. Although her body's sensitivity to chemical changes in the water generally proved to be a blessing, in this scenario, it wasn't.

Her flesh burned and itched as the first minute traces of cyanide infiltrated her lair. The octopus hoped the level wouldn't increase. She'd seen others who'd breathed the venom. Those who lived and weren't taken away by the man-tide were left changed, and never for the better.

Binti remembered a shrimp who suddenly began behaving like a squid. It swam around at night in the deep open water looking for food that it could neither catch nor ingest. She also knew of an octopus who, after breathing the venom, spent the rest of its life disguised as a clam. Both the shrimp and the octopus quietly disappeared. Binti assumed that either the venom proved lethal over time or they starved to death.

The odds were that neither was eaten, because most would never knowingly eat a creature who'd breathed the venom, one who'd been *sprayed*. Otherwise, their sickness could become yours, and that wasn't worth an easy meal.

When she felt the poison recede from her home, Binti inched her way to the sponge she'd jammed into the entrance to help keep out the venom. She surveyed the coral valley that was her neighborhood and saw the dead anemone across the way. Ozob and Agora's home. The long tentacles that once produced poison of their own now lay lifeless against the rock they once clung to.

Swimming in a crazed circle, alone, was Ozob. Half of his body was paralyzed. The fins on that one side were still. His gill cover didn't move. The eye could no longer see. As he tried to flee, Ozob could only travel in a ragged loop, going nowhere while inviting the attention of the human who wreaked this havoc. Ozob's mouth was wide open. He was screaming, but no sound came out. Yet Binti heard him just the same.

The human swam closer. Binti could see Agora, still alive, trapped in a net. There were several other creatures trapped with her.

Binti saw sacred angelfish, a goby, a very young grouper, a porgy, a pair of butterfly fish, a peacock sole, and other residents of the reef.

For a moment, Binti wondered if the man-tide were eating these fish. If they did, perhaps their own venom was affecting them the same way it would if Binti ate sprayed fish. Could they be poisoning themselves? Did they not see the connection? It could explain much of the man-tide's irrational behavior.

The human reached down with a small net and scooped up Ozob. The instant his body felt the mesh of the net, the crippled clownfish stopped struggling. Ozob just seemed to give up. He tumbled into the sack with the other fish, and Agora rushed to his side. The pair huddled close to each other.

As the human swam back to the surface, to the floating island that carried him to Makoona, Ozob's and Agora's brilliant orange stripes faded to a pasty dull pink. Their deep black bars became gray. They floated in the sack, bouncing off the other fish as if they were kelp caught in a slow current. They'd left their bodies before their bodies had left the reef. For Ozob and Agora, it was better to die together in the midst of Makoona than to have their last breath taken in a bucket.

The dark irony didn't escape Binti that these clownfish who survived because of the anemone's poison, using it to preserve their lives, had lost their lives to a toxin that wasn't part of the spirit-fish's creation, a contamination they were never meant to face.

While the human was out of the water, Binti seized the opportunity to flee. She streamlined herself, turned a sandy green with small brown spots, and jetted out of her crevice. She hugged the crusty coral cover, moving away from the seaward side of the reef to a sand shoal close by.

The cleaning station would be a good place to get information about the reef's latest onslaught, the octopus thought. Binti slid in quietly, dulled her colors, and pressed against a pile of large stones. Posed as an innocuous gray rock, Binti felt a quick nip at her mantle, which caused her to flash an involuntary orange, revealing her position to those gathered at the station.

"It's not necessary to be so secretive," Paykak said.

"I'm an octopus. It's what I do. And what's with biting me like that?"

"I saw a little sea tick on your mantle. I'm a goby. It's what *I* do."

"Next time, could you wait until I get in line before you start the cleaning?"

"It's more fun this way." Paykak swam out toward the station where several of his family members were busy cleaning a lunar-tailed rock cod who had an infected gash on its flank.

"Looks like a big job," the octopus observed.

"Sure is. This one was hooked, dragged right up to the floating island, and they slammed the claw into his side. When they lifted him out, he slipped free and swam straight here. I got my best healer on it."

"Wiff?"

"Who else? He and his crew will clean this cod up just fine. It always makes me happy when we steal one back from the mantide."

"I know what you mean," Binti agreed.

"I take it you know about the spraying?" Paykak asked.

"It happened in the valley. They got Ozob and Agora."

"I heard," Paykak said solemnly. "Makoona is as dangerous as it beautiful."

"Tell me about it. I'm the octopus with seven arms."

Paykak swam closer to the stump of the missing limb. "Let me take a quick look at this."

"Ah, don't bother," Binti said. "It'll grow back. I've been through this before."

"Seen a few of these myself. It may not hurt right now, but you might want to have Wiff look it over. It could easily get infected."

"Sure." Binti bounced a small stone on one of her arms while she looked over the clients at the station. "Looks a little slow today."

"We have competition."

"What? You don't have competition. Why would anyone go somewhere else for a cleaning?"

Paykak, controlling his emotion, replied, "Some wrasses are trying their fins at this game. They've lured away several of the morays."

"Good. You don't need them here."

Paykak raised a single fin to silence Binti. He knew where she was going. "Just by virtue of being alive, every creature, even a moray, deserves to have a profishional cleaning. As long as they respect the rules."

"Maybe," the octopus conceded sourly, "but I won't miss them."

"I will. I could use the business. Morays always have something eating them that needs to be removed."

"Don't worry, Paykak. They'll be back."

"You bet your wrasse they will. By the wave, had an octopus in here earlier. I asked if he knew you. I think he did, but I really had trouble clamprehending what the shell he was talking about."

"I've met him," Binti admitted. "I don't really get him either."

"He's a strange one. But I like him. He's reefishing, kind of catches you by surprise, like a cold undertow. Hey, do you think he got sprayed and it messed with his mantle?"

Binti considered the thought. "No," she concluded. "I think there's something else going on in that squishy mantle of his." The octopus paused. "I can't believe Ozob and Agora are gone."

"Yeah, it's always terrible to lose a good friend, not to mention a good neighbor. And to lose them to the spray."

"I haven't seen either Hootie or Ebb. Any word on them?"

"Haven't seen them, but a stargazer named Smyke was in here for a little trim, and he mentioned a farmer who was all fuzzed up about his algae getting sprayed. Sounded like Ebb to me."

At that moment, Paykak noticed one of his gobies sending a bass on its way before the cleaner had completed its job. From Paykak's point of view, that was unforgivable, very unprofishional.

The senior goby flew at the offending cleaner and issued a blistering gill-lashing for the lazy effort, claiming that it violated a sacred trust between the fish and the cleaner. He went on to predict that oversights like these would lead to other undesirable habits that would ultimately threaten the delicate beauty and the very existence of the cleaning station.

Binti could plainly see that the stress of the wrasses' operation would produce dire consequences for any slacking gobies working under Paykak.

The octopus morphed into a pale yellow with thin blue streaks and crawled slowly toward home, relieved that Ebb, at least, had survived the spraying. But in the back of her mind, she couldn't shake the sight of Ozob and his silent scream.

As she reached the outskirts of the cleaning area, she was bitten again, this time right between the eyes.

"Stop doing that!" she yelled.

Paykak smiled at her.

"Another sea tick, I suppose?"

"No, I just felt like biting you this time. How about we take a little off around the suckers before you leave? You'll feel better."

"Some other time, okay?"

"Sure," her friend responded. "Hey, don't worry too much about Agora and Ozob and their anemone. What's done is done. Their lives—and their deaths—are all part of the balance."

"That's what bothers me," Binti said as she continued crawling. "It's not part of the balance."

Back on the surface, Bao beamed over the catch. He gazed down into several buckets that contained a very impressive variety of sea life. Kemar had netted an array of small fish that the Filipino broker would pay good money for. The young refugee, however, was not as satisfied with the results. He really couldn't understand this type of fishing, but when Bao boasted about the ensuing pay-off, saying something about a bonus, Kemar didn't anchor himself with too much reflection.

A rumbling deep in his belly interrupted his thoughts. Without thinking, the boy reached into the bucket and pulled out one of the small fish. It was swimming slowly, still stunned from a hefty dose of cyanide, but the boy didn't pause to consider that either. He held the fish between his fingers and bit out the soft dorsal muscle.

Kemar swallowed and tossed the rest of the fish back into the sea. When he reached back into the bucket for another dorsal morsel, a swat from Bao's oar interrupted him.

"Not eat!" Bao chided.

"I'm hungry, and we have fish," Kemar countered.

"Worth more in bucket than in belly." Bao smiled, aware of the boy's hunger. "Give choice. Boy do good job today. Bao give one dollar bonus or can of Spam." The man held out both. He was anxious to see what urge was stronger, hunger or greed.

Kemar looked at Bao suspiciously. Then he said, "I'll take fifty cents and half a can of Spam."

"Done," Bao said with a laugh. He cut the Spam in half with a dirty bait knife, laid two grimy quarters on it, and handed both to the boy.

While they ate, the two picked out the dead fish from the bucket and tossed them overboard. Birds gathered to pluck the cyanide-laced catch from the surface, where other fish also floated as a result of the earlier spraying. Occasionally, an opportunistic jack or a torpid white-tip shark would join the feast, swallowing the dead or near-dead fish that struggled on the sunlit surface, thus ensuring that the poison would work its way further into the food chain, perhaps returning to its source one day.

Bao started the hiccupping motor and moved off to another fishing spot. On the way, Bao explained that the boy was a little too heavy-handed with the spray. Too many fish were dying, and the supply of cyanide wasn't lasting as long as Bao had hoped it would. So, in a twisted version of conservationism, the fisherman showed his assistant how to get the most fish using the least amount of poison while they prepared for another run.

When Binti returned home, two things saddened her. First, her neighbors and their anemone were no longer there. The octopus grieved; losing good neighbors can be like losing family. In fact, for Binti, good neighbors were really as close to family as she would likely ever get, having not actually known or even met any of her octopus relations.

The other thing that saddened Binti was the coral. The living rainbow that was Makoona was now flecked and patched with a dull gray wherever the cyanide had come into contact with the coral. Soon, it would bleach a lifeless white.

With its vibrancy now muted, the octopus was reminded just how precious and fragile her home actually was. She was reminded that the structure was alive, that it had taken ten million years of coral polyps secreting limestone to build the community that she lived in. It was something she knew but couldn't explain how she knew it.

Binti dragged herself up to her hollow. From behind a pale, sagging wisp of what was once purple fan coral, Hootie appeared.

"Hey," the blowfish blew. "You didn't get sprayed, so why so blue?" Hootie was speaking literally, as the octopus had turned a dark, sullen shade of blue.

"Ozob and Agora weren't so lucky. I was worried about you and Ebb too."

"Ebb's fine, although his algae doesn't look so good. Paykak told me about your neighbors. Sorry things worked out like that. I'll miss them. But what can you do? It's the way of the water."

Binti shook her mantle. "No. Paykak said something like that too, but I don't agree. If it really was the way of the water, I wouldn't mind so much. I can deal with whatever the balance brings, but this didn't come from any creature who knows the spirit-fish."

As Hootie and Binti sat for a moment, gazing at the deflated, defiled anemone that earlier in the day housed their clownfish friends, they heard a voice. It seemed to come from a blue sponge nestled between three crusty rocks.

The sponge said, "One or two moments. A piece of your time is all I'm asking, and I'll give you mine."

The blowfish and the octopus froze. Hootie inflated himself—it was an involuntary defense reaction. Binti, who was already the color of the sand, backed herself under a rocky overhang, lowered her mantle, filled her ink sack, and prepared for the worst. Neither of them had ever spoken to a sponge before. And Binti didn't recall that there had ever been one in this spot between the rocks near her home.

The sponge spoke a second time, saying, "There are things you can replace and others you cannot. The time has come to weigh those things. This space is getting hot. You know this space is getting hot."

And at that moment, the sponge pointed at the deceased anemone.

Hootie whispered, "Have you ever seen a sponge point before?"

The octopus replied, "Shell no!"

"Ask it a question," Hootie dared.

"What do you ask a sponge?"

"I don't know. Ask it if there's something we should do."

And then the sponge spoke again. "Don't turn away. Step up and see what I can do when you believe . . . Some folks trust in reason, others trust in might. I don't trust to nothing, but I know it come out right."

Binti hesitated. She stammered, "T-T-Trust? B-B-B-Believe? In what, b-b-blue sponge?"

The sponge turned yellow, green, and sky blue. "Oh, friend of mine, all good things in all good time."

"Do you want us to do something?" Hootie asked.

"Reach for the sun, catch hold of the moon. They're both too heavy, but what can you do?" The sponge burst into a fiery display of orange and red. "Here is fire and bloody slaughter written on the leaves of the water."

It was obvious to Binti and Hootie that the sponge was referring to the anemone and the spraying that had taken place a tide before.

The octopus thought she understood. "We don't like what happened either. It's happened before. But what can we do? One octopus, a blowfish . . . and a sponge?"

"It's even worse than it appears, but it's alright," the sponge replied. "Maybe that's 'cause it's midnight, in the dark of the moon besides. Maybe the dark is from your eyes. You know you got such dark eyes."

"I don't see what you mean," Binti said, confused.

"Let's see with our heart these things our eyes have seen and know the truth lies somewhere in between."

"The truth of *this*," Hootie whispered.

There was silence. The current picked up the flaccid arms of the anemone, and for a moment, they seemed to be alive once again. But as the current swept past, the tentacles settled back down, lifeless on the rock below. They stirred again, and out crawled a small spider crab housed in a dirty, brown, algae-covered shell. Gracefully, carefully, the crab stepped off into the reef.

The sponge spoke again, "Slip out of your shell, you said. Where else you got to go? You been there and back again. What do you really know? . . . It's all a dream we dreamed one afternoon long ago."

Although he was in total awe, Hootie was becoming a little impatient with the cryptic conversation. He blurted out, "You're a little tough to understand, you know? Could you say things a little more—"

The sponge interrupted, "I will go with you wherever the sun reflects on the shining blue sea. . . . Maybe the sun is shining, birds are winging, or rain is falling from a heavy sky. What do you want me to do, to do for you to see you through?" The sponge turned a deep, dark green, left a small black cloud, and disappeared behind the rocks.

Binti and Hootie glanced at each other and swam over to where the sponge had been. The only thing left was a wisp of the black cloud as it dissipated in the water. And then they heard the voice call out, "You can catch the drift, but not the drifter!"

Al stood alone on the sand in front of his unique home. He lived in a shack that resembled something the Swiss Family Robinson might've built. The walls were made of corrugated sheet metal he'd "salvaged" from an "abandoned" USAF hangar. Several function-ing portholes were cut into the walls, which were partly secured by a roof made out of the hull of an old fishing boat.

With a capsized craft as his ceiling, Al's hut was dry, had ex-ceptional pitch during monsoons, and left plenty of headroom underneath for a tall American with good posture. When the oc-casional coconut dramatized Newton's Law, it always bounced off the boat with indifference. The heavy wooden hull that had once withstood whatever the sea had thrown at it could still han-dle almost anything Mother Nature might drop on it as well.

Al breathed deeply. The ocean air was thick and not nearly as salty as usual. The sky was a grayer shade of blue, one that more closely resembled the sea below it, a sea that churned restlessly. A storm was coming. Al was pleased. Had he been out on the ocean, he would've felt differently, but facing the storm on land was another story.

A bit of a hermit, Al enjoyed weather—all types, as long as it wasn't too cold. He especially liked heavy weather. The quiet fisherman believed the weather was every bit as alive as the flora and fauna of Makoona. And when a storm blew in, it was like an old friend had come to call. For Al, the storms were female. He fantasized that the weather embodied the passionate spirit of a woman. And so he welcomed the storm, inviting it to touch him.

Rolling in gradually from the east, this event was in no hurry. The lady would arrive when she was ready, paying no heed to whatever man might place in her path. Al liked that the storm could be unpredictable, uncontrollable. It was a force of nature whose wildness appealed to something deep within him.

Al sat on an aluminum-framed lawn chair, oblivious to the thunder that rumbled in the distance. He rested his feet on an old lobster trap that had been repurposed as an ottoman, its life changing direction and purpose as much as Al's had.

The wind rose, and the rain began to fall. It covered Al quickly, wetting his dry clothes and body, and then soaking him, sustaining him, cleansing him, washing the salt from his skin and the sin from his soul. The clouds had come to Al, and in his mind, he believed the weather would heal him as only a woman can heal a man.

While the wind and the rain refreshed Al, it put an end to the day's cyanide fishing for Bao and Kemar. The two secured their catch and stored their gear, racing the storm to see who would arrive at the island first. At moments like this, Bao really appreciated Meela. Even though the boat was propelled by a borrowed engine, it was one of Meela's children. One pull and he knew exactly why he tolerated the old mechanic's eccentricities.

The boat beached minutes before the storm struck. Bao and Kemar rushed to unload. Kemar put all the gear and fish away while Bao returned the outboard and its extra tank—a little light on gas—to the man he borrowed it from.

Bao assured the fisherman, "If not for storm, tank be full. Better to have motor low on gas but not broken. Will fill two tanks for you tomorrow."

The man, who knew Bao all too well, mumbled an insincere, "Two. Sure, bahala na."

Although Bao's motor was still with Meela, Kemar tugged his boss's boat further up the beach and lashed it to a sturdy palm tree. When Bao returned, he checked the lines; slipped Kemar two more dollars, what remained of the Spam, and an orange; and said, "Good work. Tomorrow, see if old witch finish with motor. Then use last bottles of spray for fish."

Bao picked up two five-gallon buckets of fish, draped one on each end of an oar, laid it across his shoulders, and walked off. At home, he'd drop the valuable fish into plastic bags, add water and a little food, and pump air into them so the fish would be ready for his Filipino financier.

The rain was falling in sheets as Kemar trotted to Bao's side. "Can I wait out the storm at your home?" he asked.

Bao smiled and laid his hand on Kemar's arm. "No," he said. "Still need deliver catch. Not much storm. Boat secure. Boy be fine. See in morning." And with that, Bao trudged away.

Kemar was disappointed with himself for asking Bao to help him. He wasn't nearly as displeased in his employer's uncaring response as he was with his own display of weakness. Kemar stuffed the money deep into his pocket and crawled under the overturned boat. Back in Cambodia, he'd survived much worse than this.

He spread out a tattered tarp beneath him, wondering whether he was becoming weaker as his life became easier. The boy looked out at the sea. The water sliding off the boat made him feel like he was peering out from a cave whose entrance was guarded by a thin waterfall. Kemar ate his food and fell asleep.

Unlike Al, Meela never enjoyed storms. They meant two things to her, danger and extra work. She didn't see the beauty of heavy weather. To her, storms were about as useful as the flu. They only made life more difficult. This attitude went back to Meela's flying days. She mumbled disapproval as she struggled to move tools, parts, and motors out of the storm's way. Meela knew that if she didn't do the work now, the potential clean-up could be twice as bad later on.

The old mechanic didn't expect the rain; it really wasn't that time of year. But at her age, she knew that life was as much about the unexpected as it was about the expected. Certainly, she'd never expected to live this long and find herself alone, fixing outboard motors on a speck of an island in the south Pacific. Another thing she didn't expect was how happy all this would make her. Now, chewing on a tattered cigar, covered in grease and grime, dragging a dolly across uncooperative sand, Meela had never been more contented.

Whether the locals cared to believe it or not, her stories about dancing with presidents and dining with kings were true, every word. Well, almost every word, but the old mechanic wasn't nearly as senile as the residents of Makoona assumed she was.

Meela cursed herself for daydreaming rather than working, something she found herself doing more frequently as she aged. Returning to the task at hand, struggling with the black forty-horsepower Mercury outboard felt like she was pulling against forty actual horses who didn't want to return to the barn. Suddenly, the load felt strangely lighter. Looking up, Meela saw Al. He was holding a small motor under one arm while lifting the disagreeable Merc with the other. Al carried the two motors into the leaky shed and placed them next to a shiny Evenrude.

Meela, now gathering up tools, said, "I would have bet that you'd be sitting on that lawn chair, hoping to catch a cheap thrill from a stray lightning bolt."

"That's exactly where I was, but how could I enjoy this wonderful weather knowing you had all this work to do? It's kind of like being on the couch with your date while mom's slaving in the kitchen. What fun is that?"

"For your own sake, I hope you're not suggesting that I'm like your mom," she said, with her cigar bouncing up and down in the corner of her mouth.

"It's that or the date. Take your pick."

"No other choices?"

"Nope." Al reached out and plucked the stressed stogie from her lips, inserting in its place a slightly improved version.

"Selling fish to the hotel again?"

"They have good cigars. You know, my mom didn't smoke too many of these, although I had a few dates who did." Looking Meela over, Al continued, "And the only grease I remember seeing on Mother came from draining the frying pan."

Meela flashed her wonderful gap-toothed grin. "Well, my boy, we're just two different women in two different places."

"*Vive la différence,*" Al added.

The rain picked up, and the lightning cracked over the jungle behind them. The wind blew angrily. Meela and Al spread out tarps and lashed down loose ends before he said goodbye and loped back down the beach to his hut.

Along the way, he glanced at the boats to see if any needed tending. Al wasn't especially friendly with their owners; he was just the type of fisherman who recognized the value of reliable equipment. So every now and then, he'd stuff a loose bucket under a canvas, tie a line to a cooler, or tuck a net into a hold, hoping that someone might do the same for him one day.

But the more the lightning boomed around him, the less Al stopped. When the thunder instantly followed the flash, Al knew he was standing in the heart of the storm. His own heart raced. His adrenaline flowed. He breathed deeper, then fast and shallow like the water invading the beach. He savored the rush, but any potential pleasure was undone by the thunder. The random blasts, the pounding boom, the blinding flash, carried him back to Vietnam. And that was a place he vowed he'd never return to.

Although the thunder was unsettling, Al lingered in the downpour as he walked home. The crash-swish of the waves, the low whistle of the wind, and the grinding of the palms touched him deeply like a great orchestra moves its listeners. While the storm returned Al to the war, it also brought him home, back to Makoona.

Al looked up the beach to a spot where the sand subsided and the mangrove began. He noticed the light blue fishing boat that he knew belonged to Bao, someone who usually didn't go to such great pains to protect his equipment. Al wondered why Bao was suddenly so attentive to his gear.

Looking closer, the American saw two shoeless brown feet, toes in the sand, heels to the sky, sticking out from under the curved bow. Al approached the boat. For a moment, he wondered whether the person attached to the feet was alive.

Even though the storm was winding down, sleeping under a small fishing boat near a stand of tall palms wasn't a good idea. The feet looked small. "Maybe there's a woman or a kid under there," Al thought. Most people who lived on Makoona would pay no attention to someone sleeping under a boat, storm or no storm. But Al wasn't from Makoona. He knocked on the hull as if he were knocking on the door of a neighbor back in the states.

"Anyone home?" he asked.

There was no answer.

Al knocked again, with a little more gusto this time. "I can see your damn feet. You okay?"

Still, there was no reply.

Al bent down carefully, slipped a strong hand under the boat, and lifted the bow over his head. The curious American twisted his neck to get a good view of who was underneath, his free hand sliding up his thigh, closer to where a fillet knife hung from his belt. Al always carried the knife. He was a big man and probably didn't need to carry a weapon, but he reasoned that if a tiger with claws was more intimidating than one without, the same would be true for a man and a knife.

Looking under the boat, Al saw a boy face down in the sand, apparently asleep. The skinny youngster was shivering and soaked to the bone. The American nudged Kemar several times with his foot until the boy woke.

Kemar stared into the man's eyes. The boy's face was expressionless as he reached slowly under the sand where he'd buried his own fillet knife for just such an occasion.

Shifting the boat to his other hand, Al said calmly, "I'm not here to mess with you, little man. I just wanted to see if you were okay. You understand me?"

Strangers who mean to harm you don't usually begin by announcing their nefarious intent. Oftentimes, the first thing they say is that they don't mean you harm, so Kemar still didn't speak. He also didn't remove his hand from the sand.

Al frowned. He knelt down closer to the boy and said, "It's important to protect yourself, but don't be a chump. Whatever you're reaching in the sand for, you won't need. If you like sleeping under Bao's smelly boat during a storm like this, then go ahead. Suit yourself, bro. You know what I'm saying. I can see it in your eyes." Al stood up, lowered the boat, and stepped back a few paces.

The hull fell back onto the wet sand with a muddled thud. The boat didn't roll or bounce. After a second or two, Kemar's face peered out from the side of the craft. In the shadows, like a lizard in a hole, he clutched his knife. It was an interesting situation. The boy might or might not be able to protect himself, but he was absolutely willing to do so.

Al, on the other hand, possessed certain skills of his own. His size and strength also presented a walking warning. The barracuda had stumbled into the moray's lair. But this barracuda was well fed and meant no harm.

Al looked down at the boy and asked, "You want to come stay at my place? You can dry off and have a good meal."

Kemar raised one hand slightly as if to say, "Thanks, but no." And then he rolled back under the boat.

The American returned the wave with a nod, a sign that he both understood and respected the boy's decision. As he turned to continue his trek home in what was now drizzle, Al said, "Yeah, I live under a boat myself. I know just how special it can be. I'd offer you a rain check, kid, but it's already raining."

Kemar peered out once more, watching Al stroll down the shore. The Cambodian had no idea what a "rain check" was and wondered if the American knew he'd prefer cash.

Below the surface of the sea, the inhabitants of Makoona paid little attention to the storm. Surface water churned, sand swirled in the turbulent shallows, and clouds cast a thick haze over the sun, but the residents of the reef were relatively untouched.

Binti decided to check on Ebb. One of the best things about having a damselfish as friend is that they're always home. Ebb virtually never left the farm. Binti loved this. She could pop in on him at any time, and he was sure to be around. On extremely rare occasions, Ebb would ask Binti or Hootie to tend his algae while he rushed to the cleaning station for a quick gill-raking. The fussy farmer felt that his two friends were good choices to tend his crops for two reasons: Either of them was capable of defending the algae, and neither of them had any desire to eat it.

At the cleaning station, Ebb waited in line in an advanced state of algae-tation. Only the absolute necessity of the cleaning could tear the aquaculturist from his fields.

Binti liked to sneak up on her friends. It was a safer way of entering a new place, and sometimes, she saw or heard things that she might not otherwise see or hear. This did, however, pose a slight dilemma with respect to the ethical use of octopus cloaking skills, since this application of stealth really had nothing to do with defense or predation. It was more like spying, which wasn't exactly why the spirit-fish gave her these abilities. Still, the octopus particularly enjoyed sneaking up on Ebb. It was a game they played.

Because Ebb rarely left the farm, he knew every coral, crack, clam, and crevice that belonged on his homestead. Anywhere else on the sea, Binti's abilities would be too much for him. But on aqua-firma, his home turf, Binti needed to be perfect to pass unnoticed. In fact, she'd never snuck up on Ebb successfully.

The octopus was feeling lucky today. The storm had presented her with a unique opportunity. The wind-washed water had ripped loose several sizeable patches of dark green seaweed, which just happened to be floating over Ebb's fields. It would be tricky, but Binti reasoned that if she could swim above the weed and match its color, with a little luck, she might be able to float the patch over Ebb and pounce before he knew what hit him.

Binti blended into a grove of staghorn coral. She waited for the perfect patch to float by. Patience came as naturally to the octopus as cleaning to a goby. Binti was tan and brown. Several of her arms twisted upward and outward, mimicking the contours of the coral branches. She delicately puckered her skin to match its texture. A clownfish she knew, Gabbagoo, swam right through her arms and never raised a fin. Binti was invisible among the coral.

A lobster scuttled across an arm that Binti used to anchor herself to the bottom. The crustacean froze as it suddenly touched soft coral where none should exist. It was so important to Binti that she surprise Ebb, she allowed one of her favorite meals to scurry off untouched. If she could pounce on Ebb in his own backyard just once, she would have bragging rights for a very long time. Ebb would finally be forced to eat something other than algae: He'd have to swallow his words. And Binti yearned to serve up the meal.

It was drifting toward her, an oblong stretch of seaweed a few feet below the surface, undulating with the swells. In an instant, she became dark green and hovered above the meandering patch. But Binti needed to steer the seaweed, to position it directly above her target. And it would have to look natural.

The octopus lowered herself into the patch, careful not to break through it. She grasped the slippery weed with several suckers and relied on her siphon to propel her toward Ebb. Intent on his chores, the farmer never even glanced up at what was approaching overhead. In fact, Binti was so close, she could hear her friend talking to himself.

"How's this stuff supposed to grow in this light?" he grumbled. "I need sun!"

As if the sun heard Ebb, it steadily emerged from behind the storm clouds. A single bright ray cut through the ocean and landed on Ebb, marking him as Binti's target. The octopus smiled, satisfied that today, she'd get the better of her friend. She nudged the seaweed a little closer.

Ebb began his lunch break. He quietly grazed on some brown algae with no clue as to what lurked just above his relaxed dorsal fin.

Poor Ebb, Binti thought. *This algae-eating simpleton is no match for a superior cephalopod like me. It's shame that I'll have to burst his bubble, shatter his misplaced notion that a damselfish could ever escape the hunt of an octopus*. The cephalopod giggled to herself.

Binti pounced, bursting through the seaweed, spreading her arms wide so that she could envelop Ebb. It was essential to achieve maximum embarrassment, because Binti wasn't sure when an opportunity like this would appear again.

She slammed onto the rocks where the algae grew. Pinning her prey beneath her, she turned a proud, radiant red. Of course, she didn't bite, paralyze, or poison her friend, but Ebb must understand just what Binti could do if she wanted to. The octopus could feel the fish beneath her. Trapped like a killie in a clam, Ebb was at Binti's mercy.

It was such a satisfying moment, she held on a little longer. And just to add insult to injury, the octopus slapped a sucker on Ebb and dragged him toward her razor-sharp beak, which she twitched teasingly.

Something didn't feel right. The fish wasn't moving. There was no struggle, no fight. And certainly, Ebb would resist. Yet her catch just laid there. Had she hurt her friend? Was he in shock? What if he had gill-stroke or fin-itus and couldn't tend his fields anymore?

All this just so the octopus could catch a cheap thrill? What had she done?

Binti released her suckers and relaxed her grip. Her prey didn't twitch. No heartbeat, no gill flutter, no finning, no electrical impulses—there was no life beneath her. The octopus turned a pale, lifeless gray, weeping, "Spirit-fish, what have I done?" She knew what death looked like and was afraid to gaze upon Ebb. "Please breathe life back into my friend."

The tears that oozed from Binti's eyes reminded her of an old reef-belief which claimed that in the beginning, Makoona was covered with fresh water, but when the man-tide began fishing with nets and killing creatures on such a massive scale, so many tears were shed that the ocean became salty.

Binti spotted Hootie swimming over an orange sponge-covered ridge. The blowfish swam over to his friend. "Look at you, you're all gray. What're you doing?"

The octopus shook her mantle in shame. "I have just done a terrible thing."

"What could you do that would be so terrible? It's not like you killed someone or something."

Binti couldn't breathe. All she could do was lift up her arms, turn her mantle away from the corpse, and mutter, "Look, look what I have done."

Hootie peered under the octopus. He swam closer. The blowfish disappeared beneath Binti for a moment. When he emerged, he was chewing. "Hey, that's pretty tasty. Did Ebb know about this?"

"How can you ask that?" she screamed. "How can you eat Ebb? He was our friend!"

"I hope I still am," the damselfish said from a few fins away. "And if you take another bite of my algae without asking, Hootie, you're gonna be the one who's dead. Get my drift, blowfish?"

"Hey, I . . ."

Binti jetted over to Ebb, ready to lay a seven-armed embrace on her resurrected pal.

"Stop it!" the farmer commanded. "Mind your distance." Ebb hated emotional displays.

"But you're alive!" Binti bellowed. "You're alive!" She turned to Hootie, who'd snatched another algae hors d'oeuvre. "He's alive!"

"What's she talking about?" Hootie asked Ebb. "Did she just get sprayed?"

"Nah, she thought she was gonna pounce on me. Made a pretty good try too. But you gotta be smoother than sunlight to catch me, which is, by the wave, what ruined your plan."

"How?" Binti asked as she adjusted to the dual realization that Ebb was alive and she was apparently still inept.

"Well, it seemed a little humany that one patch of seaweed would come directly at me while all the others floated out to sea."

"I figured that might be a problem."

"You almost got away with it . . . Take another bite of that algae, blowfish, and I'll be using your scales as fertilizer." Ebb turned back to Binti. "When you were hovering over me and that ray of sunlight broke through the clouds, it not only lit me up, but I could see the silhouette of a strange seven-armed octopus just above the seaweed. *I wonder who that could be?* I says to myself.

"Oh, it took a lot of thought for a simple farmer like me, but I must've guessed right, 'cause suddenly, this big, stupid octopus crashes down and murders . . . my lunch, a ball of algae. Yep, looks like you really showed me who the ultimate reef creature is. Must be *me*. Thanks for confirming what I already knew." And with that, Ebb swallowed a big bite of his lunch and went back to work.

Later in the day, Binti was still feeling blue about her failed attempt to pounce on Ebb. She was so deflated that Hootie suggested she visit the gobies. "Go get cleaned. You'll feel better. There's nothing like being pampered when you feel down."

"I don't feel like a cleaning," Binti said, pouting.

"Sure, you don't now, but wait until those little gobies get going on you. Wait `til they suck your suckers, massage your mantle, and tweak your beak. You'll forget all about that little episode."

"Ya think?"

"Trust me, you melancholy mollusk. A good cleaning will give you a whole new outlook on life." As they swam to the cleaning station, Hootie asked, "Are you still upset about the last shell?"

The octopus didn't answer.

"Let it go, Binti. Didn't your last experiment teach you anything?" Hootie didn't mind trying new things, but he also prided himself on knowing when to quit. He felt that there was nothing inherently wrong with being a quitter. It could be the perfect course of action, provided the quitter knew what to quit and when to do it. For Hootie, it boiled down to timing. And he believed it was time for his friend to give up looking for a shell.

"I just picked the wrong shell last time. I should know better. I'm not a trident. A worm could see that a trident shell would clash with my arms. I need a different shell, something a little more . . . me. Maybe a bailer."

"I got news for you." But before he could utter another word, the sand erupted in a silent explosion, the water swelled, and Hootie disappeared, swallowed by a deceptively banded wobbegong. The large shark was half-buried in the sand beneath some weed-covered stones.

Binti went into her freeze and blend mode, stunned by Hootie's loss. She watched the wobbegong sway its strong tail as it swam off. Then the shark paused, choked, gagged, and spit the blowfish's bile-covered remains onto the sand. The remains spoke.

"Wobbegong, a stupid name for a stupid fish. What's wrong with you? You should know better than to test a blowfish. You can't swallow me. I'd make you sick if you did, fool. And they say *I'm* toxic. Now back off and let me continue my conversation. A barnacle has more sense than you."

"My bad," the shark mumbled. Then it flashed its teeth and went on its way.

"You bet your bad! Think before you swallow!"

Hootie waited until the shark was gone before he spoke to Binti. Had the wobbegong swallowed the octopus instead of the blowfish, he would've enjoyed a much more palatable meal.

Binti asked, "Are you okay?"

A little unsteady on his fins, the blowfish declared, "I'm fine, I'm fine. I'll just swim it off. No big deal. Better fish than that have tried to swallow me . . . Now, what was I saying?"

"Something about news."

"Right, right. I got news for you. *Any* shell is the wrong shell. You're an octopus. It's time to face the current."

"I'm also a mollusk."

"Well, that argument's getting old. A squid's a mollusk. Where's its shell?"

"Maybe one of them is looking for a shell too. Maybe I'll start a trend. Someone has to be the first."

"Yeah? Well, as long as we're being honest, lemme tell you what I think will happen. You'll waste a whole lot of time—yours *and* mine. You'll never be comfortable in any shell. And you'll wind up getting eaten by an eel or a wobbegong 'cause you're paying attention to shells instead of survival."

They'd arrived at Paykak's. Binti's goby friend slipped her in front of the line, claiming it was an emergency case. The octopus hovered over a violet sponge, spread her arms out wide, and turned a relaxing shade of green while several tiny gobies went to work. Paykak floated next to the octopus.

"If I stay here and talk to you, you'll get a much better cleaning," he said. "It's a sad reefality of the practice, but when the boss is around, all the cleaners become more gilligent."

"Ah, it's only natural."

"Is it? You'd think they wouldn't need the extra inducement, that there wouldn't be another level they could rise to, that they'd always clean the best they could, but that's just not the way it is anymore. Today, there's no pride in one's craft." Paykak turned from Binti and shouted, "Hey, open your eyes! I can see that leech from here. Come on, fish. Suck 'em up!"

"Maybe if they were happier," Binti mumbled as two gobies trimmed plaque from her beak.

"Happier? Who could be happier? Is there a more noble occupation for a fish than this? What other job can you do and be on a perpetual meal break at the same time? All they have to do is eat." Again, Paykak turned from Binti. "Pus! I see pus! Make it disappear!"

"Well, you're kinda tough on them, Paykak."

"Tough? Me, tough? I'll tell you what tough is. When I swam to my first cleaning station way out on the edge of the reef, every day I had to swim into the current, both ways. Why, I . . ."

"How could that be? Into the current both ways?"

"It's a rather technical tidal event, just trust me on this. Like I was saying . . . Oh, yeah. Tough. Let me tell you, I earned this lateral stripe by being tough, swimming over a rock all day with no help and no fish waiting in line, flashing this blue stripe until you're so tired you turn belly up and start floating to the surface. Then the only one who stops in for a cleaning is an ill-tempered reef shark who just ate a sprayed angelfish. You know what happens to a shark who just ate a sprayed angelfish?"

"No. I don't eat angelfish, sprayed or otherwise."

"Me either, but I'll tell you what happens. It makes the shark twitch. You want to go inside the mouth of a twitching reef shark? Ever seen those teeth up close and fishonal?"

"Ah, no. And I don't really want to."

"That's my point. And once you get into that twitching teeth trap, you know what you find? Nothing. There's next to nothing 'cause those pain in the tailfin—"

"Paykak!"

"I'm sorry. Didn't mean to use the t-word. Gee, you'd think *I* could keep it clean." The goby laughed. "Heeh, heeh . . . get it? I'm a cleaner, but I used a dirty word. Heeh, heeh, that's pretty funny."

Binti laughed, more out of awkwardness than amusement. She was starting to wonder about her friend.

"Okay, let me finish. There's nothing in the shark's mouth because of those scab remoras. For years, they've been cutting into my business. They're the biggest suck-ups in the sea. Sharks wind up with their own private cleaners attached to them night and day. How can you compete with that? It's not right." Then Paykak returned to his original point. "Would any of these do-littles go in there and clean that shark?"

"I bet if—"

"No wave! In my day, gobies were gobies. I don't know what's going on today. Look at 'em. They're like barnacles. 'Oh, let the current carry the food to me.' Ah, they need to get off their fins and get their scales dirty."

Paykak shifted his attention to a tiny goby working on Binti. He calmly asked, "Do you see that lesion?"

The cleaner froze, petrified by Paykak's question.

"Oh, spirit-fish save me! Do I have to show you everything? Take some fishnitiative yourself."

As Paykak swam out to the youngster, another little goby emerged from behind Binti's mantle and whispered, "He's a legend, you know."

Binti smiled, "Him?"

"Really, he's a finspiration. It's an honor to say that you studied under Paykak.

"But he's so tough on you."

"Sure, but what's a little yelling? He's passionate about cleaning. One day, we'll all be great cleaners like him. He's my fishtor."

Paykak drifted up behind the little one, shocking him with, "Hey, are those jaws doing something other than cleaning? There's a line back there, in case you haven't noticed."

The tiny goby winked at the octopus and then hurried back to work.

Paykak resumed his conversation. "That's the trouble with you, Binti."

"The trouble with *me*?"

"Well, now that you bring it up, you go around thinking a shell is going to make you happy."

"I didn't bring that up," the octopus pointed out.

"You, me, what's the difference? It would've come up anyway. You invertebrates are all alike. You need a backbone."

"It's a little easier to get a shell, don't you think?"

"Yeah, do what's easy. Settle. You're like all the rest. I shouldn't even be telling you this."

"Telling me what? All you're doing is insulting me."

"I know someone, a turtle named Sev. He might be able to help you."

"You mean help me find a shell?"

"No, I mean help you grow gills. Hello! What have we just been talking about here?"

"So how do I find Bev?"

"It's Sev, not Bev. Hootie will take you. He knows the turtle better than I do."

"Hootie knows the turtle? And he didn't tell me about him?"

"Sounds like a question for a blowfish, not a goby."

Kemar was soaked when he woke. The sand surrounding the boat was hard and cold. It had crusted around his eyes and on his hair. The boy squinted at the daylight, although the sun hadn't yet risen above the mangrove.

He rolled out from under the boat, sat on an upturned five-gallon bucket, and pulled an unsealed can of Spam from beneath his kremar. The boy brushed his breakfast off, dining on the Spam, a banana, and a crushed single-serving box of Cheerios that Bao had left in the boat. It was an absolute feast compared with how he had eaten before leaving Cambodia.

The boat people used to joke, "You can only eat so much fish." But in Cambodia, they said, "You can only eat so much dust." The meal that he now enjoyed helped him feel further away from the past, as if he'd turned a corner.

After breakfast, Kemar flipped the boat over, slipped three round pieces of wood—which he used as rollers—under the keel, and worked the boat back into the surf. When Bao arrived, they loaded up their gear and rowed to Meela's shop. The fisherman expected his motor to be ready. It wasn't.

"Said problem with motor not big. Said it be ready today. Why not ready?"

Meela sucked on her cigar. She grinned and released the smoke through the handy gap between her front teeth. The sight made Kemar think of a tiny smokestack releasing steam from a boiler that burned deep inside her.

"A funny thing happened," she began. "You see, Mr. Bao, I stored your outboard way over there. And right next to it—I didn't want to lose track of your valuable property—I placed that old box of grenades you asked me to hold for you."

"Took grenade! Bao not ask you hold grenade."

"Could be. At my age, sometimes, events get a little foggy. Either way, they were *your* grenades, right?"

"*Are* my grenade," Bao corrected her.

"Were," Meela countered.

"Were?" Bao inquired.

"Were," Meela repeated. "You see, I kept them together. The motor, the grenades, it was all your stuff. But the strangest thing happened. What are the odds of this happening? The lightning popped that palm tree over there. I know my eyes aren't what they once were, but I saw it myself. A coconut dropped off and landed right in the box of grenades. And wouldn't you know it? One of 'em exploded.

"Then another exploded and another. The good news is—and I know it'll be your first question—I'm fine. My hut's okay, and none of the other motors were damaged. But the bad news is, you lost all your grenades. And that pile of twisted metal under that tree, well, that's your motor. I'm not even sure *I* can fix what's left of it."

"No motor?" Bao asked blankly.

"That would seem to be the situation." Meela winked at Kemar, who looked on, fascinated. Just for effect, Meela blew a little more smoke. "I guess if you weren't fishing with those darn grenades, none of this would've happened. Oh well, live and learn." Meela turned to the boy. "That's my motto, son. Live and learn."

"How Bao fish now?"

"Looks like you're gonna have to rent one of my boats—very expensive. Or you could paddle a dugout like most people here."

"Can paddle, but not catch enough fish."

"That is a problem . . . Got a sail?"

"This not sailboat."

"That's right. How about fishing from shore? There's all kinds of fish running in the surf."

Bao just stared at Meela as he became aware of her sarcasm.

"I see, not good business fishing from shore . . . Got another outboard?"

"Not have engine." Obviously agitated, Bao repeated, "Not have engine."

"That is unfortunate, Mr. Bao. Hey, wait a minute. I got motors. Want one?"

Again, Bao just stared at the old woman while Kemar briefly flashed his white teeth.

When it was all said and done, Bao had his outboard . . . kind of. Meela promised him an old Yamarudeson, a mishmash of parts from an old Yamaha, Evenrude, and Johnson. The mechanic claimed that with a little work, the motor would run just fine, perhaps a little sluggish at twenty-five horsepower, but it would do the job.

Meela had cautioned Bao before about damage to coral from excessive wakes and speeds, unattended props, and anchors, so neutering his craft with the puny motor was how she responded to his indifference.

She also forced Bao to agree to buoys and tie-ups wherever he fished the reef, keeping his anchor off the bottom. And certainly, if

Meela ever heard that Bao was fishing with grenades or anything else lethal to the reef, she would refuse to service any motor that he used or borrowed. On Makoona, this was no idle threat. No one could avoid depending on Meela at one time or another. She was something of a goby in that respect.

As long as Bao kept his agreement, he would remain in Meela's good graces. He would, however, have to wait two days before the mechanic could make his custom creation seaworthy.

Kemar helped Bao secure his motorless boat on shore. Then the frustrated fisherman trudged off down the beach. His young associate ran up to him, asking, "What are we going to do for the next two days?"

Bao replied, "*We* do nothing."

"But what will *I* do?"

"Ask you, not me."

Kemar stared at the man, confused.

"No fish. No money. No food. Two day, we fish again." And as he continued down the beach, Bao spoke loudly, "Be good for you. Will appreciate more what Bao do for you."

Kemar knew exactly what Bao did for him. He didn't need the next two days to point that out. He also knew that once again, he was going to be hungry and cold. Then the boy heard an outboard running. He looked over his bony shoulder, back to Meela's workshop, where he saw the motor reserved for Bao running like new. The Cambodian approached the mechanic.

"This motor runs nicely," he said.

"Of course it does, it's a Meela motor. As a matter of fact, I have to put a governor on it and slow it down."

"But why won't you let us fish with it now?"

"I won't let that bilge-for-brains Bao fish with it now. He needs to be grounded for a few days."

"Yes, but I, too, am grounded."

Meela hadn't considered that. Assuming Kemar was a half-pint version of a pint-sized Bao, she also hadn't considered that she would like the boy. The woman raised her arm and extended her index finger. She wanted quiet while she considered the situation and chewed on her cigar.

"What's your name again?"

"Kemar."

"Kemar, how about this? The storm left me with some heavy work. I don't like heavy work. Can you move a motor without getting sand in it?"

The boy studied the motor mounted in an oil barrel next to him. It was a coin toss as to whether the boy or the motor was heavier, but Kemar's desire to work was absolutely bigger than the barrel, as Meela saw when the boy answered, "I can move these."

"Well, head into the hangar and start hauling them out. I'll tell you where to put 'em. Kick the chocks out from under that dolly, and it'll make the job a little easier."

Meela had a long, flat path—a mini boardwalk that ran a loop through her yard—passing within a foot of each oil drum. A motor would be laid onto a raised dolly, then wheeled to a barrel or into the shop. Meela's track made the job easier.

The Cambodian stood his ground.

Meela smiled. "Apparently, we need to come to terms."

Kemar tilted his head back, listening.

"What's Bao paying you?"

"He pays me to fish. You want me to move motors."

"Good! Never tell anyone how much money you make. I'll give you two dollars up front to start working. When the day is over, if you've done good work, I'll give you a bonus of my choosing, okay?"

The boy nodded his acceptance.

"No negotiation? Well, let's get to work."

Kemar peered into the hangar, which was what Meela called her workshop. It did resemble a hangar. The structure had a rounded roof of bent sheet metal with a tattered but functional windsock mounted above the wide doorway. There were as many tools and parts as one would expect to find in a hangar, but this building was strictly for boats and their motors.

Kemar stashed his two dollars and disappeared into the shop. He spent the rest of the morning lugging motors, parts, and tools.

After a quick lunch—provided by Meela, of course—he held parts in place for the mechanic while she turned screws and made adjustments. Kemar did whatever was asked of him and several other helpful things she never requested.

At dinner time, Meela told the boy that she was waiting for a friend to stop by with a "doormat" for their meal, and, as a gratuity, she invited the youngster to dine with them.

Kemar asked, "How do you eat a doormat? I have eaten many things—insects, rats, bait, other people's garbage—but I have never eaten a doormat. Aren't there better things? I still have some food. I could share."

Meela laughed and hugged the boy. "That's a good one, kid! Don't worry, this doormat won't taste like dirty feet."

The boy and the mechanic sat on a crate eating fruit while they waited for Meela's friend. She casually questioned, "What's a kid like you doing on Makoona, fishing with that lowlife Bao?"

"Mr. Bao saved me from drowning and gave me food and work. He lets me sleep under his boat."

"That Bao's a real Albert Schweitzer," Meela mumbled.

"Who?"

"A famous humanitarian. So, where were you before Bao saved you?"

"On a boat."

"Before that?"

"Cambodia."

"You escaped the Khmer Rouge?"

"Once you live under them, you can never escape. When I was the last of my family, I left Cambodia. But I will never escape what happened."

"You speak English very nicely, kid. You're educated?"

"I speak and read English and French. For a boy my age, I am educated. My parents were teachers, my father a professor at the university."

"He opposed the Khmer Rouge?"

"In the beginning, he spoke against them. He warned people that bad things might happen, but no one, not even my father, dreamed our cities would be evacuated. No one dreamed we would be in forced labor, growing rice that we weren't allowed to eat. No one dreamed that we would fall like leaves from the trees. It was easier to speak out before they took control. To do so after was crazy."

"Your father spoke out?"

"No. My father died because he wore glasses."

"What?"

"The Khmer Rouge believed that glasses were a symbol of the educated class. Anyone caught wearing them, especially reading or writing, could be killed. My father lost his life because he put his glasses on to read me a story. A cousin turned him in."

Kemar untied his kremar from around his waist and opened it up in front of Meela. "Look," he said, smiling. Gentle fingers untied a small velvet sack. It was stained and faded. He parted the top, pulling back the dark blue material. The bag jingled with the sound of a few coins and other unseen treasures. The boy's fingers slid into the sack and emerged with a pair of shiny wire-rimmed glasses. Kemar handled them as if they were the most precious things on Earth. To him, they were.

The low sun reflected off the metal and glass as the boy raised them to his face and lifted the ends over his ears. He smiled his brightest smile, saying, "Every day, they fit my face a little better."

"Your father would be proud," Meela whispered.

"I like to wear them. I can't see straight with them on, but that's what I like about them. When I wear Father's glasses, I see the world a little differently. He always saw things differently but clearly. It's kind of like seeing the world through his eyes."

"And what kind of world do you see?" Meela asked.

Kemar removed the glasses from his face and hesitated. The old woman thought that perhaps she'd asked too many questions.

The boy reached out both hands and said, "Would you like to see for yourself?"

When Meela opened her bony fingers to accept the gesture, the two were interrupted by a call from the mangrove behind the shed. "Dinner has arrived," they heard.

In an instant, the glasses disappeared into Kemar's hand, which was thrust into the velvet sack that was tied tightly and then wrapped in the kremar.

The woman was relieved by the distraction. It gave her a chance to wipe the tears from her eyes. She didn't want the boy—or anyone, for that matter—to see them. It had been a long time since Meela had cried. She stood and called to the trees, "Don't come in here unless you have the doormat."

Out of the brush stepped the other American on Makoona, the man who'd spoken to Kemar the night before. He walked with confidence, although most of the locals interpreted the gait as arrogant. But Al wasn't an arrogant man.

"If you know how to ask, the sea will give you anything you need," he said.

"And you certainly know how to ask. Hey, I'll bet the sea can't give me a case of tomato juice. I really miss tomato juice."

"I bet a case or two of tomato juice has washed up from the sea before."

"Not in front of my hut," Meela teased.

"Maybe the sea has decided you don't really need tomato juice," Kemar interjected.

"Luckily, I'm old enough to decide for myself."

"Then get it yourself," Al added.

"That's it. You guys are teaming up on me. I'm outnumbered. Tell you what I really need—dinner." Meela asked Kemar, "Do you know my friend here?"

"We've met, but I do not know him."

He extended a large hand to the boy. Fish scales clung to the fingers. "I'm Al," the man said. "Didn't mean to scare you last night. Just wanted to make sure you were okay."

"I'm Kemar. I was not scared. And I am all right."

"Well, I can see you and Kemar go way back, so let's eat first and chat later," Meela remarked.

A stringer was pulled tightly across one side of Al's chest. His fingers filled a loop at the end of a line that stretched over and dug into the skin on his shoulder. There was something heavy slung over the American's back, but Kemar couldn't see it.

It must be a very large, dirty, smelly doormat, Kemar thought. Suddenly, the boy wasn't so hungry.

Al extended his arm, placing a wide, flat flounder onto an up-turned barrel. It covered both ends of the barrel easily. Had it been made of rattan or rubber, it would've made an impressive doormat indeed.

Meela looked at Kemar and said, "This, my boy, is a doormat."

He smiled, suddenly hungry again.

That evening, under the stars of Makoona, with the music of the surf shimmering across the sand, Kemar, Meela, and Al shared an enormous fillet of flounder, dressed in fruit and spices.

Kemar spent that night sleeping in Meela's workshop on a cot, serving as her night watchman. In return, Meela would provide either dinner or a dollar, sometimes both. Kemar was pleased with the arrangement. Meela was pleased too. She hoped that soon she might get the boy out from under more than just Bao's boat.

A Shell Game

Hootie not only knew Sev, he knew where to find him. Ancient and reclusive, Sev inhabited one of the many wrecks that littered Makoona. Most of them were cloaked with coral, barnacles, weed, and sponges. Many no longer resembled what they'd once been. Countless creatures used these carcasses for homes, hunting grounds, and breeding cover.

Sev's home, however, was unusual among wrecks. It didn't have open decks, a mast, a thick propeller, or a rudder trailing behind it. Even though it had been in the sea longer than many of the others, the turtle's home was still much shinier than most wrecks. In a sense, it resembled a barracuda: long, lean, silvery, and tubular, with fins like a flying fish that spanned out as long as its body. To the inhabitants of Makoona, this was a mysterious shape. Everyone pretty much stayed away, except for Sev.

The aged turtle had lived inside the silver shadow for as long as anyone could remember. Having little need for the protection of the wreck, he dwelt there for other reasons. Sev claimed that his home dropped out of the sky one day, splashing down in its current location. The turtle said that he actually witnessed the event, that he saw one human swimming above the wreck. Another was still inside.

Sev emerged to feed and breathe. On occasion, he would visit the cleaning station or just float wherever the current carried

him. To Sev, the reef was a theater, and he enjoyed the show. He'd even been known to take a bite or two of the sponges in Ebb's field.

A confident yet relaxed turtle, whose shell was chipped in spots and embellished with patches of barnacles, Sev's thoughts were as clear as a glass shrimp. His expression, however, was not so clear. The loquacious leatherback only asked questions, and yet he'd been known to provide others with guidance, despite his circumspect manner.

A lifetime of eating jellyfish and being stung in and around the eyes had left Sev's vision somewhat blurred. Still, the timeworn turtle recognized Hootie from a respectable distance when the blowfish and the octopus approached.

Hootie knew that Sev had a fondness for sponge, so he instructed Binti to bring a large one. The octopus also hoped that a little pre-discussion nosh might lead to a more enlightening result.

"What brings you youngsters to my neck of the coral?" the leatherback greeted them.

Hootie introduced Binti and explained her quest for a shell. Then the octopus made an offering of the sponge.

Sev smiled. "So you've heard that the best way to a turtle's thoughts is through its stomach?" He gathered the meal with his front fins and added, "Do you mind if we speak while I dine? Would either of you care to join me?"

Binti raised three arms and said, "No, thank you," while she slapped a sucker on the blowfish to keep him from accepting the invite. It was a gesture that didn't disappoint the turtle, since it left him with the entire sponge.

But Hootie wasn't giving up. He expelled any trace of water from his system so that he appeared emaciated, leaned toward the meal, and said, "I'd love to . . ." When he felt Binti's grip tighten on him, he got a grip on his own gluttony and grudgingly mumbled, " . . . see you enjoy that entire sponge." The blowfish turned to the octopus and added, "Binti will find something for us to eat later."

The turtle looked pleased. "Well?" he asked, slices of sponge slipping from his jowls. "What can I tell you about a shell?"

"*You* have one," Binti answered, "so you must understand how I feel when I say that *I* want one."

"I must? Have you ever seen a turtle without a shell?"

"No," the octopus responded while Hootie nosed around Sev's floating scraps.

"Then why would you presume that I would understand your shellfishness?"

"I just meant that by having a shell, you would obviously understand its benefits, its allure."

"So you believe I enjoy having a shell?"

"Yes."

"Could there also be detriments to having a shell?"

Hootie joined in. "Sure. Like without a shell, Binti can feel things all over her body that many of us can't. She can fit into places many of us can't. She can change color. She's lighter—"

"We catch your drift, Hootie," Binti interrupted. Then she whispered, "You're not helping," while pushing a scrap of sponge toward the blowfish, hoping to distract him from the conversation.

"Doesn't Hootie make sense?" Sev asked.

"I suppose, but being an octopus, I could shed my shell anytime and have the best of both worlds."

"So you're not *truly* interested in having a shell?"

"Of course I am," Binti replied, indignant that her conviction was being questioned.

"Can I give up my shell as the mood moves?"

"No."

The turtle pointed a fin and asked, "Can that snail?"

"No."

"Then why should you be able to?"

"Because I can."

"Can you?" the turtle probed.

"Yes, I can."

Sev pressed. "Can you put your shell on right now?"

"I don't have a shell yet."

"Then you can't put your shell on and take it off as you please, can you? Isn't life often about making choices and sticking to them, swimming in the scales you've been dealt? Isn't life really about taking what the spirit-fish has given you and making the most of it?"

"But I believe the spirit-fish has given me the inspiration and the ability to wear a shell."

"Then why do you need to speak to me? Why not let the spirit-fish provide the shell?" Sev spoke without interrupting or diverting his attention from his meal.

Frustrated, Binti said, "No one in the sea has looked harder for a shell than me."

"Could your difficulty in finding a shell perhaps be an indication that you shouldn't have one?"

"Well, it seems to me that you don't like my idea and that you're not going to help me."

"Haven't I already helped you?"

"How? You just keep asking me questions. I need answers. Where can I find a shell?"

"Don't you really mean, where can I find the right shell, the shell that will bring me closer to the heart of the spirit-fish?"

The octopus turned an intense orange. Sev was finally telling her something she wanted to know. "Yes, that's exactly what I mean. Where will I find the shell that will enable me to become one with the spirit-fish?"

The turtle stopped chewing. He smiled. Sev had a flair for the theatrical. He paid great attention to his delivery, his timing, his posture, and, of course, his pronunciation. The leatherback's dark head glistened, illuminated by shimmering shafts of light that penetrated the sea. "Have you ever hunted for crabs in the shallows?"

"Yes, I have."

"Have you ever seen shells washed up on Makoona's shores?"

"Yes. Yes, there are shells, all kinds of them, scattered along the entire shoreline, of course. But they tend to be small, broken. Do you think there will be one big enough and beautiful enough?"

"Do you know the beach where the sand is softest, where the female turtles choose to lay their eggs? Is it not a place where all types of shells come alive, where the water tickles and they dance, where animals crawl into their husks and find homes, where little ones break out and start their lives?" Sev, playing to the drama of the moment, cocked his smooth head and waited for a reply. "Are you afraid of the danger?"

"It *is* a dangerous place, with birds, man-tide, and others."

The sagacious sea turtle smiled. "How badly do you want a shell, restless octopus? Are you prepared for what you'll find on that beach?"

Strings of indigo pulsed through Binti's orange flesh. "You have spoken with the spirit-fish about this. You know what I will find. Tell me, please."

"Who said you will find anything? Could it be that something will find you?" Sev sashayed closer to Binti. He laid his head against her mantle and whispered, "Do you think my shell is what enables me to know the spirit-fish?" And then, Sev turned toward his silver home and swam away, picking up the last shred of sponge as he passed over the remnants of his lunch.

Hootie appeared on the other side of Binti's mantle and said, "Let me guess, you'll be taking a swim over to the shore."

"You're not coming? It's where the turtle told me to go."

"I'm not sure he *told* you anything. Sounded to me like he might've warned you not to go. Besides, I'm not looking for a shell. And the shallow surf isn't the safest place for me—or you."

Unlike her friend, Binti was not very afraid of the shallow surf, and although she didn't make a habit of it, she had, on occasion, hunted crabs in tidal pools left by receding water. Those little puddles were a hunting haven for the crabs and, by extension, for those who hunted crabs. It was easy for the octopus to surprise and corner her prey where the land met the sea. An added benefit was that the water was so shallow that larger ocean predators who might have a hankering for octopus couldn't hunt there.

There were, however, dangers. Pelicans, hawks, gulls, and others were known to swoop down on creatures in the surf. The mantide also plucked meals from the wet sand. And when an octopus is not completely submerged, as Binti might be while she dragged herself from puddle to puddle, her defenses diminish. Binti would be more sluggish, less buoyant, feeling the full effects of gravity.

She would also have to keep mindful of the sun. Her flesh wasn't equipped for too much exposure. Once on the beach, she would become a fish out of water. But for a chance to find the divine shell, Binti was ready to accept the risk.

As she came closer to shore, Binti crawled along flats of turtle grass. The ocean's depth lessened dramatically while the turtle grass quickly gave way to a clear, clean stretch of sand. The octopus shifted from light green with yellow streaks to grayish tan with small clusters of brown and yellow spots.

Binti continued crawling across the sandy plain until she felt the unmistakable burn. Her mantle had broken through the water's surface. The sun beating down on her naked flesh both warmed and chilled her. The chill came from the thought of what would happen to her if she were trapped and exposed to the power of the burning orb for too long. Binti had seen jellyfish baked on the sand.

The octopus emerged from the sea. The surf rolled but didn't crash. The sand was hard, wet, and warmer than the water. Binti would use any moisture as a buffer. When she felt dry, flaky sand cling to her skin, she would retreat, dragging herself back, closer to the sea. But what if she spotted her shell further inland, perhaps at the base of a sun-seared sand dune? Would she abandon the shell or her plan for survival?

Sev was right. The beach was a virtual treasure trove of shells. Binti was ashamed that she hadn't thought of this herself, but she didn't give Sev all the credit either. The octopus believed that the turtle had help, that he was a conduit used to carry directions from the spirit-fish, directions that led her to land.

In a way, it made ironic sense, Binti observed, that a mollusk who didn't have a shell would have to leave the ocean to find one on land. An insight like this, she optimistically decided, had to be a sign from the spirit-fish that she was on the right track. Binti began examining shells.

There were so many to choose from that the octopus established two guidelines. First, because she was going to live in it, the shell must be a good fit. Most of what rolled around the beach was obviously too small and could be ignored. Secondly, and more importantly, the shell must be perfect. It must be chip free and without cracks—no barnacles, algae, or damage of any type. In short, the shell must be stunning. Since the spirit-fish was perfection, could one really hope to come closer to the spirit by adopting anything less than perfect?

The octopus conducted her search, paying particular attention to her two guidelines. With so many shells automatically eliminated, and with seven out of eight arms in good working order, the search went quickly.

The mollusk casually disqualified scallops, clams, conches, a trident, angel wings, razor clams, mussels, and a shoal of other shells. Finally, after hours of chasing the changing tide and digging out shell after shell, Binti crawled into a shady pool, stretched out, and considered whether something in Sev's message had eluded her.

The way the turtle had talked, only asking questions, she might've missed a vital clue. The loony leatherback could be as annoying as sand in your siphon, but Binti believed that if she were really worthy of the shell, she would understand the turtle and why she was sent to the shore.

Her solitude was broken by a question. Binti heard a muffled, "What are you going to do?"

It sounded to Binti like the voice came from inside of her, but it definitely wasn't *that* voice.

Again, she heard the voice. "Eat me or let me go, but this is ridiculous."

Afraid of what danger might be attached to the source of the sound, Binti was reluctant to move or answer. In need of a better vantage point, the octopus carefully slid to the other side of the small pool.

Across from Binti, smashed into the sandy wall she'd clung to moments before, an engulfed hermit crab peered out. Apparently, when Binti had plopped into the puddle, she'd pushed a hermit crab into the depression's sandy side. The wall was fairly soft, and the crab was well protected by her shell but was pinned against a wide, flat rock within the wall. Naturally, the crab assumed she was about to become dinner. So when the octopus merely sat on top of her for such a long time, the crusty crustacean became cranky.

"So what's the deal?" the crab questioned. "If I'm supposed to be lunch, let's get it over with. But if you're not eating, could you try not to sit on me anymore?"

Binti, who had other things on her mantle, replied, "You would be wise not to worry about what I do. Just be glad that I'm not eating right now."

"What is that? A threat?"

And then, perhaps it was the power of suggestion, but for some strange reason, Binti got hungry. She thought back to her last meal. It was well before she'd spoken with Sev. The octopus saw the hermit through new eyes—hungry ones.

"Normally, I wouldn't be overly concerned with what someone else was doing, but when you slam yourself on top of a crab and prevent her from breathing, not for nothing, it does tend to pique one's interest." The crab stopped speaking. She noticed that hungry look in Binti's eyes. "You did just say that you *weren't* eating?"

The octopus pounced. She spread herself wide and crashed down a second time on the diminutive crab, who buried herself deep within her shell. When Binti probed inside the armor with the tip of an arm, the hermit went wild, snapping and crushing whatever her claws could grab. The crab was no pushover. She dug deep into Binti's flesh, turning and twisting a massive claw.

For the oppressed, victory would not be measured by the octopus's death. That was beyond the crustacean's capability. All she hoped to do was show the predator that there would be a painful price for her flesh.

Binti wrestled her arm free and backed off.

"So that's how you feed yourself? You introduce yourself to your meals, tell the victims you're not hungry, give them false hope, chat for a moment, and then when they're feeling safe, you attack? I know octopuses don't have bones, but I didn't think they were without hearts too."

"Actually, I have three hearts."

"Well, they certainly don't feel anything, do they? What? You introduce yourself to your meals? You're one sick cephalopod."

The blushing Binti responded, "No, I didn't mean—"

"Your kind disgusts me." The crab backed into a corner and waved her claws menacingly at the octopus. "You think you can take me? You want a piece of this? Come on back. I got a little something for you. Ever been decked by a decopod?"

Binti stretched out an arm just beyond the hermit's reach. "No," she said quietly. "I'm sorry. I know the code of the kill as well as anyone. *Don't meet who you eat.*"

The crab lowered her orange claws. Her carapace was dusted with white spots within larger black spots. Two eye stalks studied the octopus. "Ahhh, no harm done, I guess. I'm okay. It'll hurt more in the morning." But the crab quickly raised her large claw, opening it, and then snapping it shut. "You're not setting me up again, are you?"

"No, no. I'm not really myself right now. Maybe I've had a little too much sun, a few too many shells. I don't know."

"You eat shells?"

"No. I'm looking for one. Don't ask."

"Name's Elaber," the crab volunteered.

"You're a tough old crab, aren't you?"

"Remnants. Remnants of a glory that once was. But there's still plenty of pinch left in me." Elaber sat quietly with Binti for a moment or two. Even though they were situated at different ends of the pool, the crab could see that the octopus was sullen, troubled. Elaber crawled toward Binti. "I know I should be minding my own sand, but it doesn't take eyestalks to see you could use a friend. I'm gonna take a snap here. If it's a shell you're looking for . . ."

Binti brightened. This was the moment. This was why the turtle had sent her here. She could feel it coming. "Yes."

"Like I was saying, if you need a shell for some reason, I have a shell for you."

Binti was hanging on Elaber's every bubble. "Where is it? What do I have to do to get it?"

"Clam down," Elaber said as she waved a claw. She bent over, looked out from under herself, and said, "Could you just help me get it off? It's a little tight right here."

Binti was speechless. The crab was talking about her dilapidated shell.

By now, Elaber had managed to wriggle out of the puny shell herself. She held it up and looked it over one last time. "I know it's got a few waves behind it, but it's a good shell."

Binti mumbled, "Well, thanks, really, thanks a lot . . . but I couldn't bear to—"

"Stop. I won't hear of it. It's nothing. I can find another. It's easier for me. Take it. I want you to have it."

A blushy pink began to overrun Binti. "I could never accept this."

The crab paused. "Is something wrong with it?"

"No. Nothing."

"At least be honest."

"It's just, I don't know. I guess it's a little too small for me."

"Yeeees?"

"And it's kind of cracked right there . . . and there. The colors aren't quite right either. Actually, it's tough to tell what color it is under all that algae and those barnacles."

"I *sea*."

"Not that I don't appreciate the gesture. It's quite overwhelming. But I think I'm just looking for something else."

"Oh, I get it," Elaber quipped. "A shell has to be like an octopus—smooth, colorful, form fitting, flashy. Its worth is determined by how it looks. That's a pretty narrow view coming from one with such a large mantle."

"And how should my view change? Wouldn't my shell—an octopus's shell—need to be all those things?"

"Try not to judge a shell by its luster."

"How should one be judged, Elaber?"

"If you really believe what you're saying, then maybe you're better off without a shell. Trust me, the shell I'm offering you is unlike any other you'll find. It may be smaller, older, dirtier, but so what? A shell is as much a concept as it is a thing. A shell is an understanding, a state of mind. While this removable carapace might not look like much, it can take you where you want to go."

Elaber grinned. She leaned the shell upright on the sand between the two of them. A small piece of seaweed floated by and stuck to a tiny barnacle that clung to the shell.

"It can take me where I want to go?" Binti repeated. The octopus lifted one of her arms to pick up the shell.

Elaber interrupted Binti by holding out her larger claw and saying, "There is always a price to pay."

The octopus nodded pessimistically. "I should have known. What do you want for your shell?"

"First, this is not *my* shell. It is *a* shell. Secondly, I give it to you because I must. Lastly, once you have accepted this gift, let it guide you. Agreed?"

"Yes, of course."

Elaber backed off and allowed Binti to approach the shell.

The octopus asked, "Are you sure you haven't been sprayed recently?"

The crab climbed out of the tidal pool. She sat high on a sandy ridge and looked down at Binti. "I've been sprayed by the spirit."

When Binti heard that, she reached for the shell. The husk rose by itself from the sand to her arm and nestled snugly into a sucker. A flash of light shot out of the shell's twisted tip. It spread and flowed into the pool, filling it, illuminating it. Algae and barnacles attached to the plastron turned into fine white sand and fell to the floor of the shallow where it radiated out to the soft walls that encircled the water. Soon, all of the sand in the tidal pool was white.

The shell, now clear of its dirt and debris, sparkled like a little rainbow of mother of pearl. Its soft colors spread soothing up Binti's arm. Red, blue, yellow, indigo, violet, orange, and green swirled from arm to arm, then up to her mouth. The colors converged at the base of her mantle, rising until the entire octopus was dressed in a rainbow. Binti gazed up at Elaber and into the sky above her. She tingled.

Relaxing, she saw the beauty of what Elaber had given. The crab she'd tried to kill only moments before had stripped herself of her best defense, her most valuable possession, to help an octopus she barely knew. Bathed in golden sunlight, Elaber nodded from atop the little sand cliff.

"Sometimes it's easy to miss something that's everywhere," she said.

A lone cloud, nudged by the breeze, blew across the sun, eclipsing it momentarily, muting its glare and revealing a disturbing sight. Something was diving at the pool. A bird that had hidden in the brilliance of the blazing orb was attacking. Binti didn't know whether she or the crab was the intended target. In a moment, the question would be answered.

The octopus knew what to do. She stretched an arm out of the puddle toward Elaber so she could return the shell, Elaber's protection. Binti tried to slip it back over her, but the crab, apparently unaware of what approached, scurried away, laughing.

"No re-gifting! It's yours now!"

Elaber stood tall on the sand, raised her gaping claws to the sky, and faced the sea. Her eyes were opened wide. Binti prepared for the strike in her own way, yet she continued to watch her friend until the cloud that covered the sun blew on, unmasking the full face of the star. Blinded by the light, she instinctively covered up and hunkered down, turning black and releasing ink into the pool so she couldn't be seen.

There was no splash. The water was undisturbed. The bird hadn't seen the octopus. Binti peered out from the tidal pool and saw nothing. No Elaber. Then she spotted a solitary gull flying over the ocean, chasing the cloud that had abandoned the sun. Was Elaber in its beak? she wondered. Was the crab a meal being digested or perhaps a minion being welcomed home? The octopus couldn't decide.

Binti lowered herself back into the dark water. She tucked the shell into a large sucker at the base of her arm. It was the most secure place on her body. Through her flesh that surrounded the shell, she saw gentle flashes of rainbow and could feel the warmth radiate from it.

Suddenly, her wonder was replaced with panic. She felt something she'd never felt before, something she prayed she'd never feel in her lifetime. Fingers! A human had plucked her from the pool.

With nothing left to do for Meela and with Bao boatless, Kemar decided to stroll the shore. He hoped to find enough food so that he could return the meal that Meela and Al had given him. It was a good day. The boy already had a dozen crabs, a pair of lobsters, and an assortment of shellfish stuffed into a canvas bag.

Gathering seafood from the surf and shallow tidal pools reminded Kemar of visiting his uncle Neang, who lived on the banks of the Mekong River. When the water spilled out onto the flood plain, the fish followed. They gorged themselves on insects, plants, and other food that the flood enabled them to reach. But when the waters receded, thousands of fish always wound up stranded in little pools all along the plain.

Kemar and his family would scour the muddy puddles for fresh fish. He'd always found this to be the most enjoyable fishing. He needed neither bait nor net, so in a sense, it was a free meal. To Kemar, it was as if the river had delivered the fish to him. Scavenging along Makoona's shore reminded the boy of better days in Cambodia.

On his way back to Meela's shop, he ran into Al, who was also combing the shoreline, but for a different reason.

"Hey, kid. Looking for treasure?"

Kemar answered the question with one of his own. "You are not fishing today?" The boy laid his bag on the sand, a sign, Al noticed, that he planned to chat and an indication that the youngster was getting more comfortable with those who lived on Makoona.

"I don't fish every day."

"Why not? Bao does. That's how you make money."

"That's Bao, not me. If I thought life was about money, I would not live here."

"But you sell fish."

"You sound more American than I do. Yeah, I sell fish. But I try to strike a balance, you know?" Al opened his arms and waved them to encompass the totality of their setting. "Can't put a price on this."

Kemar enjoyed hearing people's different philosophies, their variety of beliefs. He asked, "So you take, but how do you know when you've taken too much? What is the limit?"

"I just know." Al dragged his foot through the sand and nodded. "Well, maybe it's not something I know. It's something I feel. And it starts with knowing that there is a limit. There has to be."

Kemar spotted a crab moving along the rim of a puddle. He poked at it with a stick, backing it up against a waterlogged piece of driftwood. When the crab latched onto the boy's twig, Kemar picked up the crustacean and dropped the crab, stick and all, into his sack.

Al smiled. "Looks like you're gonna eat well tonight."

"It's not one of your door knobs, but it will make a nice meal."

Al gave the boy a friendly shove. "Doormat, not door knob. They call 'em doormats because they're big enough to wipe your feet on."

"You wiped your feet on our dinner? Wouldn't your feet get all slimy and full of scales? I bet they'd be dirtier *after* you wiped them."

"No, I didn't *do* that. It's just an expression."

"It makes no sense to me, but I did enjoy the meal."

Al nodded. "Thanks, we'll do it again sometime."

Kemar held out his bag. "I am hoping you and Meela will share this with me."

Al took a corner of the bag and opened it. "Let me see what you have in there." He closed the bag, saying, "Only if you let me do the cooking. And don't let the mechanic touch a thing. Every time she tries to cook, it comes out tasting like it was marinated in crank-case oil."

"You are a good cook."

"Catch it, cook it, eat it. That's what I do."

Several thin streams of water rising from the sand wet Kemar's face. Al dropped to his knees and dug briskly. A few seconds later, he held three clams in his hands and deposited them into Kemar's bag.

"Pisser clams really liven up a bouillabaisse," Al observed.

"A bouillabaisse? You cook an *awful mess*?"

Impressed with the boy's mastery of French, Al explained, "Not everything's literal, kid. It really means a collection of sea food, kind of like an ocean stew."

The Cambodian and the American walked on. Al stopped, picking a piece of plastic out of some dried seaweed. He cut away a tangle of fishing line with the fillet knife that hung from his belt and stuffed the monofilament deep into a pocket. When he was done, he passed a piece of bright yellow plastic to Kemar for further inspection. Perplexed, the boy handed the trash back to Al.

"It's a lure."

Kemar just stared.

"You've never fished with a rod and reel?"

Kemar shook his head.

"Really? You'll have to come with me one day and try it. It's the only way to fish. One on one."

"How does the plastic catch the fish?"

"This probably wouldn't catch any fish right now, but when I'm done with it, it'll work just fine." Al tossed the plastic up and down in his hand while he walked.

"What will you do to it?"

"You see that boat out there?"

Out on the horizon, where the curve of the planet dipped the sea from sight, a white speck bounced on the water. It flashed as it danced, the sun reflecting off its brass and glass.

"Rich people fishing," the boy commented.

"Rich people fishing with rod and reel. Some fishermen. They can't find the fish, tie a leader, or clean their own catch themselves. There's really no skill or sport in what they do. Fishing's about eating, not terrifying and exhausting some creature.

"They lose tackle all day. When they get back to the dock, they buy more. The more they buy, the more they lose. The more they lose, the more I find. The ocean carries everything I need—lures, sinkers, hooks, leaders, swivels—right to the beach."

"But it's all broken and tangled."

"You pick it up, clean it off, paint it, attach another hook or two, and it works just fine."

"That's a great way to save money. I'll bet you could even sell some of it."

"It's not about money."

The boy pressed, "You just said it was. You said that they buy and you get for free. That's about money."

"It's not the main reason I do it."

"Well," Kemar said with a grin, "why do you do it if not to save money?"

"Every time I pick up a plastic plug, a lead weight, a rusty hook, I remove garbage from this beautiful beach. No bird will get tangled in that line. The beach is a little cleaner, and the wildlife is a little safer. And if I reuse this stuff, I'm not asking the planet to produce more. Again, less waste, less consumption, less pollution. If I happen to save a couple of bucks in the process, that's fine too. You can do well by doing good."

"And if all this reduces your needs," the boy said, following the logic, "then you will have to fish less often to fulfill your needs. So you use less fuel, kill fewer creatures, and your equipment lasts longer."

Al nodded. "Less is more. I'm telling you, Kemar, this island is a regular education. I didn't always—"

The boy raised his arm in warning, a gesture that required no elaboration for Al. The veteran froze, his senses heightened.

The Cambodian quietly dropped his bag, moving swiftly and silently across the sand. He knelt at a tidal pool, leaned to his left, and thrust his hand into the cloudy water. His other hand followed in a flash with a splash. And when the boy stood up, he displayed his prize with pride.

"Nice octopus," Al said while he untied the sack.

Kemar nodded. He held up the octopus for a moment as he recalled the day in the ocean when he'd let go of the scare line and later when he dropped the hand net. And then he dropped Binti into the wet sack.

The first thing that struck Binti was the darkness. Her eyes, much more sensitive than those of her human captors, adjusted quickly. She realized that she was a prisoner and that her only hope was to escape. But how?

Then she noticed that she shared her confinement with crabs, lobsters, clams, a snail or two, and mussels. Had she been in any other situation, she would have been in octopus heaven, stuffed in a container with all her favorite foods. They had nowhere to run. Unfortunately, the same was true for Binti.

As she was carried along the beach, the mussels and clams settled beneath her. The crabs and lobsters backed into corners and locked onto each other in some strange pursuit of security. Occasionally, one would nip at Binti. Everything was clamoring to breathe. The only relief came when the bag was lowered into a pool. The animals fought to breathe the water while the human gathered another creature.

Binti thought, *I finally find my shell, and this is what happens.* Feeling a sense of doom, the octopus pondered her life. She'd never mated. She'd never mothered. She'd never even surprised Ebb. As an octopus, Binti felt that she was an utter failure. To make matters worse, she'd likely perish out of the sea providing sustenance for the man-tide. She would rather die in the jaws of a moray eel than end her life like this.

Binti tried to position herself so that she could get ahold of the canvas with her beak and bite a hole into the bag. But the constant bouncing of the human's gait and the heavy load inside pulled the sack taut, preventing her from getting a grip with her beak. She looked up. The top was held closed. There was no way to get out.

The octopus felt something against her skin. It wasn't anything in the bag. It was something from the outside that touched her—light. In the bottom corner of the sack, under the crabs, beneath the lobsters, light somehow found its way in through a small hole. Binti crawled to the hole. Most of the crustaceans moved away easily, preferring the false security of the darker corner. The octopus used her suckers to move the clams and mussels out of the way. All the while, she clung to her precious shell.

Binti watched several insects fly in and out of the tiny hole. For these little creatures, the space was wide enough to fit a family through, but as Binti settled into the corner, she saw just how miniscule the opening really was. There was plenty of room for insects and light, but an octopus was another story. The smallest mussel in the bag couldn't fit through the hole. The lobster would have trouble getting a claw into the opening. And even the clams were too wide to reach the beach below the bag.

But Binti had something going for her that none of her sackmates could claim. The octopus had neither bones nor shell to speak of. All she really needed was an opening large enough to fit her beak through. The rest of her flesh would squeeze out somehow. There were, however, two other problems. Binti would have to accomplish her escape before the humans reached their destination, and she would have to exit the sack without being noticed.

Wasting no time, the octopus began pressing one of her arms through the opening. It went through smoothly. When she felt the hot sun on her flesh this time, she was overjoyed. Five other arms reached out of the pouch in succession. The hole seemed to widen a tiny bit. Then she dragged her mantle through. She held onto the bag from the outside, hid under it, turned dark green to match the canvas, and was careful not to touch the human. Soon, she had only one arm to remove. That was the problem.

In order to pull it free, Binti would have to relinquish her shell. The shell was too big for the hole. It was the moment of truth. She would die with a shell or live without one. And then the bag came crashing down on her. Binti was pinned under the sack, which had been dropped onto the sand. It was the perfect opportunity. If she slipped free now, the human would probably not notice the loss of her weight when he lifted the bundle once more.

The human opened the sack and dropped in several more shellfish. As he picked it up, Binti made her decision. She released her shell, pulled her arm free, and slipped into a small puddle. Binti turned brown and hugged a shaded wall. She didn't grasp the irony that she'd escaped because she had no shell and the others were doomed because they did have shells.

The octopus's next decision was an important one: hide or flee? Had there been a corridor of water or a wave washing over, Binti

would've risked fleeing. But the puddle was stagnant, and she didn't know what was beyond, so she waited.

Eventually, the octopus began her journey back to the coral. She thought about Elaber as she crawled from pool to pool. One by one, they got deeper and larger, and the water became cooler until Binti was in the surf, jetting toward home. The shell was gone, but perhaps its effect wasn't.

Just before dawn the next morning, Kemar was in a boat, heading back to the fishing grounds. The craft chugged along steadily. Using a sharpening stone, he put a fresh edge on a fillet knife so he could cut bait. Kemar was happy to be on the ocean again. He was happy to be fishing. And he was happy that he'd chosen to leave Bao.

Bao arrived just as the sun rose to the low branches of the treeline behind him. It was early enough for him, but for Al and Kemar, the day had begun hours earlier. And when Bao saw that Kemar wasn't waiting at Meela's shop, he became suspicious.

"Where boy?" the anxious fisherman asked.

The old mechanic lifted her head out of a crate of parts and answered, "Your motor's almost ready."

"Where boy?" he asked again. "Need mount motor. Need start fishing."

"You miss your helper? You can't work without him?"

"Not Meela concern what boy do with Bao. He not work for you now."

Meela smiled. "You're right, and you're wrong."

"Boy not work for Meela," Bao countered.

"I told him he could help me clean up the heavy stuff in the evenings. And he could sleep here and watch the place at night. Who knows, I might even teach him how to overhaul an engine."

Forgetting about his percentage of Kemar's pay and irate that Meela would be Kemar's employer, Bao bellowed, "Don't care of that. In day, boy fish with Bao. Boy owe that."

"See, there's where I think you're probably wrong. And here's why I say that. You see, it's day right now. Do you see Kemar?"

"Boy do what Bao say."

"Kind of tough to do that since he's not here. He's actually out fishing with—"

"American!" Bao hissed.

"Precisely. I'm guessing that he'll be doing that for a long time. I'm also guessing that you won't want any problems with me . . . or Al. So why don't you just mount your motor yourself? Spray your poison and throw your grenades yourself."

"Ah, Meela, now *you* right and wrong. Right Bao take motor. Right Bao not want trouble with old soldier. Wrong Bao afraid of Meela. Only you and Bao here now. Old lady easy to step on. Brittle, like dried driftwood. Could die anytime."

"I see what you're saying. It's a good point." With her back to Bao, Meela continued working. She leaned into another wooden box, removed a length of copper pipe, and laid it on the ground. She dropped an aluminum rod on top of it. Still rummaging through the crate, she said, "Here it is. Glad I saved this."

"Why keep working? Will not finish."

Meela laid her find on a workbench and untied the burlap that covered what looked to be two more lengths of greasy pipe. "I had a feeling this was here. It may not look like it, but I know where everything is in this shop." When she turned back to face Bao, she held a vintage double-barreled shotgun in her hands. It looked twice as old and nearly as big as Meela, who leaned against her bench to support herself. Her arms shook, and her hands trembled with the weight of the weapon.

Amused by the sight, Bao asked, "Meela shoot Bao?" He began to laugh. "Meela can barely hold gun."

"I'll pull the trigger before I drop it."

A little more concerned, possibly because he realized that she was serious, possibly because it dawned on him that there weren't many on Makoona who would care if he disappeared, Bao said, "Cannot aim. Will shoot own boat."

"So you think my shaking makes me *less* dangerous? I'll be honest with you. I've never fired one of these before. Does that make you feel safer? You know what? I'm not even sure the gun's loaded. What do *you* think?"

"Put gun down before Meela hurt Meela."

"Now you're worried about me? How sweet. But you should worry about yourself. You see, my inexperience should make you very nervous. It means I'm unpredictable. I could hit anything. For an old person like me with such poor aim, I imagine a shotgun can be very forgiving." Meela wedged a dirty lifejacket behind her back. "You know, I'd never admit this to anyone, but I'm not only shaky, I don't see as well as I used to. So when I pull this trigger—wait, there's two of them? That's great. Looks like I get a second chance."

Bao tried to appear relaxed, but by this time, he, too, was shaking a little bit and sweating quite a bit.

Pow! The shotgun went off. Bao slammed his eyes closed, turned his head away from the blast and raised his arms to ward off the flying lead. The pellets exploded a large container of grease, which flew in every direction, covering the left side of Bao's face and torso.

"Sorry about that," Meela said. "It just went off. I guess that's what they call a hairtrigger. Packs quite a punch, doesn't it?"

Bao was frozen in the doorway.

"That's okay. No need to answer. I have good news, and I have bad news. The good news is I only have one shot left. The bad news? Looks like the shotgun is loaded. Hey, now you know what it's like to be a fish that has a hand grenade exploded next to it."

Bao screamed, "Crazy old witch!" He spun around and dove out the door.

As he ran into the mangrove behind her shop, Meela admitted, "Maybe I am crazy." Then she called to him, "Tell you what, I'll let you keep the motor if you leave Kemar alone! We'll call it even!"

Bao stepped out from behind a tree. Meela lowered her weapon as he approached his motor. He laid the outboard into his boat without bothering to mount it. Quietly, he pushed the boat into the lagoon and rowed off. Meela heard him mutter, "*Tianoboto*," a Makoonan word for crazy.

The mechanic replied, "You just better hope that motor runs forever. Thanks for stopping by. This was a lot of fun. I'll tell Al you were looking for him."

Fishing for an Answer

Al piloted his small boat to the ocean side of the reef. The water was a bit choppy, but Al knew it was a good spot for snapper and black jacks. He was also hoping to hook a tuna or an albacore without going too far out to sea. The fast ocean swimmers often chased baitfish along this part of the reef. As he slowed the outboard, Al pointed to a blue jug that bounced on the surface. It was almost the same color as the water and could easily be overlooked. Kemar glanced back at the American, puzzled.

"Grab it and tie us up," Al said.

"Why not just drop anchor?" Kemar questioned.

"There's coral down there, buddy. You know what anchors do to coral?" As the boy tied the line, Al asked, "Why would I want to destroy something that makes fishing easier? That stuff down there is a fish factory."

"Coral never made fishing easier for me," Kemar countered. "Fish hide in there. Nets get caught and ripped. It gets in the way." He wanted Al to see that he was experienced in these matters, that the *boy* really was a fisher*man*. But the more he expressed a lack of concern with what lived below, the less he impressed Al.

"Yeah, they hide in coral. And sometimes it slices right through my line, but the bottom line is the fish need the coral. They breed and grow and live in there. What's more important than that to a fisherman? So whenever I find a good spot, I run a mooring line, secure it to the bottom, and tie the end to a jug or two that floats on the surface. No more anchor effect down below."

"If you used bigger orange jugs, you could find the spot even easier."

"So could everyone else. For every jug that's floating in a good spot, I got two set up in horrible spots, just to throw off any squatters."

Kemar rubbed his forehead with the tips of his fingers. "It's a different way."

"It's the only way."

Al selected a pole and handed it to the boy. He tied some tackle on the line, explained the reel mechanism, and had Kemar make a few practice casts. He explained that he used a lighter sinker than he really should have because sinkers smash coral too. Then he showed the boy how to hook strips of squid that Kemar would use as bait. The American pointed out that their color, smell, and action in the water would attract a lot of attention. Al added two small orange beads above the hook to dress it up a bit more.

He cautioned Kemar to keep the tip of his pole up and to make sure he didn't rest the rod on the rail. Next, Al demonstrated the proper way to set the hook, relaxed the drag a touch, and invited the youngster to "wet a line." Then the American did the same.

Just as fishermen had done since two humans first shared a raft, Al and Kemar talked while they bobbed on the swells.

For many, the ocean has a soothing effect. People become calmer, more contemplative. And although they're often more quiet initially, the ocean soon spawns discussions about dreams, philosophies, beliefs, feelings, and memories that gather dust in the closets of the mind. It was as if the waves washed inhibition, insecurity, and distrust from the soul. On a boat, surrounded by the shimmering sea, truth flows out like surf finding shore.

"Have you ever seen Cambodia?" Kemar asked the American. "Have you ever seen my past?"

"I've seen more of Cambodia, Laos, Thailand, and Vietnam than I ever thought I would. I know a little about what you left behind, just as you probably know a bit about what I saw, what I left."

Kemar nodded and asked, "Why are you here and not in America?"

"I'm not sure I know, but I'll tell you this. Makoona is the only place I've been to since the war that I didn't feel like running away from."

"Yes," the boy agreed quietly. Even though he'd only been on the island briefly, he believed he understood what Al felt. And while Al hadn't really answered his question, Kemar didn't press any further. It was part of the unspoken etiquette of conversations in a boat, as much a part of fishing protocol as not getting tangled in your companion's line.

Then the jacks began to hit. Powerful swimmers with powerful jaws, they often hunted in small schools or packs, somewhat like wild dogs of the sea. Kemar enjoyed the challenge of trying to hook and land the fish.

The boy made mistakes. He lost several fish and a fair amount of tackle, which Al noted silently. Yet the older fisherman refrained from criticizing his companion. There were two things that made it easy for Al to hold his tongue. First, regardless of the result, the boy was intent on fishing correctly. He studied Al, trying to mimic everything the American did. Secondly, Kemar rarely made the same mistake twice. He was quite skilled at learning from his experience.

When the boy asked Al's advice, the American gave it, briefly, gently. And when Al sensed that Kemar was getting frustrated, he smiled and offered a solution.

For the first time since he was a small boy, Kemar learned while he fished. He enjoyed the learning as much as the fishing, maybe more. He quizzed Al about the creatures he caught, their habits and habitat. Although Al was no marine biologist, he was very knowledgeable about the sea. It had been a long time since Kemar had been educated about something other than his survival.

The youngster felt a tug on his line. He'd already taken up the slack in order to feel this type of action. Clumsily, the boy popped the tip of his rod higher, hoping to set the hook firmly into whatever grabbed at his bait. His enthusiasm, however, only served to rip the strip of squid from the fish's mouth, frightening it off from another strike.

After a few moments, Al suggested, "Check your bait, buddy."

The hook emerged from the water, naked and glistening in the sun.

Al smiled. "Tough to catch a fish without any bait. I know, I've tried." Then he tossed Kemar a fresh strip.

When they'd filled a cooler with fish, Al asked Kemar to untie

the boat. He fired up the motor and crossed over the massive reef to try his luck beachside. With sandy flats and calmer surf, shielded from the ocean reef, Al hoped to hook a flounder or two, a coral cod, or a couple of sea trout. As they prepared their lines, the American grasped a pair of pliers and squeezed the tip of his hook. When the boy asked if he should do the same, Al explained that he was snipping the barb.

"It's too easy," he said. "A real fisherman can land his catch without the barb."

"But it's much less efficient," the boy pointed out, wondering if Bao might actually be the superior fisherman. "You only lose fish and waste time."

"I certainly lose fish and waste time . . . but not *only*. Besides, there's plenty of fish and plenty of time. In the end, the fish has a fair chance to escape, and I get better at fishing. What's wrong with that?"

"In the end, you make less money for the same day's work."

"You've spent too much time with Bao. It's not *the same day's work*. I do things differently. I go to the hotel *before* we come out here. I find out what they need, and then I get it. I catch fewer fish, but I get paid more for them. If I catch something they haven't asked for, I put it back in the ocean so it'll be there when they do ask for it. And if I'm not using a barb, the creature isn't all torn up and injured.

"The way I fish, the stronger, smarter fish don't wind up in my boat. I probably catch the slower, dumber ones, so in a sense, I'm providing a service by culling the weakest from the gene pool, leaving the strongest . . . Besides, I live on Makoona. How much money do I need?"

Kemar, who left his barb intact, tossed his line out onto the sandy flats a fair distance from the coral. Al had suggested earlier that dragging it slowly toward the boat, which was moored to yet another jug above the reef, might catch a fish's attention. Kemar reeled the line slowly along the bottom, pausing now and then, hoping a fish would strike and he would impress Al.

Though the morning on the sea had ignited conversation, the two fishermen enjoyed an afternoon of relative silence. Hearing only the testy terns, restless swells wafting against the hull, the whine of line peeling off Al's reel, the click of the bale, the grunt of the fight, and thumping of the catch dancing on the deck, all served to soothe the Cambodian. It was music—a *sea*nota, if you will.

While fishing the reef, the Khmer Rouge, the boat people, and Bao were all momentarily forgotten. This was a different type of fishing. It was less industrial, less dependent on great numbers of dead. This was less like a harvest and more like a hunt. It was one person seeking one fish at a time. Kemar had to be patient, determined, skillful, and creative—much like the fish he hunted—to be successful.

The goal wasn't to destroy or exploit; rather, the pace and the results of rod and reel seemed to complement the harmony of the reef. And so, Kemar was drawn closer to the wildlife, closer to the spirit-fish, even if he did belong to the man-tide.

At one point, Al reached under a seat and pulled out a tackle box. He opened it carefully and showed the contents to Kemar. There were lures the likes of which no one, not even experienced salts, had ever seen before.

The American said, "Beautiful, aren't they? They're the big guns."

"Where did you get them?"

"I made them. Most of them are those reconditioned plugs I found on the beach. But these are special." Al removed a smaller box tucked inside. He flipped the lid. The lures sparkled like treasure in a pirate's chest; gold, silver, and bronze, with frayed ribbons of blue, red, white, and yellow.

"Do they catch fish?"

"They catch fish."

"I've never seen anything like these. Are they valuable?"

"If you're hungry, they're priceless. Otherwise, they're not worth much. They're really just medals from the war."

"Yours?"

Al nodded. "Medals aren't very good for anything, but I'll tell ya, little bro, hang a hook from `em and they catch fish."

Al had trimmed, flattened, filed, drilled, and embellished his citations with hooks, swivels, feathers, and beads that he found on the beach. The result resembled some type of pop art fishing icon. Kemar was anxious to see if Al's creations really worked.

"Pick one," Al coaxed. "Go ahead, any one you want. Give it a toss."

The boy poked through the box with the tip of his knife. Kemar knew how dangerous a box filled with hooks could be. But when he selected a lure—a reconditioned silver star married to a purple-heart ribbon—and began tying it to his line, the boat rolled on a swell, and the hook lodged in the youngster's palm between his thumb and index finger. For an instant, the boy tried to pull the hook out. He gave up quickly. The point was imbedded.

Kemar complained, "I thought you clipped your boobs."

Al winced at the image and then explained, "They're called *barbs*. Must've missed one." He continued, amused by the situation, "I can help you with that."

Kemar slowly, reluctantly presented his hooked hand to Al, who picked up a pair of needle-nose pliers and then grasped the boy's hand in his own. The colorful lure dangled from Kemar's palm, spinning slowly, glinting in the sun.

Al held the pliers near the boy's face, opening and closing them like a crab's claw. "Do you trust me?" he asked. Then Al lowered the pliers and clutched Kemar's wrist firmly. He gripped the shaft of the hook with the pliers. It looked like he was going to yank it out of the boy's hand. Instead, Al quickly pushed the point through the skin above it and snipped off the barb. The lure fell onto the floor of the boat.

"Now you know what it's like to be a fish," Al said. "Maybe we better stick with baited lines instead of lures today."

Later, as they began to pack up, Al said, "Fishing like this might teach you things. You wind up a little more in tune with the sea and the reef."

Kemar grimaced. "I've already learned what I need to know about fishing like this. You wind up with small meals, small profits, and holes in your hand. I have lived with less long enough. I want more."

"Do you want more, or do you want to be more?"

" . . . Both."

"It's difficult to have both, buddy."

"How do you know?" the boy asked, suggesting that perhaps his ambitions were beyond Al's.

"Yeah, what do I know? But it seems to me, if you first become more as a person, then you might survive getting more afterwards. Getting more and being more are two very different things. Take fishing, for example. All you have in front of you right now are the fish in this cooler. Your arms ache, you're hungry, and you're tired. That's what you have. But what have you become?"

"Nothing worth mentioning. That's why this fishing makes no sense."

"So you've become *nothing*?"

"Nothing more than when we began."

"That's because you see these fish, you see this ocean, and it doesn't touch you. It's nothing to you, and so you get nothing from it. When you appreciate what's beneath the surface, what's happening on the reef, you will become this ocean. And that, little bro, is surely something."

Kemar was getting confused, but somehow, Al's rambling caused him to recall that moment when he dropped his scare line and the fish escaped from the nets of the boat people. He wondered if that was an example of becoming the reef. It was pleasing in the moment, but it didn't seem like good *business* to the boy.

The youngster's thought was interrupted when Al reached into a bucket, slid his pliers behind the gills of a strange-looking fish that Kemar had caught himself, and lifted it out of the water. It was a stargazer, and it had already regained a little color and life after its exhausting battle with the boy.

Al said, "This is what you have. And to you, it is next to nothing?" He returned the fish to the bucket.

"I guess I do have something." Kemar nodded. "I have a victory. I conquered the fish. It is *my* fish."

"A lot of people would agree with you. Those rich people on the big boats certainly would. But I don't."

"Why not? How am I wrong?"

"The way I see it, it's never *your* fish. It belongs to the reef, now and forever. And you should never be proud that you ended someone's life."

"Someone?"

"I mean a fish," Al explained. "Some*thing*."

"But I am pleased that I will now eat, that I will get paid."

"But don't forget the price. It's not just about you. Every time you take a fish, this is diminished." Al moved his head slowly to sweep the horizon. "Even with a fish, a lost life is no small thing."

The boy's eyes narrowed. "I know about lost lives."

"I know you do. Can you extend that feeling to the loss of this life?"

"I think I understand what you say, but I don't understand you."

"Me?"

"If you truly feel the death of this creature—this stargazer—how can you be a fisherman?"

Al paused. He stared the boy in the eyes and said, "Who better? Rather than abuse or conquer all of this, I try to be part of it. I kill to eat, just like much of what's down there. I'm proud of my skill as a fisher-*man*, but I'm never happy to take something from these waters."

"Talk is talk. You sell fish for money. You prepare them for tourists."

"So you see me as a hypocrite. Luckily, I live my life based on how *I* see me. I'm not worried about making sense to everyone else. I'll tell you what I do know, bro. I know I'm not bigger than this." Al gestured to include the vast ocean around them. "Are you?"

Kemar shook his head thoughtfully. "No, I am not."

Al reached into a tackle box. He wrote something on a frayed pad, removed a red wire, noted a number, and snapped it onto one of the stargazer's fins. He picked the fish up once again, saying, "I'll tell you what, buddy. I learned in the jungle that there's two ways to take a life. One is from a somewhat safe distance. The other is up close and personal."

"Why do you speak to me as if I know nothing of this? I already know more about this subject than I ever want to."

"You're right. My bad. Let me put it another way. If you can hold this fish in your bare hands, then his life is yours, not the ocean's. But if you can't, then he belongs to the ocean and must be given back. Want to play?"

"You think I can't hold my fish? I have probably caught more pounds of fish in my life than you have."

"But I'll bet I learned more from my experience. As a matter of fact, I'll sweeten the deal. You hold this half-dead fish for five seconds, and I'll let you pick any piece of equipment on this boat to keep."

Kemar instantly forgot the fish. He scanned the boat with the eye of a practiced scrounger. There were riches to be had. He noted the fillet knife hanging from Al's belt. He noted the belt. He saw the shiny black pole with the well-oiled reel that Al fished with and wondered how much it could be worth. He admired the tackle box stuffed with lures, hooks, bobbers, rigs, and other riches. And then he saw what he wanted. Now it was Kemar's turn to test Al's courage.

"Anything on this boat?" Kemar repeated.

"Anything."

"The motor."

Al looked back at his outboard and winced. It was like someone asking for your dog. But after a moment's consideration, Al nodded and said, "Sure." Then he dropped the stargazer into the bucket one last time. Al wanted him slippery and energetic. He turned toward the boy and instructed Kemar to stretch his hands out over the water.

Smiling broadly, almost giddy at the thought of having his own outboard, the boy did as he was told. Kemar couldn't remember the last time he'd had fun like this.

"Ready?" Al asked.

Kemar smiled, rubbed his hands on his kremar until they were bone dry, spread his fingers, and nodded.

Al presented the gazer to the boy. "Five seconds for the fish and the motor," he reminded his young friend. Then he placed the fish onto Kemar's hands, which were held out over the sea.

Norton didn't know what was going on. He'd blacked out for a while and wasn't sure whether he was dead or alive. However, when he saw nothing but water underneath him and felt those human fingers around him, well, even a conch could see the opportunity. The gazer wriggled like his life depended on it, which it did, hoping that he could scrape a stinging dorsal spine or a sharp gill slit across those soft hands.

And then it happened. The fish couldn't believe his luck. The silly human slipped a finger on top of Norton's head just behind his eyes. It was the stargazer's last chance, and he was now in a position to use his secret weapon.

Al began to sweat as he counted, "Three-one-thousand, four-one-thousand, fi . . ."

"AhhhHHH!" Kemar screamed. The cry grew louder as the fish fell into the sea. The boy squeezed his injured hand and tried to shake the pain from his arm.

"Oh, soooo close," Al taunted.

"What was that? You knew he'd do that. My hand feels like it's on fire."

"Don't worry, it's not . . . This is the difference between having more and being more. Gain insight, not objects. Instead of asking me for an outboard, you should have asked me for information about the fish. You might've held on for that extra half-second and won the motor if you knew more. Knowledge is power."

"My hand is burning!" the boy bellowed. He slammed his palm on the boat's rail, hoping to swat the pain from his fingers, but the gesture only ignited a new level of agony. A rogue hook had found its way back into Kemar's hand. Fortunately, it was one of Al's and the barb had been clipped, so the boy removed himself this time.

Al couldn't help even if he wanted to. He was bent over the outboard, hugging it, laughing hysterically.

"What did the fish do to me?"

"Don't worry, you'll be fine, bro. He just gave you a little shock. If you touch a gazer behind the eyes near the top of its head, it can give you a decent jolt. The one you caught was pretty big. Must've been quite a blast." Al paused, looked at the boy, and started laughing all over again.

Kemar sat down and began chuckling as well. "You must think you're pretty funny."

"Not half as funny as you. I'll bet that fish is laughing it up right now."

They untied the boat from the jug line, fired up the motor, and headed back to Makoona.

"I'll tell ya," Al said, "you almost didn't get zapped. You had me sweating."

"Would I have won the motor?"

"We had a deal." After a brief silence, Al added, "Sorry I talked so much today, but I'm not used to having company. I thought I liked fishing alone, but I gotta admit, you're okay. Can I tell you one last thing?"

"Yes, please."

"That fish deserved to go home."

"You confuse me like the priests and monks when I was young. Why should I release a fish that I worked so hard to catch?"

"Two reasons. One, I don't see many gazers. If something's scarce, why kill it? That only brings it one step closer to being gone. And then how many will we catch?"

"That's a good reason, but you said you had two."

"The other one's a little more personal, but, at least to me, it's just as valid."

"Yes?"

"Well, that fish was a real fighter."

"I know. My arms still sting."

"Just stop for a second and think how hard that fish fought for its life. I fought that hard. I'll bet you have too. And when I've fought like that against impossible odds, all I wanted was a break."

"A break?"

"A little help, a little luck."

"Good fortune?"

"Yes, exactly. As far as I'm concerned, this fish earned his freedom. I'm a little nuts anyway, but it's actually an honor for me to put him back in the sea."

"You are a crazy American."

"No argument there, but we're in my boat, so I'm entitled. Besides, there's nothing that says once you go fishing you can't have honor or mercy. For me, there's something incredible about anything that's alive, like the spirit that lives in it isn't all that different from the spirit that lives in me, in you. So if you fish with a little integrity, you might wind up feeding your own good karma."

"I'd rather feed my family."

"One doesn't exclude the other."

After they motored on a few more minutes, Kemar asked, "What was that red wire you attached to the fish? Was it something to help it shock me? If it was, I believe the motor might be mine."

"Nice try, Kemar, but all I did was tag the fish."

"What is *tag the fish*?"

"Well, there's a professor from Queensland, Australia that I met in Vietnam. Name's Campbell, an ichthyologist."

"A what?"

"It's a fancy way of saying she studies fish. My pal asked me to tag and record some of the special fish I stumble upon."

"Actually, *I* stumbled on that fish."

Al smiled. "Let it go, little bro. A couple of times a year, Campbell pops up here to work on some kind of study."

"A fish study?"

"Yeah, it's part of the job."

"A fish professor?"

Al nodded.

"Is your friend trying to help the fish?"

"I guess so. The study certainly helped that gazer. Campbell's trying to do something for the reef."

They motored on a few more minutes with Kemar lost in thought. He considered several things: his father, how fishing with

Al was different. He was also reminded of the octopus, the one that had escaped him several times.

Kemar blurted, "I would like to meet Professor Campbell." And then he returned to his rumination while the small boat sputtered and chugged its way back to Makoona, fleeing the sinking sun behind them.

An Under-Estimated Prophet

On her way back to her lair, Binti passed over a site that some-one had fished with explosives. The coral was obliterated. The des-olate plain was murky with dust that rose and fell in the churning water. Occasionally, a small fish would swim by, but the area was basically barren. It stood in sharp contrast to the lush lifeforce that fueled the healthy reef not far off. Binti wondered if the man-tide knew what was left after they exploded the fish from the sea.

It was quiet crossing the gray patch. It was also dangerous. There was no cover, no place to hide. Every move along the bottom stirred up sediment, an announcement for predators to take no-tice. It was an easy place to catch a meal and an easy place to be-come a meal. Most fish avoided these desolate patches.

Binti maintained a dull, lifeless gray color, became flat as a flounder, and moved along slowly, looking for the occasional ditch or valley wall to keep her out of sight. She raised her eyes above the sediment to see if she could spot danger. Seeing none, she contin-ued to cross the killing field.

Almost to the living coral, a craggy run of rocks and debris came into view. That was when she spotted him. At first, she was alarmed because the creature blocked her entrance into the reef, but when she realized who it was, Binti could only smile.

Molo was perched on a solitary black boulder that stood like a monument to nothing. He said solemnly, "I hear the cries of chil-dren and the other songs of war. It's like a melody that rings down from the sky. Standing here upon the moon, I watch it all roll by. Standing here upon the moon with nothing left to do, a lovely view of heaven." Then he turned and looked at Binti and continued, "But I'd rather be with you."

The eccentric octopus was bursting with vibrant colors, waving his arms all around him. Molo had an explosion of his own going on. It was as if he believed that since an explosion destroyed this place, another might restore it.

He grinned at Binti and waved three arms, inviting her to crawl closer. "Walk into splintered sunlight," Molo said, "inch your way through dead dreams to another land. Maybe you're tired and broken, your tongue is twisted with words half spoken and thoughts unclear."

His display of vibrant colors and patterns revealed the energy that flowed within him and stood in stark contrast to the dull lunar void that surrounded him. The octopus had gone psychedelic.

He chanted, "Picture a bright blue ball just spinning, spinning free. Dizzy with eternity. Paint it with a skin of sky, brush in some c'ouds and sea. Call it home for you and me."

Binti wondered if Molo had some strange power, if he could actually bring the dead sand back to life. And for a brief instant, she thought she saw the rock below him flash with color. A thin vein of electric blue shot into the boulder and danced around it. Binti crawled closer.

Molo, it seemed, was picking up pieces of lifeless coral, rolling an arm around them, injecting them with different colors, and then tossing them into the austere field as if they were seeds of life. The octopus was glowing, beaming, bursting as he grappled with the gray. A living palette; a pinch of peach, a sheen of green, and a wink of pink all spilled from his arms, swallowed by the bland sand.

When Binti approached, he chanted, "A peaceful place, or so it looks from space. A closer look reveals the human race. Full of hope, full of grace is the human face. But afraid they may lay our home to waste."

Molo faced Binti, nodded to her, and continued, "There's a fear down here we can't forget. Hasn't got a name just yet. Always awake, always around . . ." Molo gestured to the obliterated coral, " . . . singing ashes to ashes, all fall down."

"You're one sprayed octopus," Binti responded. "What the shell are you doing?"

Molo grinned, every arm splashing colors on coral all around him. Like a living fountain, pastels streamed from his suckers. "She comes shining through rays of violet. She can wade in a drop of dew."

A small bubble of violet dew dropped from the tip of his arm and gently settled on Binti's mantle. When it touched her flesh, it burst, and she was bathed in the color. For an instant, Binti was carried away to the place where Molo found his finspiration, but she quickly returned to the reefality of the moment.

"Listen, boulder-brain, get down off that rock and stop that finsane display before something grabs you."

Molo wouldn't be distracted from his enchantment of the barren field. "Let me lie, let me lie. I don't need no alibi. The fault of this crime was none of mine. I was the victim of the crime."

"We all were," Binti agreed. "But you're not going to bring life back to this spot. And you might lose your own if you don't come off that rock and get gray."

"Tell you what I'll do, I'll watch out for you," Molo whispered.

"I'm not the one who's making a spectacle of himself. You're the one who needs to be watched out for."

Molo tilted his mantle to one side and countered, "The future's here. We are it. We are on our own."

"Are we on our own?" Binti asked, touched by the thought, wondering if perhaps the mysterious Molo knew something she didn't.

He warned, "By and again, the morning sun will rise, but the darkness never goes from some men's eyes." Molo waved his arms to point to the dead field as evidence of man's darkness. He leaned down to Binti and calmly said, "Inspiration moves me brightly. Light the song with sense and color . . . All around her, the garden grew, scarlet and purple, crimson and blue." The colors poured over her as Molo named them. "Just one thing, then I'll be okay. I need a miracle every day."

"That's a lovely thought, but I'm not going to become a moray meal over a patch of dead sand. Good luck with whatever you're doing." Binti blasted herself into the rocks and living coral that waited just beyond Molo. She hunkered down among some brain coral to think and get her bearings.

When she looked back to see if Molo was safe, all she saw was the large rock. Dull streaks of blue grudgingly pulsed through the stone, reaching down into the sand beneath it. Then she heard, "Sometimes, we walk alone. Sometimes, the songs that we hear are just songs of our own."

"Okay, where are you, Molo?" she asked.

"You poured a cup of moonbeam and assumed a thoughtful face. Just such a look as angels have before they fall from grace." And with that, a large round of brain coral uncoiled and stood up, becoming Molo.

Although Binti was shocked, she was starting to learn not to be shocked by anything involving this octopus.

Molo crawled closer and whispered, "From the other direction, she was calling my eye. Could be an illusion, but I might as well try, might as well try."

"Try what?"

"Once in a while, you get shown the light, in the strangest places if you look at it right." Molo extended a gentle arm and touched Binti. He slid the tip of the arm along her soft sides. He lifted one of Binti's arms and extended it, barely touching it. He turned it so that her suckers were exposed. And holding his own arm over hers, he dropped something onto it. It was Binti's shell.

Molo rubbed it once, and it sparkled like a small star. "Slip out of your shell, you said. Where else you got to go? You been there and back again. What do you really know?"

Binti, surprised and pleased by the gift, didn't know what to say.

Molo continued, "If I had a star to give, I'd give it to you long as you live. Would you have the time to watch it shine, watch it shine, or ask for the moon and heaven too? I'd give it to you.

"Well, maybe I got no star to spare, or anything fine or even rare. Only if you let me be your world could I give this world to you, could I ever give this world to you."

Molo closed her arm over the shell. "I can tell you fancy, I can tell you plain. You give something up for everything you gain."

The male slid two arms down one of Binti's. She responded by wrapping hers around them. Their suckers touched, grasped, and a faint purple pulse began to beat through their sand-colored bodies. It started in the intertwined arms, spread to the others, and gradually rose up into their mantles. The pulse beat identically in both of them, uniting them until Binti pulled away.

Molo spoke softly. "One or two moments, a piece of your time is all I'm asking, and I'll give you mine. One or two moments out of all you have got, to show how I love you, believe it or not."

She'd never done this before. Part of her wanted to swim with Molo more than anything she could imagine, but there was also a

quiet sadness welling up inside her. The octopus was confused by the emotion. She backed off but not away.

As she considered the moment and smiled at Molo, the male reached out once more. He turned deep-water green—an honest color—and said, "If you could see my heart, you would know it's true. There is none except for you. Except for you. I swear on my very soul, if I lie may I fall down cold."

Binti reached out to Molo. They touched and intertwined. Two other arms followed, and then two more. Soon, the pair looked something like a giant starfish. They turned and spun dreamily in the sea, churning and changing color—red, yellow, peach, plum, until they finally became white with dusty traces of violet, blue, and pink, like living pearls.

Their suckers released, save for one arm each. Binti's other arms slid between Molo's, his between hers. They wrapped themselves around each other's mantle, exploring and tasting as only an octopus can. There were fifteen arms and no mantles to be seen.

Molo seized on Binti's proximity and whispered, "Where there is no pebble tossed, nor wind to blow. If I knew the way, I would take you home."

Binti considered where that was. Even she could see, despite her obvious bias, that he was no ordinary creature of the reef. Where did Molo live? Where had he come from? Where was he going? Hootie had called Molo "a prophet on the burning shore." Was he a prophet?

Her attention, however, returned to the more pressing matter of Molo pressing himself closer. With modest trepidation, Binti gave herself up to the moment. She knew that this was how it must be for her, she could feel it. Molo was a special mate, a special friend. He was gentle, vibrant, and unlike anything she'd ever seen in the sea. Molo, like her shell, was one of Makoona's jewels. Binti returned his embrace.

This time, it was Molo's turn to hold Binti at arms' length. He looked deeply into her eyes and said, "All I really want is you. No one else will really do." And then he cautioned, "But never give your love, my friend, unto a foolish heart."

The male was giving her the chance to leave, to deny his advance and his love. It was this gesture of understanding and care that finally drew Binti to complete the union with her newfound love. They drew together once more, arm-in-arm-in-arm-in-arm.

This time, Binti cooed in Molo-speak, "Let the world go by like clouds a-streaming. To be with you is my best dreaming."

They grasped each other firmly and jetted off beyond the reef, out into the deep, dark water where it was dangerous but private. Later, they glided into the sandy starlit shallows, and by the time the sun and the tide rose, Binti was in her lair.

Molo laid his mantle next to his mate's and snuggled her. They both knew he would leave. It was the way of the octopus. He rose reluctantly, saying, "I fare pretty much as I please, roll with the waves and ebb with the tide by the edge of the shining blue sea."

Then he slid close and wrapped his arms around Binti, whispering, "Wake up to find out that you are the eyes of the world. The heart has its beaches, its homeland, and thoughts of its own. Wake now, discover that you are the song that the morning brings. But the heart has its seasons, its evenings, and songs of its own."

Binti knew what must be. It was hard-wired inside her—instinctual, just as it was inside of Molo. For much of its life, the octopus is solitary. *But why be solitary?* she wondered, *when being together is so wonderful?* Sometimes, Makoona's ways were difficult to understand, difficult to live. They would separate.

By being a little less in tune with the ways of Makoona, Molo seemed to comprehend them better, the way an outsider might better appreciate what insiders take for granted. Molo flashed a confident expression and wore a confident color. He recalled the evening and drew strength from it, as both he and Binti would in the future.

Molo crawled into the coral crease that opened onto the jungle that was Makoona. He peered back at his mate and said, "A walker after midnight and my destiny is grim. Staring at the starlight till my eyes are growing dim. I still see well enough to know the path

I must pursue. If we meet again before the end, I'll share my fate with you." Molo slid out onto the reef, changed color, and was gone.

Binti curled up around her tiny shell and tried to dream her way back into his arms. She drifted into sleep, thinking, "Like the morning sun, you come, and like the wind, you go." It was the way of the octopus.

Having fished with Al for several weeks, Kemar's routine had become quite familiar. The boy was pleased to have a routine in his life. In the evenings, Kemar would secure the boat with Al, clean fish, and tend to tackle and gear before his day was done. He'd collect a little money and a fish or two from the American. Then he would return to Meela's shop, where he helped her tidy up and bedded down in her hangar.

Kemar usually gave her the fish. Meela wasn't the best cook, but compared to the grasshoppers and grass he ate as a boy in Cambodia, Meela's fare was downright gourmet. Still, as settled as he'd become, another part of Kemar was growing restless to move on.

By the time the boy was through policing the shop, Meela was usually done cooking. They'd sit at an upturned crate overlooking the still lagoon and talk. For Kemar, that often meant a discussion of the day at sea.

Meela was always interested in types of fish he and Al caught. She liked to hear the boy explain the creatures' lives, and he enjoyed telling her. Her eyes sparkled as Kemar retold much of what Al had explained to him. Kemar's eyes also glittered as he passionately presented the information, trying to outline each fish's position in the web of ocean life.

Rarely did Meela discuss her past. But when she did, the boy didn't know what to make of it. According to the old woman, who many of the locals believed was *tianoboto*, loosely translated as "nuts," she'd had quite a life before coming to Makoona. The old mechanic claimed to have lunched with the president of the United States several times, danced with the king of England, owned her own airline, and been married to a wealthy publisher. She quickly pointed out, however, that the publisher wasn't nearly as rich as everyone thought and, with a trace of bitterness in her speech, said that his love of money was much greater than his love of her.

Kemar didn't believe that Meela was *tianoboto*, but he also didn't believe all her wild claims. The one claim he had no doubt was true, however, was the claim that she was an accomplished pilot.

"In the newspapers, they used to call me an 'aviatress,'" she'd say, "but I was a pilot, damn it! The plane doesn't know what sex you are! Ahhh, don't get me started." Then she'd wave her hands as if to dispel the memory and return to her meal.

Eventually, Kemar asked the obvious question. "Meela," he said, "if you were as rich and famous as you say, why live here on Makoona? Why not live with your family? Why not live where life would be easier?"

Meela put down her beloved tomato juice, which Kemar claimed he had "scrounged" from the hotel, and rubbed her eyes. Without looking up, she spoke. "I do miss my sister. And yes, I miss my husband." The old woman thought for a moment. "Being rich and famous isn't what people think it is. No one realizes that until they get there, and then it's too late to do anything about it. But it wasn't too late for me."

Kemar did not comment, so Meela continued.

"Rich, famous, it's all lies. We're all just people. No one's really all that different from anyone else. Rich might've made me appear better to some, but I wasn't. The world believed I was the greatest woman pilot who ever lived. Truth is, I probably wasn't. I crashed a lot of planes. And when I raced, I had an advantage. I flew the best planes there were. I better win. Still, I lost a lot of races. Yet the public loved me and hailed me as the best. The truth was, there were plenty of women who flew better than me . . . and plenty of men who flew worse."

"I don't understand."

"Well, I was living a lie—actually, lots of them. And it seems to me, life is about truth, finding it in yourself and living with it. I was tired of the hustle, the hype, the publicity. I spent more time begging for money when I was rich than when I didn't have any. So the last time I flew a stunt . . ."

"A stunt? Is that a type of plane?"

"No, it's an event, a show. I was going to be the first woman to fly around the world. That's a stunt. But the real stunt is how my husband, G. P., promoted the flight." She paused and settled deeper into her lawn chair. "The result was always the same. This wouldn't have been any different. More fame, more money, more planes, more flying. Leading to more money, more planes, more flying. It's a brutal cycle.

"I guess it started when I was giving an interview to a journalist, Martha Gellhorn. I liked her. I guess we were kindred spirits, two successful women in a man's world, both with famous husbands. She was actually married to Ernest Hemingway."

"Who?"

"A famous author . . . Well, one of her questions was what would happen to me if I didn't return from the flight. It got me thinking. Later, I was on the last leg of this world flight—doin' pretty well, I might add—and wouldn't you know it? I crashed. Right into the ocean, didn't even catch an island. Couldn't call for help 'cause I never learned Morse code. That's what a great pilot I was.

"Well, I was floating around wearing a life jacket, hanging onto another one. I couldn't find my navigator anywhere. He was usually more gassed up than the Elektra. I'm guessing he's still in that plane. By the time I washed ashore, I knew one thing for sure: I wasn't going back. I figured sooner or later, they'd forget about me. I'm betting it was sooner.

"Now I'm Meela. I live on Makoona. And I'm the best damn outboard motor mechanic you'll ever meet. It's simple. It's true. And I love it."

"Meela," Kemar began, "I feel I must tell you this, and I hope it doesn't upset you too much."

She stared at the boy. "What?"

"I met a man," the boy said with a grin, "who lived on Tonle Sap, Cambodia's largest lake, who I believe was a better outboard motor mechanic than you."

"Don't even start that, you little cockroach! If he was better—and I know he wasn't—it's because he didn't have a slimy octopus like you putting all his tools in the wrong drawers. That kind of stuff can ruin a good mechanic."

"It can also provide a good excuse for a bad mechanic," Kemar added.

They laughed together, the young Cambodian and the grizzled American pilot. Both had found Makoona and each other.

Binti hadn't seen Molo since they swam together. It seemed like a long time ago, and yet the memory was vivid, as if he were still with her. But of course, he wasn't. She was at the cleaning station when Paykak approached. He found an infection in a large sucker at the base of one of her arms. It was the sucker she used to hold the shell.

The residents of Makoona had all heard about Binti's shell. Word travels fast on a reef, and everyone knows how much fish like to gossip. Most were in agreement that Binti had, in fact, been given a spirit shell. But now the question was, what should the octopus do with it?

The shell had already changed her. She seemed to have a deeper understanding of life on the reef. She had a broader perspective. She was more secure, relaxed, not all up in arms so often. One could say that Binti had matured. And everyone attributed her growth to the shell.

Paykak called Wiff over to talk with Binti about the infection. "Had a manta ray in here once. He had a spirit shell with a hole in it and slipped it through the spine on his tail. It's a real safe place for a ray to keep a shell. Saw the same infection on that tail. The ray said he'd have to pass the shell along soon."

"Why'd he say that?" the octopus inquired.

"He claimed that in order for the shell to keep its power, its spirit, it had to reach different fish. Said it had to be constantly passed along to others who needed it."

"So you think I should give up the shell?"

"Not necessarily. I'm just sharing what the ray told me."

"What if I just hold the shell with a different arm?"

"The infection might go away, but it could also spread. The ray said the spirit shells get weaker the longer one holds onto them. Who knows? At some point, if you get shellfish . . ."

"Are you calling me shellfish?"

"Clam down. I'm just saying if you hold onto this shell too long, it might turn against you. It's not a normal shell."

"You know what they say—" Paykak interjected.

"Yeah, yeah," Binti replied. "Be careful what you fish for, you just might catch it."

"The ray also said if you give the shell away, it must be given sincerely. Sounds like the hermit crab understood that too."

"Wonderful, maybe the ray was mistaken," the octopus said, searching for a reason to keep her precious shell.

"Maybe," Wiff said, clearly unconvinced. He dipped his head under Binti and asked, "How does this feel?" Then he bit into the tender sucker.

"AHHH!" What are doing to me?"

"Sorry, did I touch something sensitive?" he asked smugly and continued, "If that ray was mistaken, would that sucker be so infected?" Wiff shook his head and swam off to a crevalle jack who was next in line for a cleaning.

Paykak said sarcastically, "I'll bet that manta had no idea what he was talking about."

Swimming toward the crab-infested shallows, Binti hoped she'd find a hermit who needed a shell so that perhaps she could unload hers before it did any real damage. But part of her still believed the shell was precious. An unfamiliar voice whispered to her to keep it a little longer. Could the shell be talking to her? Yet she had to admit that having a shell—even a small one—wasn't what she'd hoped it would be.

Binti's hunger distracted her from her thoughts. She was looking forward to a good feed. Lately, she was eating more and getting larger as a result. There would be crabs in the shallows.

Binti never made it to the shallows. On the way there, she became queasy and ill and lost control of her coloration. The octopus began to turn pasty shades of red and gray that didn't match her surroundings at all. She forgot about feeding and raced back to her lair.

Inside her home, Binti felt safe from predators but still wondered what was happening to her. This was a sickness she'd never encountered before. She felt compelled to move rocks, shell shards, and other debris from her home.

In her haste, Binti even launched her spirit-shell out onto the sand with the rest of the clutter. As she cleaned her living space further, her appetite disappeared, and Binti lost her desire to socialize with friends on the reef.

She was hot and then cold, restless and then tired, joyous and then pensive. The voice inside her—the voice of instinct, the voice of her ancestors—spoke. It told her to relax and reassured her that everything was fine and what was happening to her now had happened to octopuses before. The voice sounded old, like a grandmother speaking to a nervous child.

Confused, Binti tried to do as she was told. She climbed up on her rock ceiling and wiped it clean of growth and dirt. When it comes to cleaning, seven arms can make for light work. Finally, when she felt as if she'd finished, the octopus took stock of her efforts. Her home was sparse and sparkling—perhaps a little less comfortable or cozy, but really clean. Whatever the sickness was, Binti thought, her den had never been more sanitary.

As tired as she was and wanting to rest, Binti was surprised to find herself stretching. She reached three arms up to the ceiling and stood tall on four arms beneath her. Then the sickness and the intense cleaning suddenly made sense. Binti began to lay eggs. They came out of her slowly on delicate strings, thousands of tiny eggs on each string. Binti hung the strings from a rocky overhang in a sealed-off corner of her home. She marveled at their beauty, each exquisite egg a potential life. They looked like strings of living pearls, undulating with the water. And like pearls, when the eggs hatched—if they hatched—the reef would be their oyster.

The old voice that only she could hear helped her understand the perilous paradox before her. This incredible garden of life could lead to an ominous conclusion for many. When one creature lays thousands of eggs, thousands will be lost. Those who perish pay the debt for those who survive. This was the way of life on Makoona, the way of maintaining the balance. Lives lost would nourish other lives. If only one or two of the eggs survived to adulthood and were able to reproduce, the cycle would continue, and Makoona would always know the octopus.

The voice warned that Binti shouldn't dwell on the eggs that would be lost. Being an octopus mother wasn't about death, it was about life. Like all those who came before her, Binti would have to dedicate herself to the survival of these eggs. Regardless, the octopus didn't need a voice from within to point out that she was entering motherhood, that these eggs needed her protection. Would she give them everything, even her life?

Maybe, with a little luck, five or ten might survive. Perhaps even twenty or thirty, maybe more. But the odds weren't in her favor, as there were those on Makoona who had different plans for Binti and her eggs.

When Kemar showed up at Al's hut in the morning to load the boat, he was greeted by someone he'd never seen before. Tall, thin, and with hair as orange as a sponge, the visitor walked quietly, gently, much more Asian than American. But the height, the hair, and the ruddy skin made it obvious: this person was not Makoonan. When she turned to introduce herself and said, "'Ello, mate," Kemar knew exactly where she'd come from.

In fact, the woman turned out to be the professor from Australia whom Al knew from Vietnam. The angular academic stretched out a long, thin arm toward the boy and said, "Name's Campbell. 'Eard you were taggin' a gayzah yesterday. Al says it was a real ripper and a bit of a rare thing."

"I caught it," Kemar replied, "but Al tagged it."

"Ah, anyone can tag 'em. It's catchin' 'em's the 'ard part."

With that, Al stepped out from his hull of a house and quipped, "Oh yeah? If anyone can tag 'em, why do you pay *me* to do it?"

Campbell countered, "If *you* get paid to do it, it just proves that anyone can do it."

"Anyone except you . . ."

"Aw, you know better than that, mate."

The three loaded gear into the boat, which seemed much smaller once Campbell and all her gadgets were aboard. Before they shoved off, Kemar asked, "Would you prefer that I not go with you today?" He could see beyond the good-natured kidding. He could see that Al and Campbell enjoyed each other's company a little more than perhaps two people fishing together might.

Al laughed. "No, I'd prefer that this red-headed kangaroo not go with us today, but since she's paying—both of us, I might add—we'll let her tag along. You are paying for both of us, right?"

The professor nodded. "Compliments of the University of Southern Queensland."

"What I mean," Kemar continued, "is that Professor Campbell is here to do something important. I don't want to be in the way."

Campbell and Al glanced at each other for a split second. They seemed to be able to communicate without speaking, the kind of thing that might have come in handy when they were in the jungle. After a moment, they grinned simultaneously.

"If that gayzah is any indication, sounds like you're the fisherman and Al's the assistant. Don't worry, son. We'll put you to work right enough. You might even learn something."

"What would I learn?"

Al smiled as the professor replied, "'Ow about this? Makoona's part of a chain of coral that stretches over a thousand miles. It's larger than all of Cambodia. And it's the only living organism on Earth that's visible from space."

"You can see it from space even though it's underwater?" the boy asked, trying to picture what Makoona would look like from that far away.

"This is one special place, Kemar. And I can tell you a lot more about it if you're interested. Are you keen to go now?" Campbell asked.

"If there's something to be learned, Kemar will want to know it," Al said. "Let's get going."

The boy hopped into the boat, asking, "What's my job today?"

Al answered, "Well, you won't be blowing up the reef or poisoning fish, that's for sure."

"Blowing up the reef?" Campbell echoed, blue eyes widening in alarm.

"I'll explain later. As a matter of fact, little man, today, you're gonna fish hard. And everything you catch goes right back into the sea."

"Doesn't sound like we'll make much money today."

"Luckily for you," Campbell said, "the USQ, in its enlightened approach to science, pays handsomely for fish to stay alive. You'll earn every penny locating, tagging, and gathering data on Makoona's greatest treasure . . . its life."

The boy scratched his head and bounced his foot. "I will keep no fish, but I will earn more money than when I do keep them?"

"You still have to catch 'em, mate. And you're gonna see fish like you've never seen before. Tell you all about 'em too, I will."

Kemar unsheathed his fillet knife and took out a sharpening stone. He looked at the two adults and declared, "I will try this."

The three fished until the sun was above the water but well below the clouds. Kemar proved useful on many levels and listened intently as Campbell described the peculiarities of every fish they tagged. She showed the boy how to systematically classify each fish, how to handle them safely, and how to return them to the sea so they would survive. Between catches, Campbell explained why each creature was important, pointing out the niche it occupied in the fabric of Makoona.

For Kemar, it was a revelation. He'd never really thought of sea life as anything other than a means to a meal or money. And he'd certainly never considered that someone could profit from the sea, which Campbell seemed to be doing, without pillaging it. In fact, Professor Campbell was actually making the reef healthier.

In a way, she reminded Kemar of the priests in Cambodia. There was a reverence in the way that she approached the sea that even went beyond the philosophies that Al professed. Where Al was a fisherman with a conscience and soul, Campbell took it a step further. She actually served Makoona as a custodian of the coral, and in doing that, she seemed to become part of it.

While they prepared to return to shore, Kemar realized something else. The feeling generated by the act of stewardship was so intoxicating that—for an evening, at least—he'd forgotten his journey and his past, so steeped he had become in the intricacies of Makoona.

As the island came into sight, the three sat listening to the sound of the swells slapping the bow of the boat, embellished by the steady putt-putt of the tired outboard. Occasionally, a bucket would bounce or a pole would roll noisily across the deck.

It was the young Cambodian who broke the silence, turning to Al, asking, "Can I ask you a question?"

"You can," Al said, "but I may not answer it."

"Why are you here?"

Al cocked his head sideways, running the question through his mind, deciding if he would answer. "Seems to me someone's gotta steer the boat."

"That's not what I mean. Why are you here on Makoona? Out here, people tend to pillage, some protect. You do both. Why?"

Campbell smiled a huge face-creasing grin. She ran her fingers through her thick hair and removed her sunglasses. Her eyes were soft and warm like the waning light of the sun. "Nice question, son. I can't wait to 'ear the answer."

Al unbuttoned the one button left on his shirt. This was a question that only a friend could ask another friend. The same could also be said of granting a reply. It wasn't that Al didn't want to answer Kemar, he was just struck by the idea that he'd remained so distant from others so well for so long that no one had ever asked him this before. "Sounds like you asked two questions," he said. "I'll answer one."

The boy smiled. "Which one?"

"You pick."

"Why do you live here?" Kemar asked.

"And can you tell me why you pillage and protect?" the Australian added merrily. "Please, enlighten me."

"I said one question."

"Right, one question . . . from each of us."

Al sighed. He knew when he was beaten. The fisherman began, "Bao's not the sharpest hook in the tackle box. He fishes like an idiot—takes without concern for what he destroys. Campbell fishes like she's some kind of angel—she takes nothing and is concerned about everything. I think there's a middle ground. I'm no angel, but I try not to fish like an idiot either. I'll take a life but never more than I need. I kinda fish like a fish."

Kemar nodded.

"I guess if I could get by doing Campbell's work, I'd do it. But she's a scientist, and I'm just a guy who catches fish. Bottom line, Makoona's a great fit for me. I like it here."

The scientist leaned forward, running her fingers through her hair. "I have a few more questions I'd like to pose, mate."

"Not a chance."

Campbell turned to Kemar. "Since the bodgy fisho here is apparently not entertaining questions from me, why don't you take my turn?"

"How did you get here, Al?" the boy asked sincerely. "I've told you my story. You should tell me yours."

"Oh, I should?" Al frowned. He didn't really like talking, much less talking about himself. He tried to avoid the question by looking toward land, hoping something there would catch his eye and turn the conversation away from his past.

Campbell flashed her beguiling grin. "Go on, Al. Tell 'im your story."

Al stared at the water, cut the engine, drifted for a moment, and then spoke quietly. "When I was on my first tour, standing in rice paddies, leeches getting as much of my blood as the VC, tired, sick . . . well, all I could think about was a plate of fresh pasta—angel hair with marinara, scallops, a little shrimp scampi, grated parmesan sprinkled on top, a warm loaf of fresh bread on the side. I just wanted that meal. I stayed alive just to eat that meal."

Kemar nodded. He understood.

"So after I finished that first tour, I don't know what I was thinking, I signed on for another. But before I returned to action, I went on leave in San Francisco. I went to a nice Italian bistro. I sat there in my dress blues with my two best buddies, and I ordered that meal. The three of us sat quietly, soaking up the atmosphere, enjoying the America we had missed, when this woman walked up to our table. I stood up. I mean, I was raised to be a gentleman. She reached her hand out to me. I shook it. She asks, 'You were in Vietnam?'"

"I said, 'Yes, ma'am.' All this time, I'm thinking maybe she has a brother or a husband stuck over there. Maybe my mother or sister saw a GI and went up to him in a restaurant thinking of me and offered a kind word to him. But instead of sharing a friendly thought, she looks into my eyes and pours her drink over my uniform. Then, in front of everyone, she calls me a 'killer,' a 'murderer.'

"But it's what happened next that really got to me. I reached down to my hip for my sidearm. I wasn't wearing one, but I could feel myself unhook the holster. That same lifeless glaze that I had in the jungle came over me. You feel like your life's already over and that whatever crazy thing you have to do doesn't really matter. It was a bad moment, as scary as anything that ever happened over there.

"When I ordered that meal, it was the first time I felt alive in so long. It's all I wanted. And that woman walked over and ripped it from me. I never did anything to her.

"As I lifted my hand from where I expected my holster to be, I felt another hand on mine. I didn't know the man, but the hand belonged to an officer, a general by the name of Del Anderson. He held my wrist with one hand, took out a handkerchief with the other hand, and personally wiped the drink from my ribbons. Then he said, calmly, 'Son, you would do me a great honor, and you would honor the Corps, if you would join me at my table as my guest. Please bring your two comrades.'

"For a minute, I just stared at him. I felt as though I was coming back from somewhere far away. I thought I heard rotor blades from a chopper cranking through the air. The woman was still talking, but I wasn't listening. I just walked over to the general's table. Then the owner of the restaurant—I still remember his name, John Caragiulo—came to the table. He put his hand on my shoulder, squeezed it gently, and left a bottle. I had a drink, maybe two. Never did get to eat that pasta. I knew then I could never come home. I didn't fit in anymore.

"Wanna hear more?" Al asked.

As Kemar began to answer yes, Campbell touched his arm softly, interrupting the boy, and said, "Want to tell us more?"

"A little bit."

The two nodded simultaneously.

"Near the end of my second tour, I was pretty amazed that I was still in one piece. We took a lot of fire that day, and me and this sergeant named Karl DeMasi were zipping down this dirt road trying not to get killed when all of a sudden we hit something in the road. The front of the jeep lifted up. Dirt, rocks, metal were flying everywhere. I could see the trees, then the sky, then I was laying in the bush. The jeep had turned completely over, and the sergeant was underneath.

"The first thing I did was look for my weapon. I spotted it, scooped it up, and ran for cover under the smoking jeep. Thought I'd check on Mace, that's what we called the sergeant. He was messed up, but nothing crazy. I figured we got dojoed by the VC, so I gathered some ammo and waited for them to approach.

"Well, we waited and waited and waited. No one came. Finally, I crawled out and poked around a bit. I looked in the brush and along the road. Then I spotted a big triangular hunk of metal not far from our vehicle. When I picked it up, it was still warm. At that point, I was pretty dizzy, and I noticed that blood was dripping from my ear. A drop fell on that piece of metal I was holding.

"As I wiped the blood off, I saw words, *Armorie de France 1957*. Of all things, here we are in Vietnam, and a French land mine that's over ten years old almost kills me and Mace. Don't know whether the VC buried it or the French did. Didn't seem to matter. Then I blacked out.

"So I wake up in a MASH unit with Mace a few beds away. Sittin' right next to me is a Methodist minister. I'll never forget him, Captain Morton Magee. He was this incredible combination of huge and gentle, kinda like a friendly bear. I mean, here we are in the middle of Vietnam, in the most screwed-up war you can imagine, and this minister is so serene, completely at peace. He saw all the craziness, all the crap, but it didn't seem to rattle him. At least he didn't show it. The captain was there on a mission of his own. You could read it in his eyes.

"A padre, they see the worst—the worst wounded, the worst of the war, all day. But I could tell by looking at him that it would take more than a war to shake his faith. I thought that was cool. I wanted that. That sense of peace. I think it was the most powerful thing I ever saw in the eyes of another human being. Kinda strange that in the middle of a war, the most powerful thing I saw was peace.

"The two of us have this long talk. I guess he thought I was Catholic, 'cause he ends our conversation by saying, 'Go and sin no more.' Well, that really struck me—I mean, it hit me like a physical blow. So, since the captain outranked me and I had already done two tours, I figured he had just given me a direct order. 'Go and sin no more.'

"So I just got up and left . . . left the hospital, left Vietnam, left the military, left the whole damn messed-up world. I bounced around a little bit, but when I got to Makoona, I stayed. I like it here. And one day, I'm gonna have the same peace that I saw in the eyes of Rev. Capt. Morton Magee.

"I saw this place in his eyes. The same calm blue that I see in the shallows. The same calm blue that I see in the sky. He sent me here. I'm sure of it. And I'm never leaving."

Al fired up the outboard. It replaced the silence after he stopped speaking. Once again, the waves slapped the bow while the hull bounced on the white-caps. Campbell reached out and tenderly squeezed Al's hand. He shook himself and lifted his head a little higher, and his eyes lost the faraway look of someone seeing his own past, if there is such a thing as *past*.

A Friend in Need

Binti hadn't eaten since she strung her eggs. She'd lost track of the days and should have felt famished, but the expectant octopus had no desire to nourish herself. In fact, she hadn't even left the lair, terrified that something might happen to her eggs. Hootie had stopped by several times. Once, he even brought a detail of gobies, compliments of Paykak, to tidy up the eggs and their mother. Even Ebb abandoned his fields to make quick visits. Binti was always gracious to her guests but continued to refuse food.

Although the octopus appreciated the concern of her friends, she felt disconnected from them. She was in a different place. All that mattered now were the young. She was consumed by caring

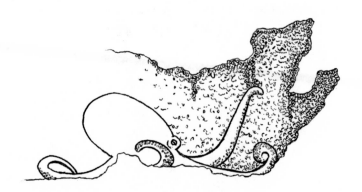

for them, summoning energy, devotion, and selflessness that Binti never knew she was capable of. Her biggest fear—indeed, her only fear—was that somehow, the eggs would be harmed.

Although Binti was never known for keeping a spotless nest, her home had somehow surpassed immaculate. It is, however, difficult to leave crumbs and shells when you refuse to eat. Yet anytime some dirt or debris invaded, Binti whisked it away, using her siphon as an underwater blower.

The octopus lost all interest in spirit-shells, searches for truth, surprising Ebb, visiting the cleaning station, and even Molo. She politely asked Hootie and her other friends to stay away from her home. She had no time for socializing, and visitors would only draw attention to her location and endanger her young. Of course, her friends all understood, except for Hootie, who spent his spare time swimming watch from the coral above Binti's den.

Executing her duties as an expectant mother, Binti began to see that her life did indeed have a purpose, and a very important one at that. Before she'd become a mother, her life was filled with a desire to find out who she really was and why she existed. She'd enjoyed her life yet had often felt troubled. Now, everything seemed crystal clear. Binti believed that life was about life—living it, creating it, preserving it, enjoying it, understanding it.

Her eggs had become her life, replacing her former habits and desires, lifting her above them. The eggs weren't merely new life for a species. They gave new life to Binti. She was reborn. But just as these tiny capsules of hanging octopuses provided a future for her kind, they could also provide nourishment for others who lurked beyond in the coral garden. For that reason, Binti wouldn't leave her eggs, not to feed, not to fight. Nothing would pull her from her lair.

Since octopus young go off on their own immediately after hatching, one might think that the newborns receive no motherly interaction, but Binti did a fine job making sure that as many as possible would feel her presence while they were with her. In-

stinct—her inner voice, the collective voice of thousands of generations of octopus mothers—directed her in how to care for the little
ones both before and after they would hatch.

Binti touched the eggs often, cleaning them, caressing them.
She told them useful things she would likely not be able to tell them
after they hatched. She studied the youngsters, watching them
through the translucent eggshells, wondering if they were also
watching her. The little ones had to survive long enough to leave
the lair. After that, instinct and common sense would guide them.

All this mothering, all this pressure and worry, drained Binti.
She began to lose the ability to change color. At first, whatever
shade she chose was muted, the vibrancy gone from her once-col-
orful chromatophores. As time went on, she could no longer change
color at all. Her flesh faded to soft green, then tan, then a pale yellow. Eventually, the octopus would become pure white, like an
empty shell lying on the beach, bleached by the sun. Binti wondered if she'd ever get her ability back.

She'd never seen a white octopus before but knew that a white
octopus wouldn't last long on the colorful reef. Sitting in her home,
she tried to diagnose the disorder. Perhaps she lost her camouflage
because she hadn't used it enough lately. Maybe it was the result of
not eating. The food might fuel the color. It was also possible that
she'd passed the talent on to her young and relinquished it in the
process. This last theory was the one Binti hoped was true. That
would be worth it.

While Binti got paler, thinner, and slower, her babies grew. She
watched thousands of minute octopuses ripening, blooming all
around her. Each one was perfectly formed in its own little bubble,
capable of performing all the tricks of a mature octopus. Soon,
they would hatch and race out onto the reef, getting bigger and
learning more every day.

Binti began removing the sponge from her doorway for short
periods of time. Her home became a bit less secure, but the increased flow of clean water added to the health of the young. The
mother watched the opening carefully, praying to the spirit-fish
to keep danger away.

Hootie increased his presence. He knew that the eggs would hatch soon. Perched inside his coral lookout tower one perilous dawn, the scaly sentry could see predators emerge and predators return. Some were bloated and ready for sleep after a night of feeding, swimming sluggishly to shelter, allowing potential meals to pass under their fins unmolested. But others woke from their slumber hungry or returned famished after a disappointing night's hunt. It was a deadly time to be on the reef.

The blowfish spotted a hole in a boulder, deflated as much as he could, and squeezed inside. Then he puffed up again, wedging his body into the crack so nothing could remove or join him. Hootie wondered what he'd do if he did spot danger. He guessed he'd try to alert Binti, but beyond that, what could a blowfish do to fend off an attack from a shark or a barracuda? Hootie hoped he'd never have to find out. But, of course, that's just when danger arrived.

The puffer spotted something nosing around a pile of coral rubble at the base of an ancient wreck. It wasn't a very threatening act in and of itself, but the digging and the activity could easily have attracted other, more formidable feeders. The sun was low in the sky. A long shadow shrouded the wreck. The foraging fish was completely covered by the rubble it rummaged through, which indicated to Hootie that the fish was smaller and not a direct threat.

Even if nothing larger was attracted, a school of small hungry fish could devastate Binti's eggs, so he felt it was a good idea for the fish to dine somewhere else. Deciding the best defense would be a good offense, he emerged from the rock, slid down the slope of Binti's lair, and hid just outside her entrance.

"Binti," he whispered, "it's me, Hootie. Don't get nervous, but something's poking around the wreck, and it could cause trouble. I'm going to swim it off."

The tip of Binti's arm, which was now ivory in color, appeared near the opening. It carefully latched onto the brown sponge and pulled it snugly into the crack, sealing the octopus and her eggs from the coral canyon beyond. She used her other arms to cover and compress the strings, shielding them from sight and scent. But what the protective mother hadn't noticed was that a solitary egg had broken free from its string and slipped out of the den when Binti reached for the sponge.

Now Hootie took over. He was uneasy. He didn't know exactly what he was approaching. Whatever it was, it was too close for comfort. The blowfish swam toward the diminutive dust cloud that marked the scavenger's location. Hootie planned to become a living decoy if necessary, luring the fish as far away from Binti as he could.

Hootie was close enough to see coral rising and rolling. Dust clouded the water and cloaked the creature within. Wanting to make an entrance that would lead to a chase, the blowfish swam closer until he was under the same shadow that spread across the coral. He puffed himself up and squeezed all the water from his body with one powerful compression, blowing the debris away, and revealing just who it was nosing around the coral-encrusted wreck.

To his complete dismay, Hootie found himself gills-to-gills with a very formidable predator, or more accurately, several predators not nearly as small as the puffer had anticipated. Three large

morays gaped open-jawed at Hootie. For a heartbeat, they contemplated each other and the situation. Then the chase began.

The blowfish fled. Instinctively, he cruised low over the coral contours of Makoona, turning tightly, unpredictably. Yet as much as he wanted to lose his pursuers, he didn't want them to give up and return to Binti's backyard. At this point, however, the morays gave no indication that they were interested in anything other than blowfish de jour.

Hootie worried about an ambush. He struggled to keep himself in the lead, with the morays far enough away so that he couldn't be outflanked and subsequently trapped. The helpful blowfish had never expected to antagonize a family of eels.

Believing that he'd lured the morays far enough from Binti and tiring from the chase, Hootie tweaked his strategy. He decided it was time for a cleaning and raced to Paykak's. Winding through weeds, accelerating around anemones, sprinting through sponges, Hootie reached the cleaning station with all his scales intact.

Although it was a practice that was frowned upon, using the cleaning station as a safe haven was Hootie's only chance. He hoped that when Paykak realized it was done to protect Binti, the goby would give sanctuary to the puffer and declare the morays "uncleanable" if they attacked the blowfish while he was at the station.

Paykak, however, didn't see the situation Hootie's way at all. In fact, he refused to make any such declaration, saying, "The cleaning station is not something I can use to protect my friends. The rule is intended to preserve the balance, even if it means that Binti, her eggs, and a well-intentioned blowfish suffer."

The morays waited ominously behind a wall of fan coral, listening to Paykak's judgment, eying Hootie with culinary curiosity.

"But what if I'm being cleaned?" the blowfish argued. "What I've done before I came to the station shouldn't matter. The fact that I'm being cleaned or waiting to be cleaned should protect me. The fact that I need a cleaning doesn't disappear because I'm being chased, does it?"

Paykak considered the logic in Hootie's plea. He asked simply, "Do you need to be cleaned?"

"More than I ever have in my life," the blowfish spouted. "I'm very dirty. Soooo dirty." Hootie glanced over at the morays behind the fan coral and continued, "If I don't get cleaned right now, tomorrow, one of your helpers will be sucking pieces of me out of their jaws. You bet I need a cleaning."

"That's not a legitimate reason to need a cleaning. Do you have a parasite? A tick? A lesion, perhaps?"

"Well, if I don't, I'm gonna get one."

"If you do, you get cleaned. If you don't, well . . ."

At that moment, Wiff approached Paykak. He smiled at Hootie and turned to his boss, saying, "Rhett me rhook the ruffer rover," strangely slurring his speech.

Paykak nodded, and the goby performed a cursory, half-hearted inspection.

With his life on the line, Hootie protested, "Come on, Wiff! You can do better than this. Be thorough."

Wiff resumed and, without anyone noticing, spit something under one of Hootie's gill covers. Then he winked at the blowfish, shrugged at Paykak, and swam off.

Hootie grinned for an instant. He puffed himself up, waved Paykak over, and said, "I think Wiff might've missed something." The blowfish opened a gill cover for Paykak to examine.

"Is that a leech in there?" the goby observed.

"A leech?" Hootie howled. "I'm infected! A parasite! Oh, he's sucking the life out of me. Who does a fish have to swim with around here to get a cleaning? Someone help me!"

"Okay, blowfish, you've made your point." Then Paykak commanded, "Someone clean this bag of scales."

Wiff began work on Hootie, whispering, "You owe me big-time, Puffer."

The morays were forced to either get in line for a cleaning or wait beyond the station for Hootie to leave. But the latter was risky, because one could be declared "uncleanable" merely by staking out the station. While Wiff continued work on the puffer, leaving no scale unturned, Hootie came to a shocking realization. There were only two morays behind the fan coral, a mature male and an adolescent. The female was nowhere to be found.

It was a warm night following a long day on the reef. Kemar was sleeping soundly, a king in his cot with one hundred and thirty-eight dollars stashed in a tin can buried under Meela's workbench. Makoona had been good to him. Soon, he would be asked to return the favor.

Although physically, the boy was sleeping in Meela's hangar, in his dreams, his mind found its way to water. The ocean glistened and glowed, lit by a bright moon. Kemar dreamed he was floating out to the reef on his mattress, searching for something he'd left behind, not sure just what it was. The mattress carried him like Aladdin's magic carpet, barely touching the tips of the swells. He liked this dream. It was peaceful, relaxing.

Eventually, he stopped moving. Over the bow of his bed, a long, blue arm reached out of the sea and slid up onto the mattress. Another arm and then another did the same until finally, a lone octopus crawled aboard. It sat, looking out to sea, never facing the boy. Then a lifeboat glided up beside Kemar, rowed by Captain Phan. Although the boat had holes identical to those of the lifeboat he slept in as a boat person, this one floated easily on the water.

Phan called, "Quick, boy! The Vietnamese have saved Cambodia. I will take you back. It is time to go home. Pay me and come aboard."

Kemar responded, "I have nothing but this mattress. I cannot pay."

Phan rubbed his chin and then nodded. "The blue octopus. I will take it as payment, a small gratuity for bringing you home. Quickly now!" Phan reached out to grab the creature.

"No!" Kemar yelled. He deflected the hand and pushed the lifeboat away. As it drifted off, Kemar could hear Phan murmuring, "Come, Kemar. Come now."

The octopus turned to the boy. It was Binti. He recognized her. She smiled and climbed back into the sea. Half-submerged, she clung to the mattress, flashed the truest blue she could muster, and said, "You have saved me again. Now it is my turn to save you. Welcome home, my friend."

As the blue water swallowed Binti, Kemar could still hear Phan far off, calling, "Come, Kemar! Come now!"

And then the boy was blinded by a brilliant ray of light shot right into his face. His eyes squeezed more tightly shut against the glare. When the bright beam sunk to his chest, Kemar opened his eyes and realized he was awake and that the beam was coming from a flashlight. Someone was shaking his arm, whispering, "Come, Kemar. Come now." It was Bao.

The boy pulled on a tattered sweatshirt that Meela had given him and silently followed Bao to the edge of the mangrove. There, in the thin moonlight, the man said, "Not want old witch see Bao. Try kill Bao once."

"Then you better stay away from her," Kemar advised.

"Bao want help."

"From me? Why?"

"Boy know valuable thing. Valuable for Bao and boy."

"And what's this valuable thing I know?"

"We fish tonight. You see."

"I was in a boat all day. I'll be in one all day tomorrow. I'm tired. I'd rather go back to sleep."

"Could make two month money in one night with Bao," the fisherman implored.

"I fished plenty of nights with you and never made that kind of money."

Bao tugged at the boy's earlobe. "Tonight different."

"No, it's not. I'm going back to sleep." Kemar turned toward the tool shed.

"When boy need Bao, Bao not sleep. Have short memory."

Without turning back to face the man, Kemar asked, "What do you want from me?"

"Come, help Bao tonight."

"And then, after that, I owe you nothing."

"Fish hard tonight. Ask no question. Keep quiet, and debt is paid. Hear no more from Bao."

The two walked off into the darkness.

Later, Kemar found himself mildly surprised, not so much with where Bao had asked to go, but with the fact that he'd actually cooperated with the fisherman. Seated in the same boat that had come to the boy's rescue, they bobbed on the sea over one of Al's most secret fishing spots.

"Find bottle," Bao commanded. "Tie up."

Kemar searched for the floating bottle that marked the mooring line. He didn't like the way things were shaping up, but if this one night would free him of Bao forever, the boy was willing to take the chance.

If morays are anything, they're sneaky, suspicious predators. The mother moray was no exception to the rule. Convinced that her mate and their child could handle the blowfish and skeptical that they should abandon the feeding ground, the mother returned to rummaging in the wreck.

When it floated by, her instincts were confirmed. The moray couldn't believe her luck. A solitary octopus egg drifted directly past her nose. She could smell the prey, see the tiny octopus inside the soft, transparent shell. Immediately, the moray sucked it in, swallowing with satisfaction.

She scanned the coral valley, hoping to locate what crack, what crevice, leaked the egg. If there was one unhatched octopus egg here, there were probably thousands more tucked away in some coral corner nearby. Judging from the advanced development of the one she'd swallowed, she believed the eggs would be hatching soon. And, knowing that the mother octopus would not be feeding while she tended to her offspring, the moray guessed that she was very weak at this point.

The moray's instincts were right on target. Binti was barely alive.

When she didn't see any other eggs on the coral, the moray, who isn't known for superior eyesight, became more active. She slithered out from under the wreck, felt the current carefully, and attempted to reconstruct the path the egg had taken. The predator swam into the drift, tasting, smelling, on the lookout for anything that murmured *octopus.*

As she passed above Binti's lair, a strange scent nudged her nostrils. It wasn't that of an octopus; rather, she smelled fish, a blowfish. She tracked the smell. It led her to a small stand of sponge in a coral valley across from the wreck. The moray wriggled into the sponges, coiling in the dark along their bases. The scent was strong and fresh.

Could it be the same blowfish who stumbled upon us? she wondered. *What if the blowfish didn't "stumble" upon us? Maybe it wasn't an accident. But why would a blowfish intentionally agitate a family of eels? Why would it want to commit sure scalicide?*

At that moment, a large reef shark swam overhead. It didn't see the moray, but she could see it. She could also see the remora stealing scraps from the shark's gills. And then she remembered something she'd heard at the cleaning station, something about a blowfish and an octopus who were best friends.

It's a long shot, she thought, *but perhaps this blowfish and the lone octopus egg are connected.* The moray decided to look this spot over very carefully. She'd leave no shell unturned.

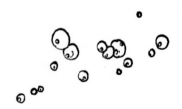

It didn't take long to trace the blowfish's scent. She located the sponge with the hole, where Hootie had hidden himself. Then she followed the scent beyond the sponges down the rock alongside Binti's den, right up to the entrance. There, the blowfish's path ended. But the moray was getting closer. She could sense opportunity lurking.

She poked around the entrance to Binti's home until something sweet reached her nose. The brown sponge that sealed off the opening gave the octopus away. Because it was porous, it allowed a trace of scent to leach out into the water. Had the moray not been hunting in that precise spot, the smell would've dissipated and never have been noticed, but it was noticed, and now she knew exactly what was on the other side of that sponge.

Kemar returned to his bunk in Meela's shed just before dawn. He expected to feel relieved to be rid of his heavy debt to Bao, but he didn't feel that way. In fact, the boy felt more burdened now than before he left. In clearing his debt to Bao, Kemar had betrayed Al, Campbell, and in a sense, Meela too.

Bao had the boy take him to one of the spots where Kemar tagged fish earlier in the week. Throwing out their nets, they'd pulled up quite a few tagged fish from the reef. Bao kept them all, claiming they were rare or special, either of which enhanced value. They would be sold to the Filipino middleman at a premium rate.

Kemar had ruined Campbell's work, betrayed a true friend, and ultimately, desecrated the sea he professed to love, the sea that had given gifts to him. The boy fell asleep, wishing that he'd drowned clinging to the cooler on the open sea.

This time, Kemar's deep slumber afforded him no rest. He couldn't escape his deeds by closing his eyes and laying his head on a pillow. Moments after he fell asleep, he was carried back to Makoona. The boy had returned to the scene of his crime.

In his dream, Kemar could breathe and swim underwater without difficulty. Like any other resident of the reef, he sat on the hull of an old wreck, watching a rare reef-dwelling bass build a nest in the sand, preparing to receive eggs from a female to create vital new lives. The male fish foraged the floor looking for food. A shadow grew on the surface, darkening the ground below. A net was lowered into the water, and the bass was removed from the sea before it could reproduce.

Disturbed by what he saw, the boy tried to swim off, but he couldn't move his feet. An octopus had reached out through a hole in the hull and wrapped its arms around the boy's ankles. It seemed he would have to stay where he was until the show was over.

A quiet *plip* caused Kemar to glance upward. He saw the bass gently returned to the reef. The creature took a second to fill its gills and get its bearings. Then it raced back to its nest. A tiny red tag dangled near the base of the bass's dorsal fin. The boy knew where it came from. Unharmed, the fish resumed its foraging. The shadow from above moved on.

Kemar expected the octopus to release him now that the point was made, but the cephalopod maintained its grip. Soon, another shadow darkened the sand. Another net hunted through the water, found the tagged bass, along with several other inhabitants of the reef, and removed them all from the coral.

This time, however, none of the fish found their way back into the sea. The only thing that was returned to the reef was the red tag, now nothing more than garbage, inviting an innocent creature to swallow it and perhaps lose its life as well. Kemar watched the tag slowly sink until it fell directly onto the bass's unfinished, abandoned nest.

The octopus reached out another arm from beneath the wreck. It picked up the tag and laid it at the boy's feet. And then Kemar heard a voice ask, "Who are you?" He looked over his shoulder and saw a flamboyant fiery red nudibranch hovering beside him.

The nudibranch repeated, "Who are you?" The creature turned black, fringed with violet, streaked with orange and white. It meandered away, strutting its splendor as only a nudibranch can.

Now it was the octopus's turn to speak to Kemar. It released the boy's legs and climbed up into the thick shadow cast by the man-tide overhead. Its mantle crinkled and creased, the octopus presented the red tag and asked, "Who are you?"

Kemar took the tag in his hand and studied it. He contemplated the bass's empty nest.

The octopus continued, "You do not see clearly. Look through these." An arm emerged from the shadow and handed the boy a pair of glasses. They were his father's.

Next, a man's hands grasped the boy's shoulders from behind and shook him violently. Kemar couldn't see the man, and his words were garbled as if the speaker wasn't actually underwater with him and called from the surface.

As the words became clearer, the dream became dimmer. Once again, someone was shaking the boy awake. This time, it was Al. The American was visibly upset, asking, "Who are you?"

The reality revived and repulsed the boy.

"How could you do that? You little bastard."

Kemar said nothing. There was nothing to say.

Binti could feel the presence of the moray eel. It was close. The octopus secured her eggs behind her. She removed two strings and hung them in a remote corner of her den, hoping the moray might overlook them and that those who would surely follow looking for an easy meal might miss these eggs as well.

The octopus didn't know how successful Hootie had been, but she guessed not very, since the moray was here and the blowfish was not. Binti slid toward her entrance, prepared to fight her final battle. If the moray smelled only Binti, then she might be able to lure it away, but if it smelled the eggs, they were gone. There'd be no way to stop the moray.

The predator approached the sponge that sealed the entrance to Binti's home. The smell of the octopus was very strong, very fresh. She would eat. The moray waved her nose around the entrance and followed the scent into the sponge.

She flashed crooked, sharp teeth, stretched her massive jaw, tensed long, powerful muscles, and prepared to burst into the coral cleft. She gazed at the sponge with cold blue eyes. Then she threw itself at the flimsy façade, laughing. But the sponge was not as flimsy as the moray had anticipated. It covered the crack and repelled her thrust. The moray withdrew and considered the problem.

Inside her lair, Binti was aware of the moray's charge. She readied herself but became puzzled when the sponge deflected the predator and it retreated. Her confusion ended when the sponge said, "There is danger at your door."

Then the brown sponge glared out at the moray, warning, "It's one thing to bark, another to bite. The show ain't over `till you pack up for the night."

The moray replied to the talking sponge, "I have no quarrel with you. Move aside and allow me to eat. Do not interfere or I will eat twice today."

Again, the barricade spoke, "Squirm, you sinner. Howl and moan. The Devil is your due."

Binti suddenly understood who the sponge actually was. She slid up to Molo, caressed him gently, and whispered, "Leave here. I will die for my eggs. There's no reason to add your life to this."

Molo answered, "A friend in trouble is a friend indeed, and what you've got here is a friend in need ... Ain't complaining about what I got. Seen better times, but who has not?"

"This *is* a bad time, Molo, a very bad time. And you're not gonna change it, so get out of here. Please."

"Tell me the cost," Molo countered. "I can pay, let me go. Tell me love is not lost."

"Don't fight the moray. The cost could be your life."

The male grinned. "When you have done your best and even more is asked of you, let fate decide the rest."

Just as she finished her plea, the impatient moray attacked her mate, this time biting into the soft sponge and removing a small piece of it. The moray chewed, swallowed, and understood what the sponge really was. She could taste it.

Molo focused his attention on the moray. Blue blood leaked from the base of one arm. He raised himself and uncoiled and shed the brown coloring, and his body became pure black with bolts of red and blue racing through his flesh. He waved his arms menacingly and taunted, "What good is spilling blood? It will not grow a thing. You know you're bound to wind up dead if you don't head back."

The moray smiled. "I'll head back as soon as I'm done eating."

Molo moaned, "And again, the hunt begins, and again, the bloodwind calls." Then he threw himself at the moray. It was a suicide leap accentuated by the kamikaze wrecks that littered the waters of Makoona.

Molo wrapped himself around the slippery moray eel, trying to constrict and hold her while at the same time attempting to draw her attention away from Binti and the eggs. The octopus shoved one of his arms into the moray's mouth. He hoped it would tear at the arm, occupying its teeth with a less critical part of his body. At the same time, Molo slid his mouth under the moray and bared his beak to her belly.

He could see the soft pale underside of the beast. He pulled his flesh back to expose his own small beak, as sharp as any barracuda's tooth and twice as hard. Molo tightened his grip on the slimy moray and pushed his beak into its supple stomach.

The moray released the arm and swatted Molo with its head, crashing him into a coral wall. It sheared an arm from Molo's flank with one swift bite, and then another. The water darkened in a purple cloud as the octopus's blue blood mingled with red dripping from the moray's underside.

Molo sat for a moment beneath the coral. He watched the female eating two of his arms. She seemed satisfied that she could grab another at will. Molo was motionless. He wanted to flee but couldn't. He wanted to attack but didn't have enough strength.

Suddenly, he was dragged from the coral, ripped out of the shelter by the other two morays who'd pursued Hootie. In an instant, two more arms were gone, and there were several deep cuts in Molo's mantle.

The morays were merciless. They removed two more arms and several other parts from the octopus. The feeding female looked down on the helpless creature, almost nothing but mantle, and taunted, "Would you like to issue any more threats to morays?"

Molo replied, "The biters were biting. The bitten were writhing . . . Paradise awaits on the crest of a wave . . . The Lord will take us when we die to golden shores . . ."

"Well, it won't have long to wait for you," the male moray said. "His mind's as mangled as the rest of him. Leave what's left for a grouper."

The eels swam off, satisfied with their meal. Molo also felt satisfaction that they'd forgotten about Binti and her eggs. In filling their bellies, he'd emptied their minds. It was a fair trade. Molo waited in the sand, powerless to prevent others from finishing him off. The octopus watched a lobster walk off with one of his suckers. Soon, it would be over.

Moments after Al stormed out, Kemar rolled off his cot. He walked outside and sat on Meela's dock, watching the water sparkle as sunlight flashed through gaps in the mangrove behind him. A patient reef egret stood in the shallows, snapping up morsels.

Kemar picked up an old shell and rolled it in his hands. Although he couldn't know it, this was the same shell Ellaber had gifted Binti. The boy contemplated his actions as he rolled the hermit's husk in his hands. Why had he gone with Bao?

Then Meela sat down next to him. Neither spoke. Kemar passed the shell to his friend. Meela held it out in front of her, bounced it in her palm, and then passed it back to the boy. She was the first to speak.

"I've felt what you're feeling now," she began.

"You know what happened?"

She nodded. "It's not as bad as you think. Someone told Al where you and Bao were fishing. It didn't take him long to figure out what was going on. Campbell got most of her fish back. She bought them from the Filipino, who was a little reluctant to sell, but Al persuaded him to accept the payment. They're returning the fish they could retrieve right now . . . So you didn't ruin Campbell's study."

"I just damaged it."

"When you spend your life just trying to survive, sometimes a choice that seems right in the moment isn't right in the long run . . . I've been there myself."

"You never fished."

"Fishermen don't have a monopoly on bad judgment. You love this ocean? Do you really love the life that's in it, all around it?"

Kemar lifted his head slightly, absorbing all the beauty that surrounded him. A ghost crab ran along the sand, tormented by a testy tern. "I would say yes, I love this sea more than anything, but my actions do not say that."

"Then change your actions. Get a new flight plan. I loved being a pilot more than anything, anyone. And some of the things I did in the name of aviation horrify me as much as what you did last night horrifies you."

"I must leave."

"That's what I did. Shame doesn't mean you have to leave."

"I don't deserve Makoona."

"Maybe today you don't. Does that mean you should leave? Bao doesn't deserve this place, but he lives here. Let me ask you, if you packed up and left today, would you ever deserve Makoona?"

"Probably not, but I couldn't hurt this place any more. I couldn't hurt Campbell or Al or you."

"You haven't hurt me. Takes more than stupidity to hurt me. So you run, and then no one gets hurt. How does that *help* Makoona?"

"I'm no longer here to hurt it. That's help."

"Too easy. It's not enough. Where's the payback?"

"The what?"

"The payback. You still haven't made things right. You've only avoided future harm. You haven't healed this place. Leaving does not right the wrong."

"How does one undo what one has done?"

"I can't answer that, Kemar."

"Then who can?"

Kemar and Meela dipped their toes into the surf. They listened to the breeze, were soothed by the slap of the swells against the docked boats, and watched a dozen giggling gulls pluck mullet from the water.

"Back in Cambodia, when a boy feels he must surrender his life to his faith, what does he do?" Meela asked quietly.

"A Buddhist boy? A Catholic boy? Either would become a monk, a priest. You think I should become a monk?"

"No, not unless *you* do," the mechanic said, chuckling. "But if you really feel as much for Makoona and its life as you say you do, then give your life to it just as a monk would give his life to his faith."

At this point, Kemar saw Meela do something he'd only seen her do twice before. She lit her cigar. The old woman blew a thin line of smoke through the gap between her front teeth. The smoke escaped, slowly rose, and dissipated into Makoona.

"Reminds me of sky-writing," Meela mumbled.

"I always thought fishing was a way to become part of the reef," Kemar said, "but it isn't. Fishing would never heal what I have done. Fishing destroys."

"Well, depends how you fish, but who's talking about fishing anyway?" Meela took a thoughtful drag on the stogie. "What's my motto, remember?"

Kemar knew it well. He recited, "Live and learn."

"There it is. Do that. Live and learn."

"Do what?" Kemar asked, confused.

"If there was a priest or a monk of Makoona—a holy person who looked at all this with reverence and gave their soul to it—who would that be?"

Kemar looked sourly at Meela. Was she trying to make him feel worse? It wasn't necessary. "Campbell," the boy answered. "The person I hurt the most."

"Then become Campbell."

"*Become* Campbell?"

"Live and learn. Yes, if anyone heals this place and protects these reefs, it's her."

"But she's a scientist, a professor. I sleep on a cot in your tool shed. If I have proved anything, I've proved that I'm unworthy."

Meela carefully laid her cigar on a stone. She reached into her pocket and took out a small, lockblade pocketknife, opened it, and cut the smoldering tip from the rest of her precious smoke. Then she returned the unlit cigar to her mouth.

"Campbell asked me yesterday if you were a good assistant to me. She asked Al as well. We both told her yes."

"Why would she ask about me? Besides, that was yesterday. Things are different today.

Meela grinned and said, "Maybe not. Ask her. Maybe she wants you to do some work for her. Maybe she wants you to get a real education. Sounds a little better to me than running away. Wanna try it?"

Kemar looked perplexed. He'd done wrong, and yet it seemed he was being rewarded. It didn't make sense. Meela reached into one of the many pockets on her coveralls, removed something delicate, and laid it on Kemar's leg. The boy looked down and saw his father's glasses, just like in his dream.

"Where'd you get these?" he asked.

"They were lying beneath your cot," Meela said. "I picked them up before one of us stepped on them. Put the glasses on. Maybe they will help you see."

The boy put the spectacles on, stretching the wire over his ears. They seemed to fit his head a little better today. And when he looked through the lenses, for the first time, what he saw wasn't fuzzy or distorted. The world was crystal clear.

"What would he have wanted you to do?"

"University school costs money, lots of it. And I have only a few dollars."

"Kick the chocks out from under your feet and go see Al and Campbell."

"I have seen them. I know what they think."

"You have seen them, but you don't know what they think. Go see Al and Campbell."

She crept up to the tattered octopus, weak herself, shocked that she was leaving her eggs even for a moment. But Binti had to speak to Molo. He'd watched over her and given his life for her eggs—their eggs.

"Molo, do not speak. I will sit with you."

However, asking Molo not to speak was like asking the current not to flow. He knew there was very little time left and yet there was so much he wanted to say.

"There are times when you can beckon. There are times when you can call. You can shake a ton of reckoning, but you can't shake it all. There are times when I can help you out, and times that you must fall. There are times when you must live in doubt and I can't help at all."

"You have helped," Binti said. "You've saved the little ones, saved me."

"If I had the world to give, I'd give it to you, long as you live. Would you let it fall or hold it all in your arms?"

Binti placed her pale arms around Molo, holding him closely.

"A hundred years on down the line, will any part of our love light shine?" he asked.

"Of course it will. There are thousands of love lights about to hatch in my den. They will shine."

"Like an angel standing in a shaft of light, rising up to paradise, I know I'm gonna shine," Molo said absent-mindedly.

The octopus sensed his end and didn't want Binti to see him go. " . . . leave me alone to find my way home."

"Not yet, Molo. Not yet."

He whispered, "Never had such a good time in my life before. I'd like to have it one more time. One good ride from start to end,

I'd like to take that ride again . . . What a long, strange trip it's been." Molo looked beyond the reef.

"I won't be far behind you." Binti sensed that she, too, didn't have long. The voice of her ancestors, of mothers before her, told her that in order to give life to her young, she must relinquish her own. Just as her mother had never seen her, Binti would almost certainly not greet her children when they were born. Having starved herself to care for her eggs, she wouldn't be nourished in this world again. It was the role the octopus played in the harmony of the spirit-fish.

As she reached this epiphany, one of the eggs deep in her lair broke open. The liquid inside the orb mixed with the seawater. A perfect little octopus emerged, flashed forty different colors, and swam toward the opening. Another joined it, and another. The tiny cephalopods gathered together and spilled out onto Makoona in a fresh, new wave of life. They instantly disappeared and blended behind whatever they could find.

Binti watched it all, holding Molo tightly. As if she squeezed the words out of him, her mate wheezed one last contorted phrase, one last exotic thought.

"My head was full of nothing but the pounding of the surf. And whirling kind of slowly like the spinning of the Earth . . . All of my fancy, all of my dreams come true just to be here with you for the last dream. All of my life starts to make sense now. I think I see what it means . . . Crippled but free, I was blind all the time I was learning to see . . . I'm going where the chilly winds don't blow."

Molo breathed in the liquid of Makoona, holding it deep inside him, hoping to bring it with him on his journey to the spirit-fish. "Fare you well, fare you well. I love you more than words can tell. Listen to the river sing sweet songs to rock my soul."

There was no life left inside of Molo's body. Binti studied it, seeing that it had become nothing more than a shell. The octopus had a shell after all, a soft one. Binti realized that what really mattered—in the end, anyway—wasn't the shell at all, but what lived inside of it and what was given to others beyond it.

The octopus left her love and dragged herself to her den to see if there was anything else she could do for her children. She turned one last time to the empty mantle in the sand and said with pride, "So swift and bright, strange figures of light. Who can stop what must arrive now? Something new is waiting to be born."

Kemar couldn't face Al, but truthfully, he couldn't face himself. For his entire life, whenever he'd been confronted with a moment of truth, he'd run.

Although many would have done the same and he was only a boy at the time, he never faced the Khmer Rouge. He ran. He'd survived being a refugee—a boat person—but had done nothing to alter his situation or the lives of those around him or the brutality of Phan. He saw how wrong Bao was in his treatment of the reef and yet had actually helped Bao commit his brutal acts. Worst of all, perhaps, the three people who'd given him so much, he'd hurt deeply.

Consumed with self-loathing, Kemar decided he would run no more. Whatever Al would do to him, he would face. It was part of the price he would have to pay for assisting Bao in the desecration of the reef, the professor's study, and the faith that friends had placed in him. Kemar went to Al.

Al, wanting to put the morning's events behind him, didn't expect the boy to behave like a man, especially after their earlier encounter, so he decided to take the initiative. The two met coincidentally on the beach halfway between Meela's shop and Al's hut. Al forced a sour grin and sat down on a long piece of driftwood waiting for Kemar to reach him.

"Sit down, little bro," Al said.

The boy sat on the sand.

"You have to know that I'm pretty unhappy, pretty disappointed in you."

"I'm sor—"

"Stop. Let me do my thing. You've already done yours. Like I said, part of me is very unhappy. But to tell you the truth, I got no right takin' the high ground. I've done worse, much worse, many times in my life. So how can I get all high and mighty on you?"

"So what do I do now?"

Al smiled another thin, bitter grin, "Wanna go fishing?"

"Please don't tease me. I did something wrong, and I want to make it right . . . so . . . so we can be friends again."

"We're friends. I believe in strong friendships, not fragile ones."

"But what you said to me earlier?"

"Heat of the moment. No reason for that. My bad."

Kemar nodded. "Meela says, and I agree, that I must heal what I have done."

"Then heal it, brother."

"How?"

"I don't know. I didn't mess things up. I'll tell ya, though, if you have trouble living with yourself after you do something bad, that's actually a good sign. Means deep down, you give a damn. And that's the most important thing . . . You wanna be okay with me? I mean really, rock solid okay?"

"Yes. I'll do anything."

"Well, don't be such an idiot. Be a little smarter next time."

"There will be no next time."

Al shook his head. "Little bro, there's always a next time. So get ready for it now."

"And how will I do that?"

"Learn from this experience, and . . ." Al stopped and let his second thought fall onto the sand.

But Kemar picked it up and dusted it off, asking, "And?"

" . . . go with Campbell."

"Leave Makoona? No, I have decided that I will not run, not this time."

"For now, one way not to be stupid—and that's an issue here—is to get smart. Go and get smart. That's not running away."

"She will take me with her?"

"I would," Campbell said as she lowered herself onto the log and sat next to Al. "I hear you can be a good assistant. Maybe I could use one."

"It was her idea," the American said. "You know, when I was back home on leave one time, I saw a movie called *The Graduate*. It was about a young guy who had just graduated college. There was a scene I still remember. When the world got too loud for him, when it was all just too much, he'd jump in his pool with scuba gear on and just sit underwater. In a way, he became the pool. It was quiet, no one bothered him, and he escaped the madness. I think that movie helped me find Makoona. I became this place, and it helped me escape the madness."

"But you did not desecrate this place."

"Maybe not this place, but I already told you, I had a life before I got here. And I did some stuff I'm not proud of. But I believe I've learned from those moments, and you should learn from your actions."

Al reached into a pocket, pulled out a leather wallet, and removed a tattered piece of paper. "Just before I went to 'Nam for the first time, my mom gave me this. She was real religious. I think she wrote this never dreaming I'd wind up in the jungle." Al read, "Your life is God's gift to you. What you make of your life is your gift to God." He folded the paper and returned it to the wallet.

"You got a chance to make your life special. Eventually, you could know these waters better than me, and you could know these fish as well as Campbell. That's cool. And that's how you become this place. Just like that kid in the movie became the pool, you immerse yourself in it. That's when the noise goes away and other things start makin' more sense."

"How will an assistant be able to pay for everything? There are too many expenses, I'm sure." Kemar shook his head.

"That's where Uncle Al comes in. I never got to go to college, but I can help you."

"You will kill more fish to pay for my education? How does that help Makoona?"

"Good! Now you're thinking. You're right, fishing's not the solution." Al laid an old army-issued shoulder bag on the ground in front of Kemar. He unsnapped the tabs, opened it up, and reached inside. The American looked into his young friend's eyes and fixed his gaze. Al produced a rusted blue can and handed it to Kemar. "Here's your scholarship," he said.

The boy breathed deeply, quickly, but felt as though no air entered his lungs. His heart pounded, but it felt like no blood reached his veins. He recognized the can instantly, even though the others didn't know its provenance. As Kemar popped the lid, he looked up to Al and asked, "How?" without actually uttering a word.

"It's amazing what you find when you pick up garbage on the beach."

The gold taels were still stuffed inside the can. It looked to Kemar as though they'd never been removed, never counted or weighed, never even touched by Al.

"Don't really know how much it's all worth," Al said. "But I know what it is, and I'll bet there's enough for all three of us to go to school."

"Then come with me," Kemar implored Al.

He smiled. "I can't leave here . . . Maybe someday, but not now."

"I break your trust and ruin Campbell's work, and you give me this?"

"We're giving you a second chance. It doesn't mean that if you blow up the reef, I'll give you more. This is a one-time offer. Take it and get an education. Do it, bro."

Kemar studied the can, rubbing the gold between two fingers. He looked out at the water and turned back to his two friends. "Okay," he said.

Kemar would go with the professor. He would do it for his father and his mother, because it's where they would have sent him. He would do it for all of his friends and family from Cambodia who lost lives and opportunities. He would do it for Mir Ta, Son Ba, and the people whom Phan extorted the taels from.

He would do it for Al, Meela, and Campbell, because it was a good way to right a wrong. He would do it for the octopus who visited him on the reef and in his dreams, because she needed a human to fight for her. And most of all, he would do it for himself, because nothing had ever felt so right in his life. He would become Makoona in thought and deed.

Binti crawled back into her den. She could feel her young swimming all around her, oblivious to the fact that their mother was among them. Like children who forget their parents when they enter a carnival, these youngsters were consumed with the carnival of life that opened before them.

The mother octopus searched the recesses of her home to see if all the eggs hatched, if any of her offspring needed help getting on their way. But Binti's job was done. She'd lived the life of a female octopus—done it wonderfully—and now was the time for her to swim with the spirit-fish, to curl up with Molo. The octopus made a final trek to her doorway. She wanted to be looking out on the coral valley while she left it. Binti laid her ivory body down and watched her children rise.

One hatchling swam by, abandoned its escape, and sat on his mother's arm for a moment. Binti was overjoyed. Many mothers never even see their young hatch. Binti not only witnessed her children emerge, but she actually touched one. It was the most enchanting moment of her life. And then it got even better.

The youngster turned white like his mother, who smiled proudly at his precociousness. He climbed along her arm, up her mantle, and stretched his miniscule limbs around her. It was an embrace so full of love and life, Binti would carry it with her to Molo and the spirit-fish. Then the little octopus whispered something to his mother. He said, "Rock your baby to and fro, not too fast and not too slow . . . Give yourself unto the light gladly. Have no fear, it gave you life."

The words warmed her cold body. Binti had given birth, in at least one of her eggs, to a little Molo. *You are like your father*, she thought, unable to speak. *And that is a wonderful thing to be.* Then she wondered if perhaps one of those babies racing into the reef was like her.

The tiny octopus clinging to her mantle said one last thing to his mother. "The seeds that were silent all burst and bloom . . . With hope in our hearts, with trust in our eyes, we arise. We have risen, we arise!" The Moloian child flashed purple, green, and gold and then streaked off into Makoona.

The End

Author's Note

Although you might have difficulty finding Makoona on the map, the undersea characters and environments certainly do exist and are based in fact. The cleaning station, for instance, is a naturally occurring establishment in waters all across the planet. The practice has even been documented in land-based communities and freshwater settings as well. Wherever possible, the story reflects accurate habits and habitats. Unfortunately, the same is true for the unscrupulous fishing practices depicted in the text.

Some of you might also recognize some of the words spoken by Molo. In fact, the octopus speaks almost nothing but lyrics written by Robert Hunter, most of which were recorded by the Grateful Dead, among others. Molo also mouths several lines from the Weir/Barlow collaboration, "Throwing Stones," another Grateful Dead gem. It would seem fitting that one of the most psychedelic creatures on Earth, an octopus, living in one of the most psychedelic environments on Earth, a coral reef, quote from one of the most psychedelic bands on Earth, the Grateful Dead. The band has agreed with this reasoning as they have given their blessing for Molo to spout their lyrics in this book. For that, I am incredibly grateful.

Thoughtful readers might see similarities between Meela and Amelia Earhart. Please keep in mind that this novel is a work of fiction in that regard. Does the author know where Amelia Earhart is or what actually happened to her? Or what her mindset was relating to her disappearance? Does anyone? At this point, who's to say that the famous aviator didn't spend time on an island tinkering with outboards and eating flounder with a refugee boy?

Lastly and most importantly, coral reefs as we know them are generally in danger, and their inhabitants are in real peril. Like with the rainforest, there is often only a superficial understanding of what secrets reside in this spectacular gift of nature. And like with the rainforest, it would surely be a tragic legacy for the human race to contribute to destroying something so incredible, so important. From a selfish standpoint, wouldn't it be reckless

to diminish this vital ecosystem before we gain a deeper apprecia-
tion of its diversity and place in the greater life of the planet?

Environmental organizations like World Wildlife Fund, the
Nature Conservancy, Ocean Conservancy, and others, along with
universities, individuals, and in some cases, governments all over
the world are leading the way to find new methods of protecting
and perceiving these marvels. This book is written in tribute to all
those who value the awesome spectacle, the compelling stories,
and the majestic life that can only be found on the coral reef. It's
not too late to save these underwater wonders, but the time to act
is now.

John Morano, 2001

Acknowledgments

Binti, Kemar, and I would like to thank the following people
for making this book possible.

Kris, for her patience and love.

Kathyrn Fuller for her contribution to this work, her dedica-
tion to the life of the planet, and for her wonderful example that
we can make a difference.

The late Roger Caras, an author who found a little space under his broad wing to mentor me.

Alan Trist, Robert Hunter, Bob Weir, John Barlow, Jerry Garcia,
and the Grateful Dead for being wildly generous with their lyrics
and for caring deeply about the planet's flora and fauna.

Mom and Dad for *everything*.

God, for giving me the words to tell stories about incredible creations.

Monmouth University, for enduring support and encourage-
ment.

Jason Aydelotte, Supreme Gecko, for being a publisher and a friend whom you can count on to live up to his word and do the right thing, one of those special people who does not separate who he is from how he does.

Hilary Comfort for directing this project through the publishing process. I know I'm always in great hands when she's on the team.

Diana Buidoso for creating such a compelling cover, one that captures not only the magic of the story, but the enchantment of the coral reef as well.

Josh Mitchell for being the most talented editor I have ever worked with. It's a joy to hand over my manuscript to someone who is such an absolute craftsman.

Sandra Van Chiles for an incredibly detailed, professional proofing of the text that would make any goby cleaner proud.

Sarah Anderson for being able to show readers what's in my mind, something I am incapable of. Your illustrations always manage to transport me into the moment.

Lastly, thanks to Vincent and John for understanding, when those rare moments occur, that Daddy can't play "rough games" because he has to write a story about an octopus and her friends.

About the Author

John is a Professor of Journalism at Monmouth University in New Jersey. He studied at Clark University, Penn State University, and Adelphi University. John began his writing career in New York at *Modern Screen Magazine*, the nation's oldest movie magazine, where he served as lead film critic and managing editor. From there he moved to Los Angeles to become the founding editor-in-chief of *ROCKbeat Magazine* before returning to New York to become senior editor for *Inside Books Magazine*.

After years of covering the entertainment industry, as an academic John became interested in environmental issues and penned his first novel *A Wing and a Prayer*. With the success of his first book, *The John Morano Eco-Adventure Series* was born, and several more eco-adventure novels ensued.

John's work has been endorsed by The Nature Conservancy, World Wildlife Fund, Ocean Conservancy, ASPCA, and other world-class environmental organizations. He has been cited for making complex environmental issues accessible to a wide variety of readers in an entertaining, uplifting way. Professor Morano is also the author of *Don't Tell Me the Ending!*, a popular how-to textbook for aspiring film critics.

John lives in New Jersey on the northern tip of the Pine Barrens in a log home with his wife, two sons, and two rescued Australian Shepherds. When he's not writing or in the classroom, John can be found hiking streams in the woods and collecting Cretaceous fossils or, when his knees let him, running up and down the basketball court.

Connect with John

EMAIL: morano@monmouth.edu

FACEBOOK: www.facebook.com/EcoAdventureSeries

WEB: www.johnmorano.com

About the Illustrator

Sarah E. Anderson is a visual artist practicing primarily in acrylics and pen and ink. She contributed the illustrations for the previous installment in the series, *A Wing and a Prayer*.

Sarah received her bachelor's degree in fine arts from Carnegie Mellon University with a focus in 2D media such as painting, drawing, and printmaking. She has also studied at the Pennsylvania Academy of Fine Arts in Philadelphia and the E'cole nationale supe'rieure des Beaux-Arts in Paris, France.

She currently resides in Columbus, Ohio and is attending Ohio State University, pursuing a doctorate degree in occupational therapy. Her other interests include playing video games, going to museums, running half marathons, and reading books, when she has the time.

Sarah would like to thank John Morano for writing such a wonderful story and inviting her to contribute to it. She would also like to thank her parents and friends, as well as Grey Gecko Press, for their continuing support.

Connect with Sarah

EMAIL: seandersonart@gmail.com

WEB: seandersonart.com

Support Indie Authors & Small Press

If you liked this book, please take a few moments to leave a review on your favorite website, even if it's only a line or two. Reviews make all the difference to indie authors and are one of the best ways you can help support our work.

Reviews on Amazon, GreyGeckoPress.com, GoodReads, Barnes and Noble, or even on your own blog or website all help to spread the word to more readers about our books, and nothing's better than word-of-mouth!

http://smarturl.it/review-makoona

Grey Gecko Press

Thank you for reading this book from Grey Gecko Press, an independent publishing company bringing you great books by your favorite new indie authors.

Be one of the first to hear about new releases from Grey Gecko: visit our website and sign up for our New Release or All-Access email lists. Don't worry: we hate spam, too. You'll only be notified when there's a new release, we'll never share your email with anyone for any reason, and you can unsubscribe at any time.

At our website you can purchase all our titles, including special and autographed editions, preorder upcoming books, and find out about two great ways to get free books, the Slushpile Reader Program and the Advance Reader Program.

And don't forget: all print editions come with the ebook free!

WEB:	www.greygeckopress.com
FACEBOOK:	facebook.com/GreyGeckoPress
TWITTER:	twitter.com/GreyGeckoPress

More from John Morano

A Wing and a Prayer

Lupé might be the very last Guadalupe petrel alive, and he knows the best way to save his flock is to find the Islands of Life and a mate. The problem is the well-meaning man-flock that's decided to keep him safe... in a cage. But Lupé has hatched an escape plan all his own!

Told in a 'Disneyesque' style, *A Wing and a Prayer* will have you smiling and laughing as you're introduced to wonderful characters but also important themes, especially the environment.

Often compared to works such as *Jonathan Livingston Seagull*, *Watership Down*, and *The Jungle Books*, this 25th Anniversary Edition also features an introduction by Mark Tercek, President and CEO of The Nature Conservancy.

amazon ⬜iBooks

BARNES&NOBLE kobo
BOOKSELLERS

grey gecko press

http://bit.ly/1YmKfQq

Recommended Reading

Horse
by Leon Berger

This bittersweet chronicle of a working horse finally gaining his freedom was inspired by a real animal and true events, yet its underlying theme is about the universal value of friendship.

The hero is a sturdy draft horse: old, eccentric, and irritable. His name, suitably enough, is Groucho. By day, he hauls a tourist carriage around the heritage streets of Montreal. By night, he goes home to a stable in a run-down, working-class district.

When his owner dies, Groucho feels the loss and is helped through it by the ancient stableman, Doyle, who is also set in his ways. This is the story of how they cope with each other, as well as the threat which endangers their entire way of life.

amazon iBooks
BARNES & NOBLE BOOKSELLERS **kobo**

grey gecko press
http://bit.ly/141V9lW

Greystone Valley
by Charlie Brooks

Greystone Valley is a land of wizards, dragons, and warriors—and one young girl who goes there quite by accident when her idle wish is granted.

Sarah discovers that not everything in the valley is as magic as she might've wished—especially the nearly illiterate wizard, the mouse-sized dragon, and the warrior who can't stand the sight of blood. Being hunted isn't helping, either. Will Sarah survive this new life of hers, and can she make it home?

And, more importantly, can she ever be the same again?

amazon iBooks
BARNES & NOBLE BOOKSELLERS **kobo**

grey gecko press
http://bit.ly/1ehaBL8